PROTECTOR

CATHERINE BANKS

Protector

By Catherine Banks

Cover design by Amalia Chitulescu Digital Art

Book Interior design by Covers by Combs

This book is also available as an ebook.

ISBN: 978-1-946301-09-3

Turbo Kitten Industries™

P.O. Box 5012

Galt, CA 95632

www.turbokitten.us

www.turbokitten.us/catherine-banks

CHAPTER ONE

After three months of living in the woods I was more than pleased to be back at the Elven Kingdom, sleeping on an incredibly soft bed in the castle. I was four years old when I came to live with the elves, after Cesar, King of the Elves, had found on me on the roadside with my family slain around me, dead ogre bodies littering the road and their blood covering my skin. Cesar witnessed me killing one of the ogres with two axes, a feat much too great for a four year old human girl.

It wasn't until last year that I had discovered that I am only part human, my real father a mystery and one that I must search to uncover. Whatever I was, I loved killing ogres and had slain over one hundred and eighty on my own in less than five minutes.

I was also the first female to not only be allowed into Macon

Academy, school for those training to be mercenaries and guards, but I was also the first female to complete it and become a Mercenary.

My best friend Favian and I had been out doing various missions across the countryside for three months since our graduation, but were ordered to come home to the Elven Kingdom by the King and Queen, my foster parents and Favian's real parents. Favian was tall with silver hair and pointed ears, your typical elf. At least he would have been had he not also been the Prince, next in line for the throne, and the male I was in love with. He also had grey eyes that had powers of enchantment, or so I believed since I always agreed to do what he said if he forced me to meet his eyes. I hid my love from him to keep our friendship and partnership strong. I cherished every moment I was able to spend with him because I knew that within the next year he would begin courting female elves and I would lose him as a partner. I was prepared for it and yet I still dreaded it.

I walked from my room, down one of the hallways of the castle in search of Favian. We were supposed to go meet the male elves at the fighting arena where they gathered to practice every Saturday. He had promised to meet me so that we could walk together, but he was nowhere to be found and the practices always began at ten o'clock, ten minutes from now. I gripped the pommels of my new twin swords, swords which supposedly belonged to my real father, and walked down the hallway. It was unlike Favian to be late. I finally spotted him coming down the hallway and hurried towards him. He walked passed me as though I were invisible.

I turned around and punched his arm hard enough to sting. "Helloooo," I said angrily.

Favian turned and stared at me in shock. "What?" he asked in a voice much more like his father's than his.

I glared at him and pushed my finger against the center of his chest. "Don't walk passed me without acknowledging me."

He stared at me in shock a moment and then shook his head and started to walk away. My anger grew and I kicked his foot to make him stumble and turn around again. Much to my surprise he whipped around, drew his sword and slashed at me. I drew my swords, blocking his attacks and then used them to dislodge his sword from his hand.

He was moving differently; his attacks and stances were not their usual fluid and gracefulness that I envied. And how in the hell had I dislodged his sword from his hand?! I wanted to think I was just getting better, but I was never better than Favian. I couldn't understand it. I couldn't understand why he was attacking me either. We may spar together and play fight, but he had never attacked me in such a fashion before.

"What the hell do you think you're doing?" I asked angrily.

He grabbed my arms and using his body, pushed me backwards against the wall of the hallway with my hands up over my head so that my swords were now useless. "I should be asking you the same thing. Why on earth would a human attack an elf?" he asked angrily in that strange voice.

I stared at him in utter disbelief. What was going on with him? He hardly ever brought up my humanness.

"Aw I see that you two have met each other. Sebastian, please release Marin," Cesar said as he walked down the hallway towards us.

"Oh, so you're the pet human my family keeps around," Favian said again using that strange voice.

"Favian, what is going on?" I asked as I stared into his eyes which were a lighter shade of grey than normal.

"Step away from her," Favian's real voice said from beside me.

I turned to my right from where the voice had come from and stared in shock at Favian. I looked from the Favian in front of me to the Favian beside me and felt the color drain from my face. There were two! Two Favians!

"She assaulted me first," the Favian in front of me said as he stepped back from me.

"What? Who? Two?" I asked as I looked at both of them.

Father patted my shoulder with a reassuring smile on his face. "Marin, this is Sebastian, Favian's twin brother."

"I realize you like your pet, but do I really need to be introduced to her?" Sebastian asked as he looked at me in disgust. I felt my anger brewing despite my extreme confusion and shock. How dare he call me a pet?!

Favian took a step towards him, but Father stopped him with a hand on his chest. "Watch your mouth, Sebastian. You will treat Marin with the same respect that you treat your mother and any other member of this family," Father said in his most commanding tone. "She is our daughter and if you cannot accept that than I will be forced to ask you to leave."

Sebastian's eyes widened and he looked from Favian, the real one who was seething with anger, to Father's serious face, in shock. "You truly accept this human as your child?" he asked.

Father nodded his head. "She is one of us, no matter what her lineage may be."

Sebastian absorbed that a moment, smiled at me, picked my hand up and then bowed over it before kissing the back of my hand. "My apologies, Marin. I was misinformed about your presence in this Kingdom. I will not make that mistake again."

"Apology accepted," I mumbled as I still tried to absorb the incredible likeness between the two brothers. I searched for any difference between them that I could use to mark them apart, but the only thing I could come up with was the slight difference in eye color. This was not good.

"Are you alright?" Favian asked me.

I wanted to shake my head and tell him that in fact I was not alright, that I was freaking out, but I nodded my head and sheathed my swords. "Yes, just digesting all of this."

"Come, we mustn't be late for the practices," Father said as he continued on his way down the hallway. How could he be so nonchalant about this? Didn't he realize how complicated my life had just become? How was I going to handle them being identical twins?

We followed behind him with Sebastian at his side and Favian at mine. "Why didn't I know you had a twin?" I asked him accusingly while feeling hurt that we hadn't discussed it before.

"He was stolen and it wasn't until a year ago that we found him. We don't exactly get along," Favian said quietly as we walked.

"He was stolen?" I asked in shock. I couldn't believe anyone would take anything from the Elves and get away with it, especially not a child.

Favian nodded his head. "The night that we were born a witch came and teleported him away. Father tried to trace it and searched for three years afterwards for him, but it was fruitless. Last year a man that you and I had worked for met Sebastian and thought he was me. After talking with him the man explained the extreme likeness between us to Sebastian. Once Sebastian knew where we were he came to the Kingdom and the family was reunited."

"Where was he all this time?" I asked quietly as we exited the castle and headed towards the fighting arena where over three hundred elves were gathered, waiting for us.

Favian shrugged. "We don't know he won't talk about it."

Sebastian was greeted warmly by the elves, as was Favian. I was greeted warmly, but also at a little more of a distance by most. I knew I had frightened many of the elves when I had defeated the ogres that had been attacking the Kingdom, but I had not realized how it would affect me until now.

Jovian, a kind, unattractive elf my age smiled at me from where he was standing near the fence. "Little Death Bringer, it has been a while since I've seen you in the fighting arena."

I smiled. "So, word of my nickname has traveled all the way to the Elven Kingdom, has it?"

"As has word of your battle with the ogres at the Academy. I'm impressed," he said, "but think you will still lose to me in the ring."

I shrugged. "Only one way to find out."

"She fights?" Sebastian asked in disbelief from where he was standing next to Father and two of the eldest elves.

"She has ears to hear and a mouth to answer for herself as well," I said angrily.

"A woman has never been allowed in the fighting arena before," he replied as though he had lived here and knew our traditions.

"True, but I am a special exception," I said with a smile as I climbed over the wooden fence and hopped down into the sand arena.

Jovian followed me in and drew his sword. "Have you learned to handle both of those swords?"

I shook my head. "Not completely, but I have learned enough to hold out against you for a little while."

"Try not to bruise her," Father said. "Amadis gets angry when she's bruised."

Amadis was the Queen of the Elves, Cesar's wife, and my step mother. Despite my tendencies towards the male arts she still tried to teach me to be a lady. It took more practicing then I liked, but I was getting better at behaving like a lady.

"Don't worry Father, he won't get that close," I said with a smug smile at Jovian.

"Your ego has grown too large for your small body," Jovian said teasingly. "Let me cut you down to size."

I pulled both of my swords and ran forward to meet Jovian as he charged at me. Our blades met with a loud clang that filled the air and I released my inhibitions and reached down for the other power that I felt within me. I had been practicing the last three months and had been able to use some of the power I felt, but not even a tenth of what was inside of me.

Jovian and I danced around the arena together in a fight much more intense than we ever had before. After ten minutes Jovian raised his arm in surrender and stepped back from me. "Where have you attained such stamina?" he asked. "You are quite more skilled than you led me to believe."

I smiled. "Deceit is one of the few skills a female has in her arsenal."

The crowd laughed and Kato, Father's guard and one of my mentors, jumped into the ring. "You think you can last more than four seconds against me?" he asked.

The last time I had fought him I would have died had he not pulled back a strike at the last second. I had no idea if I could stand against the incredibly skilled elf, but I wanted to try. "Come you old badger, let's see if you have been keeping up on your training while I was away," I said with a teasing smile.

Kato smiled back at me and then looked at Father. "You care to keep count of the seconds for us?"

Father smiled. "Of course, but remember no bruising."

Kato smiled. "That all depends on how she attacks."

"Then let us begin," I said.

He darted forward without warning and I cleared my mind, flowing from offense to defense, from blocking to attacking without thinking my moves through. It was the only way to stay alive in a battle and with the small amount of unlocked power I was finally able to fight Kato without feeling completely outmatched.

"What is she?" Sebastian asked from the other side of the fence. "Is she a demon?"

The comment stung and also pulled away some of my focus from the fight. Kato noticed my lack of concentration and took the opportunity to knock my legs out from under me and pin me to the ground. He tapped my forehead with his finger. "You can't let things distract you or you will end up dead."

I nodded my head and waited as he stepped off of me before getting up and sheathing my swords. "Thank you for sparring with me," I said with a bow to him, trying to hide my face.

Kato draped his arm around my shoulders and hugged me against him. "I don't care what anyone says," he whispered into my ear. "You will always just be my little Marin."

My pesky girly emotions reared their head, but I shoved them down and blinked away the tears before they could fall. "Thank you."

"Ten seconds," Father called out to me. "That is quite an improvement from the last time."

I nodded my head and climbed over the fence, trying to hide the sadness on my face as the elves moved a step back from me. I made my way through the crowd much easier than before since they separated like I had a disease. I had thought that I would be more welcomed among the Elves now that I was closer to their strength, but instead I was being pushed away.

"Marin," Favian called. "Where are you going?"

"I'm going to visit Fire," I called back without turning towards him. "I'll see you for lunch."

"You should learn to keep your mouth shut," Kato said to Sebastian.

"What did I do?" he asked.

I walked faster to avoid the conversation and was more than pleased when I made it to the stables. I usually liked to stay and watch the others, but now I was not in the mood. Alex, the horse master and an elf only nineteen years old despite his title, stood in front of Fire's stall, looking in. Fire was my horse, born in front of me and raised and trained by me. She was the best mare a girl could hope for and had been through many battles with me.

"Is everything alright?" I asked with worry as I walked towards Fire and Alex.

He turned and smiled at me. "Yes, everything is fine. I was just admiring her beauty."

I exhaled in relief. Aside from Favian, she was my best friend and I would have been very distraught if she were hurt. "Oh, good." I walked passed him and into her stall, running a hand along her shiny coat. She nickered in greeting and I inhaled her familiar scent.

"Having a rough day?" Alex asked.

"Why would you ask that?"

He smiled and leaned on his arms on the top of the stall door. "I've known you since you arrived at the Kingdom. I can tell when you're upset."

I looked at Alex in surprise because he was one of the quietest elves I had ever met and despite having known him for as long as I could remember, we hardly spoke and I hardly knew him. It shocked me to think that he had been watching me and might know me in such a way. "I just met Sebastian," I said as I continued to pet Fire.

He sighed. "Ah, so you met the identical twin? Things didn't go well I take it?"

I laughed bitterly. "That is an understatement. First I attacked him because I thought he was Favian and then he..." I stopped talking because I had no idea how Alex felt about me now. "You aren't afraid of me?" I asked while watching his face.

He frowned. "Afraid of you? Why would I be afraid of you?"

I looked down at Fire's coat and whispered, "Most of the other elves are."

"Just because you killed a bunch of ogres? I would think that you of all people would have the most hatred of ogres and it makes sense to me that you would want to kill them due to your awful event when you were four. And most of us have always known that you aren't completely human, Marin. No human girl could hold her own against an elf boy, no matter how determined she was and I watched you fight several younger elves when you first came here."

"I wish everyone felt like you," I whispered.

"Marin?" Sebastian called. "Alex, is Marin here?"

Alex looked at me in question.

"I'm here," I called back despite my desire to hide in Fire's stall.

"Alex would you mind giving us a moment alone?" Sebastian asked as he walked into the stable.

"You want me to stay?" Alex asked me.

I smiled. "Thank you, but I think I can handle him."

Alex smiled. "I never doubted that." He bowed to Sebastian quickly before leaving the stable, but gave me one last glance before disappearing from sight.

I turned away from Sebastian as I inspected Fire's tail and pulled out some thistles.

"Is this your horse?" Sebastian asked.

"Yes," I answered without turning around.

"She is very beautiful."

"Thank you," I said and then stepped out of Fire's stall and turned around to face him. I had to get it over with now, before I lost my nerve. "How can I help you?"

He met my eyes and I still could not get over how identical he and Favian looked. "I wanted to apologize for my comment during your fight," he said.

"What comment?" I asked, pretending I hadn't heard it even though I felt its sting in my chest.

"I am new to this Kingdom and I have not had any explanation or proper introduction to the people here, especially not regarding you. I apologize for my rude comment and want to say that I am incredibly impressed by your skill in fighting. I have never met a female who could hold her own against an elf as you can."

"I don't know about holding my own, I still get beaten in less than fifteen seconds by an elf, but I accept your apology."

He picked my hand up and kissed the back of it as he met my eyes. "I am truly sorry for offending you."

My pulse skyrocketed and I had to remind myself that this was not Favian several times. "Thank you."

"Marin," Favian called from the front of the stable with some anger lacing his voice. "Can I speak with you?"

Sebastian released my hand and turned around. "I will take my leave and see you both for lunch."

Favian waited until he was gone and then walked quickly to me. "Are you alright? What did he say to you?"

"He simply apologized, Favian. He was perfectly nice," I said and then started out of the stables.

"He looked to be behaving more than nice with your hand in his," he said irritably.

I stopped walking and looked at him in shock. "What's wrong?"

"I don't trust him and I don't like the idea of him courting you," he said with his serious face.

"I am not letting him court me," I said in shock. "How could you even think such a thing?"

He exhaled with obvious relief on his face and then smiled. "I was just making sure."

I turned and headed towards the castle again. "You are so strange sometimes," I whispered. I waved to Alex who was heading back towards the stables and he waved back with a smile to me and Favian.

"So, what else is bothering you?" Favian asked.

"Oh, just the usual."

"The others distancing themselves from you?" he asked. I nodded my head and he put his arm around my shoulders, pulling me against his side. "They will come around. Sebastian did and he hardly knows you and hasn't even seen your true fighting potential."

"Perhaps that is why he came around so quickly," I suggested.

"Or perhaps he has some sinister plot to use you against me," Favian said as he held open the side door of the castle.

I rolled my eyes at him and walked inside. "Now you sound like the paranoid human kings."

Favian smacked my arm. "How dare you compare me to a human."

I felt a twinge of anger at his comment, but ignored it and headed towards the bathing area. "I'll meet you for lunch after I get cleaned up."

Favian nodded his head and we went our separate ways, me to the bathing area so I could get clean and put a proper female outfit on for Amadis when I saw her at lunch, and Favian to speak with Father. Amadis would be surprised to see me wearing a proper female outfit since it was the first time I would get to see her since we had returned and hopefully she would be pleased by it as well.

The maid smiled at me as soon as I came in and immediately began preparing a bath. "I'm surprised you have come to me so soon. You usually wait until Amadis orders you here," she said.

"I'm planning on surprising her," I responded as I stripped my clothes off.

She grabbed a scrubbing cloth and soap and we made our way to the heated tub of water. "I'm surprised that you aren't caked in dirt as usual since you've been sleeping in the forest for the past three months."

"I took a couple baths in the rivers to remove some of the dirt."

She laughed. "Oh, dear are you finally turning into a lady?"

"That would be a sad day," I said with a smile as I climbed into the warm water.

She laughed and began scrubbing my skin with the cloth. "So, what do you think of Prince Sebastian?" she asked as she worked on a clump of dirt clinging to my arm.

"I don't know him so I don't know what to think yet." I mulled over our encounters and finally said, "He seems nice."

"It is strange how much Prince Favian and he look alike though. I cannot tell them apart," she said as she dumped water over my head to rinse my body before starting on my hair.

"Yes, I am having trouble with that as well. The only difference I can find is their voices and that Sebastian has a slightly lighter color of grey to his eyes."

She whispered, "You best be on your guard than to ensure he does not trick you by pretending to be Favian."

She had a point, but I had to hope he would not do that. "There would be no reason for him to do that, unless he wanted to go on a mission or spar against me."

"So, have you told Prince Favian that you are in love with him yet?" she asked as she combed through my hair.

I turned and stared at her in shock. "What?"

She smiled. "It is quite obvious to most of us that you are in love with him. It surprises me that he has not figured it out yet."

"You mustn't ever say that again," I told her seriously.

"Why?" she asked curiously, the smile leaving her mouth.

"Because a relationship between he and I would never work and it is something that he must never learn of. I do not want to lose his friendship because he is worried about my feelings for him."

"I think you're killing a relationship before it could start," she replied.

"Drop it," I ordered her as I stood up and pulled on a bath robe.

"I am sorry if I offended you," she said as she resumed combing my hair to ensure it was tangle free.

"I'm sorry I snapped at you."

"I understand."

As soon as she finished brushing my hair I said goodbye to her and then hurried to my room to put on one of the few light dresses that Amadis had had made for me. The dress was made from incredibly fine satin and felt like feathers against my skin when I moved. It was also a gorgeous dark blue that I loved contrasting with my brown and blonde hair and skin.

I still had on the shell necklace that Maddock had given me, a necklace that had saved my life three months earlier when I had been held prisoner by a mad man who hadn't wanted a woman to become a Mercenary. I braided my hair so that it hung in a thick braid down the center of my back, put on heels and made my way to the ballroom where my family always ate their lunch when we were all together. As I walked, I wondered if others really could see my feelings for Favian? I needed to work on hiding them better if that was the case.

I opened the doors to the ballroom and all eyes turned to me. I stared at the twin brothers who were sitting across the table from each other as I tried to figure out which was Favian so I could take my seat, but I couldn't figure out who was who. Father, Favian, Kato, and Sebastian all stood up at my presence and Mother smiled brightly at me. "You look beautiful," Mother said as I walked towards them. "What is the occasion?"

I smiled at her and then kissed her on the cheek. "I thought you would be pleased if I cleaned and dressed like a lady before you ordered me to."

"I am very pleased," she said as I looked at each of the brothers.

One moved towards me and picked my hand up, kissing the back of it softly. "You look lovely," said Sebastian's voice.

I curtsied since Amadis was present and she would have asked me to and gently pulled my hand back. "Thank you." I took my seat between Kato and Favian, but Favian was turned away from me. Did he not like how I looked? Was he mad at me for some reason?

"Now that we are all here, let's eat," Father said with a wide smile.

The chef brought in several platters of food and I was shocked to see a plate of beef. He smiled at me. "You have earned the right to eat meat here."

"I don't want to cause you issues with your beliefs," I said seriously. Elves did not eat meat because they refused to kill unless necessary. While living in the Elven Kingdom I was forced to eat as they did, but once outside of the Kingdom I always ate as much meat as possible. I just couldn't live without eating meat!

The chef patted my shoulder. "I am using animals that died of natural causes and am only using their meat so that it does not go to waste. Therefore, it does not interfere with our beliefs."

Hearing that made me feel better. "Thank you," I said seriously.

"Eat everyone," Father said.

I grabbed two pieces of beef and some of the salad that I loved and started eating while the men talked about the current affairs in the Kingdom. Sebastian listened intently, but every now and then he would glance towards me. I kept my eyes on my plate, being sure not to meet his eyes so he wouldn't think I was looking at him too. Why did he keep looking at me?

"Favian, did you tell father about the elf we met on our last mission?" I asked him.

"Yes," Favian answered shortly without looking at me.

I wanted to ask what was wrong, but with Sebastian there I couldn't. I finished my food a few minutes later while everyone else chatted pleasantly and stood up. "If you'll excuse me, I think I'm going to change and go for a ride."

"Must you leave already?" Mother asked.

"I do not wish to stay with foul moods directed at me," I said haughtily and then walked out of the ballroom.

Anger boiled inside of me and I needed to find a vent before I exploded. I climbed the stairs to my room and slammed my door closed. Why was Favian acting so strangely? What had I done wrong? Was he mad because Sebastian had complimented me? That was hardly anything I could have controlled.

I screamed in frustration and quickly changed into pants, a shirt and boots and then hurried out to the stables. Alex smiled at me at first and then asked, "Things still aren't going well?"

"I need to go for a ride," I said quickly as I grabbed Fire's bridle from the wall.

"You shouldn't take your anger out on your horse," he reminded me.

I put the bridle back and groaned in frustration. "Fine." I ran from the stable towards the fighting arena. I might by chance find someone still there who I could spar with. I reached the arena and much to my dismay, everyone was gone. I pulled my swords from their sheaths and attacked an imaginary foe, putting every ounce of anger and energy into my moves.

My skin began to sweat and I pushed myself harder, moving as quickly as I could. One of the princes approached, but without hearing their voice I had no way of knowing who it was so I ignored him. I ran to the wooden pole which was used to practice your strikes and attacked it with all of the energy I had left, only stopping when I couldn't lift my arms anymore and my breaths came in short gasps.

"Feel better?" Favian's voice asked.

I spun around and asked, "What have I done? Why are you treating me as though I have insulted you?"

"Why did you come dressed as you did?" he asked instead of answering my question.

"To make Mother smile," I answered honestly. "What other reason could there be for me to bathe and wear a dress?"

He sighed and rubbed the back of his neck. "I'm sorry, Marin."

I sheathed my swords and walked towards him. "Why are you acting so strangely towards me?"

"It's Sebastian. I am trying to get used to his presence in every aspect of my life, but I do not like it. I had hoped that you would be one of the aspects that would not be altered because of his existence."

"Why would our friendship change because of him?" I asked, not understanding his irritation and worry.

He threw his hands into the air. "I don't know. I just saw you walk in looking beautiful and watched as he approached you to kiss your hand and thought you had done it for his attention."

Had he just said I looked beautiful? I climbed over the fence and headed into the fields with him at my side. "I have not lied to you. I only dressed up for Mother."

He stopped me with a hand on my arm and stared into my eyes. "I am sorry that I'm acting like a spoiled brat and acting possessive. I just do not want him to come between us."

"That would never happen," I said seriously to him. "You are my best friend and that will be the case until I die."

He hugged me and sighed. "I feel like an idiot."

"Good," I said as I pushed him away and tried to calm the butterflies in my stomach. "Because you are."

He smiled and then tried to grab me, but I darted away from him and stuck my foot out to trip him. He expected the move though and grabbed me so that we fell into the grass together. I struggled against him, trying to pin him, but he pinned me to the ground with his hands holding my wrists above my head. "I thought you were stronger, Little Death Bringer?" he teased.

I shrugged. "I don't want to hurt you."

He gaped at me and then started to tickle me. I screamed and laughed as I tried to squirm away from him and his tickling. We hadn't had much time to play while out on our missions, so this was the first time in months that we had been able to horse around. My cheeks hurt from the wide smile I was wearing as I tried halfheartedly to get away from his tickling hands.

"Am I interrupting?" Sebastian asked from beside us.

Favian stopped his assault and stood up, grabbing my hand and pulling me up beside him. "Yes," Favian said seriously.

I wanted to smack him and tell him to be nice, but I sort of liked him acting protective of me. Although I would never admit it to Favian.

"I apologize, but Father has summoned you to the castle Favian. He has an important matter which he said you must immediately take care of. I would not have interrupted if it wasn't urgent."

I felt like I was in an alternate universe where there were two Favians. How was I going to deal with this?

"Thank you," Favian said and then tugged on my hand. "Come on Marin, let's see what task he has for us."

I smiled at Sebastian to be nice and followed Favian, pulling my hand from his. Sebastian stayed in the field as we headed towards the castle so I punched Favian's arm and said, "You should not act possessive of me. If word spreads the females will get the wrong impression and it will be very difficult for you to court anyone."

Favian looked at me from the corner of his eyes and shook his head. "I don't care about courting females right now."

We headed into Father's war room where he and Kato were looking over a map of the Kingdom. "There you are Favian. Marin, I will not be sending you on this mission."

"Why can't I go?" I asked. I was surprised at his immediate refusal towards me when I had barely come in the door.

"Because you have not mastered your powers and until you do, you are still a vulnerable human. I will not risk your life on Elvish matters when I can send Favian and other skilled elves instead," Father answered in his no nonsense tone.

I wanted to argue, but he was probably right. "Very well," I said. "Can you at least tell me how long he will be gone?"

Father stared at me in shock, probably expecting me to argue or plead my case to be allowed to go.

"About a week," Kato answered in Father's silence. "As will I, since I am going with him. Do not worry, I will protect the prince in your absence."

I nodded my head at them and then gripped Favian's arm. "Stay safe."

He smiled. "Shouldn't I be telling you that?"

I turned and made my exit. I would have to spend an entire week at the Kingdom without Favian. What was I going to do?

"Marin," Mother called. "Time to wake up for breakfast."

"Okay," I called back from underneath my covers.

"Chef made bacon for you," she bribed.

"I'm up!" I yelled as I threw back my covers and quickly put on clothes. I had watched as Favian and fifteen other elves, including Kato, left on their secret mission yesterday. It felt wrong to be parted from Favian, but I knew I needed to get used to it for the upcoming years. I had spent the last part of the previous day sulking in my room and vowed to be somewhat active today.

I made sure my appearance was at least reasonable as I looked in the full-length mirror before heading out of my room. It would not do to upset Mother so early in the morning. I skipped down the stairs and opened the door of the ballroom, running right into Sebastian, at least I was ninety percent sure it was Sebastian since I had seen Favian off the day before.

"Sorry," I said as I took a step back.

He smiled at me and took a step backwards into the ballroom so that I could enter. "No need to apologize. The fault is mine," Sebastian's voice said, confirming that it wasn't Favian.

I walked into the room and he walked beside me as I headed to the table where Father and Mother were sitting. I wasn't sure why he was following me if he had just been leaving, but I held my tongue and had to hold it inside of my mouth when he pulled out my chair for me and then pushed it in as I sat.

"Good morning," Father said with a smile.

I was still mad at Father for not allowing me to go on the mission with Kato and Favian despite knowing he had good reasons, but I couldn't be rude to him. "Morning," I replied as I draped a napkin over my lap, avoiding eye contact.

Sebastian walked out of the ballroom and I looked at Mother. "Okay, what is the sign to tell them apart?" I asked.

She laughed. "I was about to ask you the same thing. It bothers me that as a mother I cannot tell my two children apart."

I groaned. "The only difference I can see is that Sebastian's eyes are a slightly lighter shade of grey, but Favian's look like that when he is excited about something, so there truly isn't anything except their voice."

"And that won't help if you are the first one to talk," Father said.

I sighed and let my head fall onto the table with a thunk. "I'm doomed."

"It isn't that bad," Mother said. "I'm sure you will think of something."

"You think they would let me write their names on their foreheads until I figured it out?" I asked somewhat seriously.

Mother and Father laughed and I knew that I was truly in trouble and needed to figure something out. Perhaps I could find some juiceberries and smear some onto Sebastian's face. The juiceberries' juice left a red stain that took a month to get out. That had to be enough time to find a difference.

"Food is served," Chef said as he walked into the room with a cart of trays. I could smell the bacon and my mouth instantly filled with drool. He set a tray on top of my plate and whispered, "The eggs lacked a chick so they are essentially not a live animal." My shock was evident to everyone and the Chef smiled. "I have been trying for years to find ways to cook you the food you truly love and it wasn't until Sebastian came to me and talked with me that I learned of this information."

"Sebastian?" I asked.

"Yes?" he asked me back as he returned and sat in the chair across from me.

I looked at him and then at the Chef in confusion. Why would Sebastian be discussing these things? Chef set another tray onto Sebastian's plate and I watched in shock as he lifted the lid to reveal eggs, bacon and toast. "It looks perfect," He said with a happy smile to the Chef.

"You eat meat?!" I asked in absolute shock.

He nodded his head. "Yes. I was raised with humans who ate meat. They knew that elves didn't kill animals and so they found ways to obtain meat and eggs, ways that I have been teaching Chef."

It was so strange and yet I benefited greatly from it and it made me like Sebastian just a little bit more. It was nice not to have Favian watching me eat with disapproving eyes.

"So, you are an elf raised by humans and she is a human raised by elves?" Chef asked with a laugh. "That is quite interesting indeed."

I would have laughed had I not still been uneasy about the fact that I was something other than human. What was my father that gave me this incredible power?

"Let's eat," Father said as he and Mother spooned oatmeal from a large bowl.

I removed the lid from my tray and ate every piece of food despite the sour feeling in my stomach now. I stood once I was finished and said, "I shall see you for lunch."

Mother dipped her head at me in acknowledgement and I walked from the ballroom, down the hallway and out the back door to the fields. The first part of the fields were low grass and wild flowers, but the further you went, the higher the grasses grew and if you walked far enough you could disappear within their green heights. I made my way in until I found my favorite spot and sat down. Over the years I had been clearing out a small circle, just big enough for two people to lie down in. Favian and I had often hidden here after stealing cake from the kitchen or after getting in trouble. So far none had found it, not even Kato.

Now I hid here to think. There weren't too many races that existed in the world. There were humans, elves, ogres, goblins, fey, Pegasus, dwarves, and shape shifters. I gasped and stared at the ground in shock. Could I be a shapeshifter? I laughed. No, that wasn't possible. So, what could I be? A thought crossed my mind and it was truly frightening and instantly chilled me. Could I have a demon living inside of me? That would explain the time I acted and didn't remember it. I talked and yet it wasn't me, right?

"Marin, are you alright?" Sebastian asked as he sat down across from me.

I jumped, startled by his sudden and silent appearance and had to release my grip from my swords. "You shouldn't sneak up on people," I said as I tried to regain my composure.

"I'm sorry. I thought you had heard me," he said as he watched me. "Would you like me to leave?"

I wasn't sure what I wanted him to do, but I knew I had to be nice despite my true feelings at the moment. "No, it's alright. You just caught me on an off moment."

"So, what are you thinking about that has such a terrified look on your face?" he asked, sounding genuinely concerned.

I could have talked with him, but I hardly knew him and this was something very personal. If he had been Favian I would have talked with him, but he was not and I did not want to open myself up so much. "Nothing," I answered. "So, how are you liking the Elven Kingdom?"

He smiled. "I love it. Everyone here is so kind and it is so different from living with the humans."

"Where were you living?" I asked him.

He smiled. "You tell me your secret and I'll tell you mine."

I shook my head and tried to give him a smile. "Perhaps another day."

"Then you shall wait for mine as well," he said and then leaned back onto his elbows looking up at the sky. "It is beautiful here," he whispered, "How can you stand to leave it?"

"I love it here, but if I stay here too long Mother insists on turning me into a proper lady," I said with a loving smile. Mother was the most kind and loving female I had ever met and I loved her despite her not being my blood mother.

"I think you would make a great lady. You are beautiful and look amazing in a dress," he said as he gazed at me.

It was strange to have him flirt with me because my mind wanted to believe it was Favian while I knew it wasn't. "You are an awful flirt," I said with a smile as I pulled a piece of the long grass from the ground.

He shook his head and looked at me seriously. "I am only speaking the truth."

I had to look away from his eyes to tame my hormones. Was it possible that because he had grown up around humans that he would be more inclined to court one? That thought was chilling and I stood up, needing to distance myself from him. Why would I even think such a thing? I didn't know him and just because he looked like Favian, didn't mean he was him.

He stood up with me, not seeming to notice why I stood up. "Favian!" A familiar female voice called. I watched Sebastian's face as Amile stepped into the clearing, but his eyes never left mine. "Oh, I should have guessed you would be with him," she said bitterly towards me.

"I don't believe we've met," Sebastian said as he stepped forward, closer to her and I. "I'm Sebastian."

Her mouth opened in a petite circle that was incredibly cute and made me hate her a little more. "Oh, dear. I'm so sorry. I had heard that you were here, but I didn't think that you would look so much like Prince Favian." She curtsied low to the ground and said, "It is an honor to meet you, Prince Sebastion."

Sebastian picked her hand up and kissed the back of it. "The honor is mine."

I turned away from them, heading off into the fields. "I'll see you later," I called over my shoulder as I moved through the tall grass towards the smaller grass and the stables. Why was I jealous that he was flirting with Amile? I knew that she was more beautiful than I. And I knew that he was not Favian. So why did it anger me so much? I needed a job to do to keep my mind off of things and I was sure that Alex would have something for me to do.

I stepped into the barn and found him brushing Fire's tail. "Alex, you don't have to do that," I said as I walked towards him.

He smiled at me and continued to brush the tangles out. "It's alright. I enjoy it."

I stopped at the stall door and pet Fire's nose. "Do you need any help around here?" I asked.

He looked at me and laughed. "Sebastian issues?"

How did he keep doing that? "No, just need to blow off some steam since Favian isn't here for me to practice with."

"Well in that case you can muck out the stalls if you want."

I nodded my head and grabbed the pick and the wheelbarrow and headed towards the stalls on the right. The horses on the right were all used to having their stalls cleaned and each one moved over obediently as I cleaned out the poop and pee soaked straw from the stalls and put it in the wheelbarrow. I pet each horse when I entered and when I left and moved the wheelbarrow which was getting heavier to each stall. I finished the right side and moved to the back stalls where Ice's empty stall was. I inspected it just to be sure it was clean and then opened the door of Fire's stall. She moved over to the left and Alex stayed behind her as he continued to work on her tail. I mucked out the stall on the right and then flung some straw at Alex's leg. He laughed at me and I moved around him to clean behind Fire. He bumped my hip with his and I bumped him back. We laughed and I moved around to the left side, clucking to Fire so she would move to the right. It was nice to be able to do something helpful and be able to goof off with a friend at the same time. I needed to do this type of thing more often to take my mind off of Favian. I was surprised at how easy it was to be around Alex, but then again, he had to be a calm, easy to get along with person to be the horse master.

I worked on the stalls on the left and then I moved to the last stall to clean, which was the first stall on the left where a very large warhorse stood with a shiny black coat and eyes that shown with intelligence. "Hello there, boy. Move over so I can clean you out."

The horse stamped his hoof and held his ground. "Careful of him," Alex said from Fire's stall. "He's temperamental."

I met the horse's eyes and put my hands on my hips. "I don't take guff from horses. You're going to listen," I said as I opened the stall door and pushed on his shoulder. He whipped his head around and tried to bite me, but I dodged his bite and smacked his nose. "Knock it off," I told him as I pushed his shoulder again.

He snorted angrily and pushed back against me. I stumbled back a step and he stamped his hoof again, right on top of my foot and pinned it to the ground. I grunted in pain and pushed at his shoulder, but he held his ground and snapped his teeth at me with his ears pinned against the top of his head. "Alex!" I called. "I need help."

Alex hopped over Fire's door and ran to me. He took in my situation and said, "I told you to be careful."

"I didn't think he'd pin my foot to the floor," I said as tears built in my eyes. I was pretty sure my foot was broken and the pain was building the longer he stood on it. "Get him off."

Alex grabbed the horse's face and stared into his eyes. "Pick up your hoof."

The horse apparently had a sense of humor because he picked up one of his back ones and not the one on my foot.

"What's going on?" Sebastian asked as he walked into the barn.

"Your assistance is required apparently," Alex said. "He seems not to like her and is hurting her."

I hid my face, not wanting him to see the tears leaking down it as he approached and continued to push at the horse's shoulder. I hated the fact that I was crying, especially since there were other people around.

"Hoof up," Sebastian ordered the horse. The horse lifted his back hoof again and Sebastian walked into the stall and stared into his horse's eye. "You are being stubborn and I do not care for it."

The horse nickered softly and Sebastian placed his hand flat against the horse's shoulder and pushed. The horse lifted his hoof from my foot and moved over three steps. I moved backwards away from him, but sure enough my foot was broken and it made me cry out in pain when I put pressure on it.

"You need to get to the healer," Alex said seriously.

"I'll take her. It was my ass of a horse that hurt her anyways," Sebastian said as he grabbed me and picked me up. I gasped in shock and looked at him. He glared at his horse and said something in the old dialect of Elvish that I did not understand. The horse lowered its head and nickered sadly as though he felt ashamed. Sebastian turned and walked from the stable, carrying me easily. All elves were strong and carrying me was a simple task, but I still felt bad.

"You don't have to carry me," I said as I wiped at my face.

He shook his head. "I'm sorry that he did that. He is very stubborn at times. I guess I need to work on his people skills." I laughed despite my pain and Sebastian smiled. "Why did you leave when Amile came?" he asked me.

"You're supposed to be meeting everyone and she and I don't get along, so I left to keep from biasing you," I answered truthfully. Also, I didn't want to see her flirting with Sebastian.

"Why don't you two get along?" he asked.

"There are quite a few reasons," I said as I tried to dodge his question.

"Like?"

I sighed. "I'd rather not discuss it. It brings up things I can't change and makes me sad and angry at the same time."

"You can trust me, you know? I know it's difficult for you to deal with the fact that I look exactly like Favian, but I'm not the evil twin," he said with a smile.

"I don't think that," I said honestly. "But it is difficult dealing with how similar you two look. I have to remind myself that you're Sebastian and not Favian."

"Oh, I see," he said softly as he opened the door of the castle and walked to the healer's room.

The healer smiled at me and asked, "What did you do this time?"

"His horse stomped on my foot and broke it," I answered as he sat me down on one of the beds.

She tsked and pulled on my boot, but it wouldn't come off. "It seems your foot has swollen already. We will have to cut the boot off."

"No!" I said seriously. The boots had been a gift from Favian and I didn't want to destroy them.

"We have to," she said. "Your foot won't come out otherwise."

"Can't you just yank it off?" I asked.

"That will hurt a lot," Sebastian said in shock.

The healer nodded her head. "He's right and we still might not be able to get it off. Plus, it may injure your foot more."

I warred with the decision in my head and then decided that I had to hope that Favian wouldn't be too upset with me.

"He will understand the need to cut it off," the healer said quietly as she grabbed a pair of scissors.

I looked at her and then remembered that she had been present when Favian had given me the boots on my last birthday. "I hope so," I whispered.

She smiled. "He would probably be cutting it off himself while restraining you if he were here."

I laughed at the image and knew she was right. "Okay, go ahead." I closed my eyes and when the boot came off groaned in relief. She cut the sock off as well and I heard Sebastian whistle in shock. I opened my eyes and gasped at what used to be my foot. It was twice as big and already black and blue.

"Lie down. I'm going to have to set the bones," the healer said.

I laid back and grabbed the stick which was beside the bed to bite down on for pain and put it in my mouth. She pushed on a bone and I screamed as I bit down on the stick. It was an incredible pain, one that I did not wish to deal with for a while. Unfortunately, there was more than one bone in my foot and she went to work on the next ones. Fresh tears leaked down my face and Sebastian came to my side, holding my hand in his and letting me squeeze when I hurt.

I didn't want him to see me like this and yet I was glad that he was here. Why was he so nice to me when he hardly knew me, especially when he had treated me so coldly at first? Many of the elves here would have done the same for me, but they had known me almost my entire life. Sebastian had only known me a day and a half. Was it just in his personality to be nice?

"What's going on?" Father asked as he came into the room. "I heard her screams from down the hallway." He looked at my foot and whistled. "That looks bad. How did you manage that?"

"She was cleaning stalls and my horse stepped on her," Sebastian said. "I'm sorry I should have trained him better than that."

I pulled the stick from my mouth. "Don't apologize," I said as she moved to a new bone and prepared to set it. "It's not your fault." She set the bone before I could put the stick in and I screamed in pain and then clamped a hand over my mouth to quiet myself. "Sorry," I whispered before putting the stick back in my mouth.

"There are lots of bones in human feet," The healer said. "This is going to take a while. Would you rather I put you to sleep?"

The idea sounded great, but I hated to be a baby. I shook my head, but Father nodded his. "Knock her out. She's just trying to be tough."

"Father!" I gasped in shock.

He smiled warmly at me. "I know you well, Marin. Don't try to hide it. I know that you are trying to tough it out so that you do not appear weak."

I couldn't answer him because he was right so I just set the stick down to take the cup of medicine from the healer's hands. "I just want you to know that I'm only doing this because I know if I tried to refuse, you would hold me down and force me to drink it."

Father smiled. "You know me too well."

I drank the medicine and immediately felt woozy. "Sebastian, thank you."

"For what?" he asked. "Owning an ornery horse?"

"For pretending to care," I whispered as my eyelids closed in heaviness.

"Why would I be pretending?" he asked.

"Because you don't know me."

"You don't have to know someone for years to care," he said. "Now go to sleep so that the pain will go away."

"Goodnight and goodbye," Father said as he left.

"Bye," I whispered and then fall into a deep sleep where I dreamed of slaying ogres with Favian and Sebastian both beside me.

CHAPTER THREE

"Water," I whispered as I woke up with a dry throat and mouth. I opened my eyes and was surprised to find Sebastian sitting beside me. He handed me a glass and I drank it all in two large gulps. "What are you doing here?" I asked as I looked around at the empty room.

"I didn't want to leave you alone," he said. "And the healer left to eat so I stayed by your side in case you woke up. It turned out to be a good thing, right?"

"You didn't have to stay by me," I whispered as I sat up. My head was still a little loopy from the medicine and I almost fell off of the bed.

Sebastian caught me and helped me lay back down. "Easy, Marin. You don't need to act tough around me." He smoothed my hair down and smiled. "Your foot looks a lot better already."

I looked down at the foot which was wrapped and sighed. "I can't believe she had to cut the boot off."

"Were they a present from Favian?" he asked. I nodded my head. "Don't worry, he'll understand, or at least he should. I guess I need to find you a new pair of boots since my horse caused the destruction of these ones."

"No," I said as I shook my head. "You don't."

"Do you dislike me?" he asked as he leaned back in his chair.

"No. Why would you ask that?"

"You are pushing me away. It is subtle, but I can tell that you are keeping me at arm's length so to speak. I understand you need time to adjust, but I was hoping that while Favian was away you and I could get to know each other." What he said made sense, but… "How will you ever get to know me if you don't let me in?" he asked softly.

He was right, but I couldn't explain to him that I was keeping him at arm's length because I loved Favian and I was scared that I would confuse my love for Favian with Sebastian looking like him. I didn't want to end up confusing myself and making me think I was in love with him when I wasn't.

"I'm sorry," I answered since it was the only thing I could say.

"Apology accepted. Now, let's get you to your room. The healer has ordered you to bed rest for two days."

"I don't do bed rest," I said as I sat up slowly.

"You'll have to learn," he said as he scooped me up into his arms.

"What are you doing?" I asked in shock.

"Carrying you to your room."

"I can walk," I said a bit in exasperation. "I'm not helpless."

"No, you're not, but you aren't supposed to put any pressure on your foot and this is the easiest way to help you up the stairs."

"You're as stubborn as Favian," I said in exasperation.

"That makes me like him a little more," he said with a smile. He carried me out of the healer's room and down the hallway. I closed my eyes because the pain was starting to come back and I didn't want him to see it. He carried me up the stairs and asked, "Which is yours?"

I opened my eyes and pointed to the first door. He walked me to the bed and laid me down gently. "Thank you," I said despite the fact that I wished he hadn't carried me.

"Don't sound so mad," he said with a laugh. "No one saw us." I adjusted my pillows and he looked around my room. "This is not what I expected your room to look like."

I looked around at the pink draperies, lacy curtains and over the top girly décor and laughed. "Mother takes down any thing I put up that is not ladylike when I leave. I'm used to it now though."

"So, what do you do besides mercenary jobs?" he asked as he sat on the other side of my bed and faced me.

I felt somewhat uneasy with him in my room, but decided it didn't matter since I had a broken foot and couldn't leave anyways. "If we aren't on a mercenary job we are here at the castle," I said. "We have been trying to get as many mercenary jobs as possible so that we can become Protectors." A Protector was the highest rank a mercenary could attain and you only obtained the title after performing a large number of missions or a couple of high ranked missions. Some mercenaries never even became Protectors.

"By 'we' you mean you and Favian?" he asked.

I nodded my head. "Yes, he is my partner."

"So, I was right, you two are a couple."

I shook my head vehemently. "No! No, we are just friends."

Sebastian gave me a strange look and said, "So you two aren't in love with each other?"

I did not know how to answer that and I did not want to tell him the truth. "No, we do not love each other," I answered. It was partly true because Favian did not love me, I just loved him so technically we did not love each other.

"You're a horrible liar," he said with crossed arms.

"I'm not lying. We aren't in love with each other."

He stared at me a moment and asked, "Why not?"

That was a strange question and one I wasn't prepared for. "Um, because it wouldn't work even if we were," I said.

"What? Why not?" he asked again.

"Because it wouldn't," I answered a bit angrily. He was asking very personal questions which I did not want to answer. "He and I could never be married."

He didn't seem to believe me, but he let it go and asked, "What is your favorite weapon?"

The change in topic was drastic and I greatly appreciated it. "I don't have a favorite, but I hate archery."

"Only because you are terrible at it," Maddock said as he walked into my room.

"Maddock!" I said happily. "Where have you been?"

"I was with the Pegasus herd. I didn't know you were back yet," he said as he sat down on my side of the bed and kissed my cheek. "Why are you in bed?"

"My horse decided he disliked her and stomped on her foot," Sebastian answered.

Maddock looked at him and then his eyes widened. "My apologies Prince Sebastian. I assumed you were Favian."

Sebastian smiled pleasantly. "It's quite alright."

"Maddock, I owe you a huge debt," I said to get his attention back.

"You do?" he asked. "For what?"

I lifted the necklace which was still around my neck. "This necklace saved my life."

"Truly?" he asked in shock. I nodded my head and he asked, "What happened?"

I moved upwards on my bed so that I was sitting up higher and Sebastian grabbed my pillows and arranged them behind my back so that I could sit up easier. "Thank you," I said as I relaxed against them. "Okay, you remember that someone had hired kidnappers to kidnap me, and Favian and our parents brought me back?" I asked Maddock.

He nodded his head. "Yes, they chained you in the dungeon if I recall," he said with a smile.

I laughed, now able to laugh about the whole ordeal. "Yes, they chained me up in the dungeon."

"Why would they do that?" Sebastian asked in shock.

"Because they were trying to protect her," Maddock answered. "And they knew that they couldn't simply bring her back to the Kingdom because Marin would run back to the Academy to finish becoming a mercenary so they were forced to chain her up."

"And I did escape," I said proudly.

"Yes, how did you escape from the dungeon?" Maddock asked.

"I'll have to show you when I'm not on bed rest," I told him. "But it's a secret that Favian must not find out."

Maddock laughed and then he said, "Then on the mission for the Academy they managed to kidnap you and Favian was injured, right?"

I nodded my head and decided it was alright to tell them about the medallion. "They had a medallion that knocked me unconscious and stole some of my energy when it touched my skin."

"What?" Maddock and Sebastian asked in shock at the same time.

I nodded my head. "It has something to do with my true father's genetics, whatever they may be. So, three men kidnapped me and took me to a far off castle where the man who had hired them was. He wanted me to stop my pursuit of being a Mercenary because he didn't want other women trying to do the same thing. He had me chained in a cell and refused to feed me or give me water. He lied to me and told me that the medallion made me fall asleep for an entire day, so I thought I was down there for three days when in actuality it had only been three hours. He usually placed the medallion against my skin and then removed it, but the last time he tied it around my neck. I used the magic word and your necklace burned through the cord holding the necklace and allowed me to stay conscious. I then used it to melt the restraints and the door lock to escape from the cell."

"That necklace did all that?" Sebastian asked.

Maddock smiled proudly. "I made it myself and since you are probably wondering, there is no limit to how much it can be used."

"I was worried about that at the time," I said with a laugh.

"So how did you escape?" Maddock asked.

"When he came down to check on me, I ran up the stairs and out of the castle. Unfortunately, I was weakened from the medallion being used against me and he caught me." I swallowed as I recalled the next moments and tried to clear my emotions.

Maddock rested his hand on my arm and said, "If it is difficult to discuss you do not have to."

I smiled at him. "Thank you, friend, but I need to get over it." I took a deep breath and said, "He fought me and was winning. He tried to rape me and when that failed, because I injured him, he started choking me. I would have died if Favian had not come and tossed him off of me."

"How did Favian find you?" Sebastian asked curiously.

"He pretended to be one of the kidnappers and wore a hooded cloak the entire time so that even I didn't know it was him. I actually threatened to kill him at one point and probably would have tried since I had no idea it was him. He killed the man and started towards me, but since I didn't know it was him I ran away. He caught me and removed his hood." I felt embarrassed about the next part and said, "I thought he had been in on it the whole time and thought he had left me down there for days so I was furious with him. He explained that he had to pretend to be one of them so that he could find the location of the person looking for me and that had he not there would have been no way for them to have found me and I surely would have died."

"That is quite the tale," Maddock said as he absorbed it all. "I'm glad my necklace was able to help you."

I smiled. "As am I or I probably wouldn't be here today."

"How many times must I tell you not to have boys in your room," Mother said as she walked inside with a half teasing smile on her face.

"I'm on bed rest, Mother. I need some form of entertainment."

Maddock hugged her and she kissed his cheek since he was taller than her and could not reach the top of his head. "It is good to see you, Maddock. We miss you running through the castle."

He smiled. "I will be sure to visit more often."

"Please do," she said seriously. "Are you hungry?" she asked me. I opened my mouth to answer and she laughed. "I'm not sure why I even asked because I know you are since you are always hungry. Maddock will you help me get food for her?"

"Of course," he said with a smile as he stood up.

"Would you like some lunch as well, Sebastian?" Mother asked him.

He nodded his head. "Yes, please."

She turned and walked from my room with Maddock beside her. "She is going to lecture me later about how a proper lady does not allow male visitors inside her bed chambers," I grumbled.

"She is correct about that," Sebastian said. "But in the circumstances, I'm sure it is alright."

"I'm not worried," I said as more pain built in my foot. "I'm used to hearing her lectures by now."

"Are you in pain?" he asked.

I opened my mouth to say no and then nodded. "Some," I said.

"I'll go see if the healer has pain medicine for you."

I watched him leave and wondered if this was all real or if it was only an act. What could he gain from becoming my friend? I instantly felt bad for thinking such a thing and decided it must be because I was sort of an outsider like he was. Only the people here didn't fear him, but instantly loved him. I didn't doubt that by tomorrow he would be too busy with the other elves to even pay me mind.

Mother and Maddock came back with food and shortly after Sebastian returned with some pain medicine. Maddock told of his trip to the Pegasus herd while we ate and things almost felt normal. If it hadn't been for the fact that I missed Favian and was worried about him, I would have felt great. Father summoned Maddock away, which left Sebastian alone with me. He cleaned up the food mess and then sat back on the bed facing me.

"So, are you ready to get outside?" he asked me.

"I'm on bed rest," I reminded him. Favian would have been tying me to the bed instead of offering to let me outside.

"Yes, but you can lie down outside, right?"

"Yes," I said with a smile.

"Then I shall carry you to the fields where Amile interrupted us and you can nap out there."

"You are not going to carry me," I said seriously.

He picked me up and said, "You have no choice."

I groaned, but let him carry me out of the castle and to the field since I did not want to injure myself further and delay my healing. I looked around to see if anyone had watched us, but it didn't appear so. He set me down in my area of the field and I stared up at the blue sky with wispy clouds slowly moving across it.

He lay down next to me and said, "I could get used to this."

"It is peaceful," I said as I closed my eyes and relaxed.

We dozed silently beside each other until the sun began to set and then he carried me back to my room and retrieved more pain medicine from the healer. The longer I spent with him, the more comfortable I became around him. He had an incredibly quiet and gentle disposition that somehow also made me feel safe. Or was that because of his similarity to Favian? Was I confusing my feelings for one to the other?

I couldn't decide, but I shoved the thoughts away and tried to get to know him better. "What is your favorite time of year?" I asked as I showed him how to fold pieces of paper into animal shapes.

"Winter," he answered right away.

"Winter?" I asked in shock. "Why?"

"Because I love snow and having a fire in the fireplace. What is yours?"

"Spring because it is sunny and cool and the perfect time to go on missions."

"You don't like winter?" he asked.

I shook my head. "I don't like the cold. At some point every winter, I always end up in the icy river. And snow always makes camping harder when we are out on missions."

"You camp outdoors on missions in the winter?" he asked in shock.

I nodded my head. "Yes."

"How do you stay warm?" he asked.

"We use a tarp and branches to keep the new snow from falling on us and usually end up sharing a sleeping bag and lying the second one underneath us so that it keeps us warmer," I said as I finished folding a crane. I realized what I said, but it was too late to take the statement back and honestly, I shouldn't be made to feel bad because nothing intimate ever happened between Favian and me. It was only done as a survival and comfort thing. Yet, part of me worried what Sebastian would think.

"What is your favorite type of meat?" he asked, seeming to have ignored the comment or understood what I meant.

"Beef."

"Really? I would have thought pork was your favorite."

I shook my head. "I love bacon, but beef is my absolute favorite. What's yours?"

"Duck," he said with a smile.

"I've never had duck before."

His mouth dropped open. "You have never eaten duck meat?" I shook my head. "Well we are just going to have to change that."

"I won't kill a duck just to eat it," I said.

He looked appalled and said, "Neither will I, but there are surely ducks around that have died from natural causes."

"What's your favorite weapon?" I asked.

"The sword," he said. "But I also like the dagger quite a bit for close combat."

"It does come in very handy," I agreed with a smile.

He groaned in frustration and held up his mangled crane. "I cannot seem to get this right."

I laughed and flattened out the edges and said, "You almost have it. You just have to flatten it out more."

He watched me do it and then picked up another piece of paper and tried again. He concentrated very hard and after a moment held up a perfect crane. "Now I understand," he said with a proud smile.

I smiled back. "Perfect."

We spent several more hours folding various animals and then it was dinner time. I expected them to feed me in my room, but Sebastian carried me to the ballroom, despite my protests, and set me down in my chair.

"How are you feeling?" Father asked.

"Frustrated at the moment," I said as I straightened my shirt.

"Your foot will heal soon and you will be as good as new," Father said with a smile.

Dinner was delicious as always and relatively quiet. I wanted to ask about Favian, but knew no word would have returned yet. Sebastian tried to carry me back up the stairs, but I refused this time with an elbow to his ribs, making him put his arm around me and only assist me as I hobbled along, not carry me. He smiled the entire time, so at least he wasn't upset that I refused to let him carry me.

We resumed making our paper animals and I showed Sebastian how to make three different kinds. We had worked three more hours and used up most of the paper supply that I had when a yawn escaped as I worked on another animal. "It seems that my body is stealing my energy to heal itself," I said as I continued folding the paper.

"I shouldn't have kept you up so late. I'm sorry," Sebastian said.

We piled our paper animals together and he placed them on my nightstand. They looked like a little army preparing for battle and it brought a smile to my face imagining them attacking other paper animals. Tomorrow I would have to make some sinister paper animals for them to fight. "Thank you for keeping me entertained all day," I said sincerely. "And for taking me outside."

"It was my pleasure," he said with a bow. "Would you like to eat breakfast in the ballroom or here tomorrow?" he asked.

"I'm sure Mother has Elf things for you to be learning and doing. You shouldn't waste your days with me." I said it because it was true, but truthfully, I enjoyed his company.

"I think my time is being well spent," he said and then a sad look crossed his face. "Unless I'm pestering you and making you uncomfortable?"

"No," I said with a shake of my head. "I had fun today. I just know that it is important to spread out your time with the various aspects of being a royal Elf. Usually I would be taking classes with Mother on etiquette and dancing and I'm not even the Prince."

"Well I am relieved you do not view me as a pest and perhaps you are right. Amadis did mention something like that. I will speak to her tonight and find out if there is a schedule or things I should be doing. I enjoyed spending the day with you today. I'll try to make time to come see you tomorrow, if that is alright?"

"I'd like that," I said honestly.

He walked around the bed and kissed my cheek. "Goodnight, Marin."

I was too stunned that he'd kissed me to do more than mumble "night" and watch him close my bedroom door. The butterflies I felt when Favian kissed me were fluttering like crazy. As much as I wanted to believe that it was due to their similar appearance, I knew that was not the case. I had spent the entire day with him and not once had I confused him for Favian.

I laid down and rubbed my face. I loved Favian, but I couldn't have him. Could I be with anyone else? Could I let myself fall for another man?

I couldn't be with a man that I did not love. It wouldn't be fair to him and I would probably end up making myself miserable. Why did life have to be so complicated?

CHAPTER FOUR

When I hobbled down to breakfast the next morning, Father had a gift waiting for me. "I made you some crutches," he said as he held them out to me when I entered the ballroom. "I figured you were going to hobble around the kingdom and damage your foot no matter what we said, so at least with these you won't injure your foot further."

"Thank you," I said as I hugged him. "I was actually planning on getting a log to use as a cane."

Mother shook her head. "Why can't you just let yourself heal, Marin?"

"I'm bored, Mother. I hate sitting her doing nothing, especially when Kato and Favian are off on some secret mission."

Chef set a tray on my plate and then one across from me.

"Will you ask Sebastian to come see me once he is finished eating?" Chef asked me.

I nodded my head. "Okay."

Sebastian came in a few minutes later and took his seat across from me. "Good morning."

"Good morning," I replied.

"Are you busy after breakfast?" he asked.

I shook my head. "No."

"Would you join me for a quick ride?"

"She cannot ride with a broken leg," Mother reminded him.

"Normally I would agree, but my horse has an extremely smooth gait, which I believe will not jar her leg."

"His horse is very smooth," Father answered.

"I don't think your horse likes me too much," I reminded him.

Sebastian said, "I promise he will be on his best behavior."

"Where are we going?" I asked suspiciously.

He smiled. "It's a surprise."

I looked at Mother, but she was suddenly very interested in her bread, as was Father. "Okay, but I need to change first."

"You mean you have to get your weapons first," Sebastian said with a smirk.

How did he know that was what I wanted? He couldn't possibly know. "A mercenary must always be ready for battle," I said as I stabbed a piece of egg.

"Of course," he said with the same smirk.

I resisted the urge to throw my bread roll at him, only because Mother was present.

"How long will you be gone?" Mother asked him. "I would like to go over some things with you."

"A couple of hours. I'll be sure to find you as soon as we return," he said as he picked up a piece of bacon.

I finished my food and said, "Oh, before we go you need to go see the Chef. He said he wanted to speak with you. I'll go change while you do that."

"Meet me at the stables."

I nodded my head and grabbed my crutches, using them to stand up and make my way out of the ballroom. Father followed me and once we were outside of the ballroom he laid a hand on my shoulder to stop me. "Marin, I know this is difficult for you. Favian and Sebastian I mean. Just promise me that you won't do anything to cause the brothers to quarrel. We need them to get along."

"Father!" I said indignantly. "I have done nothing of the sort and won't. Honestly, how could you even say something like that?"

"I love you, Marin, but sometimes you can be very dense," he said as he ruffled my hair.

Before I could find anything to say in reply, he walked away leaving me baffled in the hallway. Parents were so strange sometimes, especially old Elvish ones. The stairs took a lot longer than I had anticipated and by the time I had changed clothes and retrieved my weapons, Sebastian was waiting for me outside my bedroom. "Sorry, I am a bit slower with the crutches."

He shrugged. "I'm in no rush."

We walked in silence out of the castle and towards the stables. As soon as we entered, Alex greeted me with a hug. "How's your foot?"

I was shocked at the affection, but dismissed it as concern since we had known each other a long time. "It's healing rather slowly."

He laughed. "You just have cabin fever," he said. "Being out in the fresh air will do you some good. You're looking a little pale."

I scoffed. "Says the pale-skinned elf."

He playfully pushed me and then turned to Sebastian who held his horse, bridled, but with no saddle and ready to go. "If your horse hurts her again, I will be forced to train him myself. I will not allow a horse in this Kingdom who does not respect Marin."

"I assure you that he will never do something like that again," Sebastian said as he affectionately petted his horse's nose. "Are you ready, Marin?"

"Yes."

Alex leaned my crutches against the side of the stall and then grabbed me around the waist. "Up you go." He lifted me from the ground and tossed me up onto the horse's back. "You good?" Alex asked as I adjusted my seat on his wide back.

"Yes."

Sebastian jumped up in front of me and gathered his reins. "Slow and easy," he whispered to his horse. His horse walked out of the stables obediently.

Luckily Sebastian was right, his horse was very smooth and hardly jarred me at all. It allowed me to ride without even holding on to Sebastian. "So, where are we going?" I asked.

"Well I know how much you hate being cooped up, so I found a spot where we could spend time outside and without anyone bothering us. Just wait until you see it."

I leaned back with my hands on his horse's rump and closed my eyes, enjoying the slow sway of his walk. "What's your horse's name?"

"Carino, it means nice."

I couldn't help it, I laughed. "How fitting."

Sebastian turned and smiled. "He generally is nice. I'm not sure why he didn't like you."

I shrugged and closed my eyes again. "There are many who are not fond of me."

He stopped Carino and dismounted, helping me down as well. We were beside the river, but weeping willow trees surrounded us and blocked us from anyone who may have been riding down the road's view. It was beautiful, as most things in the Elven Kingdom are, and exactly a place I would have picked myself. He helped me to a spot in the grass where he already had a blanket laid out and sat down beside me.

"It's a perfect spot," I admitted.

He smiled, pleased with my reaction. "I knew you would like it."

"So, what was it like being raised by humans? Were you in a town? Did you get picked on?" I asked.

"If I answer some questions about myself then you have to answer some questions about yourself as well. Deal?"

I was nervous about the questions he would ask me, but nodded my head in agreement. I needed to know more about him.

"I was raised by two elderly humans who could not have children of their own. They said they found me on their doorstep one night and believed the God and Goddess had sent me to them for their loyalty and devout worship. I was three when they found me. They taught me to farm and I helped tend to their crops and take them to town to be sold. We lived far out of town so I didn't have to deal with other humans except when we went to town to sell our crops. They knew elves don't eat meat, but it was a staple of their diet so they found ways around it. They researched the elves and made trades with some so that I could learn the important things I needed to know. It was a quiet life and I had no idea who my parents were until I ran into the man you and Favian had worked with before. Once I found out, I came here to see if it was true."

"Was it hard, not knowing who your parents were?" I asked even though I guessed the answer since it was driving me crazy not knowing who my father was.

"Of course, but I was well loved by my human parents and Cesar and Amadis have been nothing but loving since I returned here."

I smiled fondly. "Yes, they are wonderful."

"Your turn," he said as he pulled a piece of grass from the ground and began rolling it between his thumb and finger. "What was it like to be raised by elves?"

"It was difficult, but I managed."

He rolled his eyes. "Come on, give me some more insight than that."

I laughed. "Alright. Cesar and Amadis are wonderfully loving and treated me as they treated Favian. I always had issues with not being as strong as the others, but that was more my problem than it was anyone else's. I just hated being so weak compared to the others. Favian taught me in secret how to fight until Father caught us one night. I was a bit of a hellion, constantly getting in fights and despite Amadis' protests at first, she finally agreed that I needed an outlet for my seemingly endless anger. So, I was allowed in the arena. Kato, Father, and Favian worked with me and taught me to fight so that I could protect myself and at least stand up to an Elf for a few seconds. When Favian told me about Macon Academy and about being a Protector, defending the people of the lands, I knew it was for me."

"I've heard some of the elves talking about you. Did you really kill over two hundred ogres by yourself?"

I had worried he would hear about that. "Yes," I answered without looking at him, fearing the expression on his face.

"I also heard that you had killed an ogre when you were only four, when Cesar found you. Do you remember it?"

I opened my eyes to avoid the flashback, but the mind is able to see multiple things at once and despite my attempt, I was back there again. "I was only a child so I do not remember everything. I remember being incredibly sad that my parents were dead. I remember being frightened when one of the ogres came after me, but then everything turned red and the next thing I remember was holding on to Cesar, crying, and asking him to protect me. Cesar and Kato witnessed me kill one of the ogres and I remember Amadis scrubbing my body with a rag to get all of the ogre blood off of me."

I felt tears running down my cheeks and wiped at them.

"I don't even remember my mother or what she looks like," I whispered.

Sebastian hugged me and whispered, "I'm sure she was as beautiful as you are."

I pulled back from him and said, "Who could my father be? What *am* I?"

He smiled. "You're Marin, daughter of Amadis and Cesar, and one of the most beautiful women I have ever seen."

I laughed and wiped my face. "You are a terrible flatterer."

"I only speak the truth," he said.

I leaned towards him, wanting to be closer to him, to have him hold me and was saved by the sound of approaching hooves. "Greetings, Marin and Sebastian," Jovian called as he dismounted his horse and let it drink from the river.

"Hello Jovian," I said pleasantly. What on earth was going on in my head!

"Greetings," Sebastian said with a smile. "What are you doing over on this side of the Kingdom?"

Jovian shrugged. "I often ride out here and train my horse since there is usually no one here. I heard your voices and thought I would come say hello."

"How is your training going?" I asked as I looked at his horse, King. King was one of the few horses I had helped with during foal season. The poor stallion had had a hoof caught inside of his mother and she was unable to push him out. Had I not been there to adjust his legs, they both would have died. King finished drinking and walked over to me, nudging my cheek with his nose. "Hello, King. You have grown since I last saw you."

Jovian smiled. "He is still very fond of you. Of course, I guess I would be as well if you had saved my mother's and my life."

I rubbed the stallion's nose and said, "You be nice to him, Jovian or I'll get you."

Jovian laughed. "I wouldn't want to get on your bad side. I've seen what happens then."

"What happens?" Sebastian asked.

Jovian said, "It depends. Sometimes she just plays a prank on you, such as causing a bucket of mud to fall on you when you enter a building. Other times she will challenge you to a duel."

"A duel?" Sebastian asked in shock. "You've fought in a duel against elves?"

I shrugged. "Only twice and both times they deserved what they had coming."

"You won?" Sebastian asked in double shock.

I frowned at him. "I'm not a weakly human as you saw, Sebastian. I can hold my own and on occasion win against an elf."

"Especially when they think she's weak," Jovian said. "But Marin does have a kind heart and against what I thought should have been done, let them live."

"I wasn't going to kill them over insulting my lineage."

Jovian smiled cruelly. "I would have."

"Yes, you are quite a brute," I said with mock seriousness.

Jovian laughed. "You're lucky I like you."

I rolled my eyes. "You are amused by me. Which is why you have let me beat you in matches."

Jovian shook his head. "To me, you have always been one of us, Marin and you always will be. Well I better be off. Come on King."

King nudged my cheek once more and then followed his owner out of the cover of the trees and out of sight of us. That had to be one of the strangest interactions with Jovian I had yet to have.

"It seems you have quite a few suitors," Sebastian teased.

I yanked a piece of grass from the ground and said, "I have no suitors and never will."

"What?" he asked in shock.

"Never mind," I answered. I really did not want to talk about it with him. "Have you been to the Pegasus herd yet?" I asked to change the topic.

He nodded his head. "Yes, I met the herd. Their land is beautiful and their drinking hole is..."

"I'm not allowed there so I have not seen it," I said bitterly.

"What?" he asked with raised eyebrows. "Why not?"

"It is a rule that no human can ever enter the Pegasi lands."

He digested that and sighed. "Well, I am sorry. It is a place that I know you would enjoy."

"I wonder when Favian will return," I said softly.

"Am I boring you?" he asked with a teasing smile.

"Of course not. I just worry about his safety when I'm not there to guard his back."

"So, you two really aren't courting?" he asked softly.

I shook my head. "I told you, I am not being courted by anyone."

"Why is that?" he asked. "You're beautiful and I see the way many of the elves here look at you."

"Most likely because I am a human. Plus, most men like to court a lady and I am not exactly ladylike, if you haven't noticed."

"I've noticed," he said with a smirk.

Something about that smirk, a smile so unlike anything that ever crossed Favian's face, made him distinctly Sebastian. It made me want to smack him and kiss him at the same time. I jerked back at the realization that I might be falling for Sebastian. I could not fall for him.

We sat by each other in silence for at least an hour before he finally said, "Well, I guess we should head back."

"Yes, I suppose we should. You need to meet up with Mother to get started on your princely training."

He rolled his eyes. "Oh joy."

I laughed. "It is not so bad. She has a way of making even the dreariest tasks seem fun when she is there."

He stood up and held out his hand to help me up, but being the stubborn person that I am, I stood up on my own. Immediately I feel forward, straight into him when I put pressure on my foot. He caught me and helped me stand up straight. "You shouldn't put pressure on it yet."

I stared into his eyes and felt as lost in them as I did in Favian's. How could a pair of eyes cause so many different emotions in me? And why were Sebastian's causing these feelings as well? Sebastian pushed back a strand of my hair and whispered, "I am glad that I came back in time to meet you."

I smiled. "I'm glad to finally know about you."

He helped me onto Carino and we went back to the stables where Alex assisted me in dismounting. "Did you have a nice time? No foot stomping incidents?"

I laughed. "No, Carino was well behaved this time."

Sebastian put the horse in his stall and said, "And he will be every time after as well."

"Are you off to some other adventure now?" Alex asked me.

I shook my head. "Sebastian is off to lessons with Mother, but I have no plans, except to prop up this foot."

Alex smiled. "Would you mind assisting me with some chores?"

I smiled. "Of course."

"Great," Alex said happily.

"I better head off to find Amadis," Sebastian said, drawing my attention back to him.

Alex walked to the back of the stables where the tack room was and I turned to Sebastian. "Okay. Just remember that you don't have to memorize everything right away. You will have some leeway on remembering everything."

"Can I come see you after?" he asked quietly.

I wasn't sure why he was asking my permission, but I nodded my head anyways. "Yeah."

He smiled. "Great, I'll see you later." He kissed my cheek and hurried out of the stables.

"You may regret agreeing to assist me," Alex said as he set three chairs down and a pile of dirty bridles.

"Tack cleaning?" I groaned. "You could have warned me what it was before I agreed to it."

"But then you wouldn't have agreed to help me," he said with a laugh.

I sat down in one of the chairs, propped my foot up on another and then grabbed a bridle to start cleaning. "So, what do you do for fun?" I asked Alex.

"I usually play with the foals or go visit the Pegasus herd."

I sighed longingly. "I wish I could visit the Pegasus herd."

Alex rubbed the bridle vigorously, getting caked on dirt to fall off. "I'm sorry that law is in effect, but you have visited with a couple of them and ridden one."

"Yes, but it's not the same as being able to visit them. I really want to see the foals. I can just imagine how beautiful they are."

Alex nodded his head. "They are. So, how long are you going to stay here?"

I shrugged. "I'm not sure. I know I have to stay long enough to heal my foot and make sure that I'm fully able to return to mercenary work, but I am already going crazy."

"I think that is mostly because Favian is not here and you are dealing with Sebastian as well. I would probably be going crazy if I was you too."

"It's not so bad," I admitted. Except for the fact that I *was* going crazy and was very confused. We worked in companionable silence until all of the tack was clean. It was nice to have another person I could work with so easily and feel so comfortable with.

"Well, now that we are done, would you like to get some lunch?" Alex asked.

"Yes, I'm starving," I said as I stood up and hobbled on my good leg.

"Let me put this in the tack room and then we can head to the Blacksmith's building for lunch."

I smiled. "I haven't visited Baldemar in a long time. That sounds great."

"Great, I'll be right back."

I limped over to Fire's stall and pet her nose. "Hi, girl. How are you?" She nickered and nudged my shoulder. I ran my hand down her neck and sighed. "I'm sorry that I'm hurt and we can't go for a ride. I'll ask Alex to let you out in the pastures later."

"You ready?" Alex asked with my crutches in his hand.

I took them from him and started hobbling out of the stables. "Yes. My stomach is growling louder than a bear after hibernation."

Alex laughed. "Well I'm sure that Baldemar has a cure for that."

Elves waved to us or dipped their heads in acknowledgment to me, but none talked to me. I ignored my sadness and hobbled on my crutches into the blacksmith's barn, which was hot and made sweat instantly bead on my skin.

"Who goes there?" asked a booming voice from within the building.

"Alex and Marin," Alex called back. "We've come to see if you might share some bread with us."

Out of the shadows from behind the forge came an elf with muscles that only those who worked with him could boast about, muscles that one usually only saw on humans. He was tall, broad shouldered with silver hair down to his knees that he kept in a braid to keep it from getting burnt in the forge or smashed when he made items. "Marin? Little Marin who used to steal swords from my wall when she was a toddler?"

I laughed and curtsied to the famous blacksmith. "Hello, sir."

Baldemar hugged me tightly against his chest. "Don't be so formal girl. You're like a daughter to me. A pesky, sword stealing daughter."

"I haven't stolen a sword since I was ten," I reminded him.

"But you are the only one to have ever stolen from him, more than once," Alex said.

"What happened to your foot?" Baldemar asked.

"Horse stomped on it and broke it," I said.

Baldemar looked at Alex in shock. "A horse in *your* stables stomped on her foot?"

"It was Sebastian's," Alex said defensively. "And I warned her that he was temperamental."

"Dad we have the food on the table," the twins said.

I smiled at the twin male elves, Farrar and Fabron, who were almost identical copies of their father. "Hi guys."

"Marin!" They said excitedly at the same time.

I hugged the very affectionate twins and then followed them to their table on the farthest side of the barn, leaning my crutches against the side of the table. "How are your lessons going?" I asked Farrar and Fabron, not bothering to ask one of them specifically since they always answered things together.

"Good," they said in unison.

"They're getting close to mastering swords," Baldemar said as he set rolls of bread on each of our plates. The bread was hot and I could smell melted butter on it. "Please, eat."

I took a bite of the bread and felt a smile on my face instantly. "This is delicious."

"I made it," Farrar and Fabron said with broad smiles.

"Are you sure you won't become bakers?" Alex asked them half seriously. "This is great."

"They bake on the side a lot. They spend any more time doing it and they will be bakers instead of blacksmiths," Baldemar teased his sons. "So, Marin, how are you liking being a Mercenary?"

"I love it," I answered him between bites. "Favian and I have been traveling all over doing missions. Although, I have to admit that it was nice to come home for a little while and sleep in a real bed."

"How long will you be staying?" Farrar and Fabron asked.

I shrugged. "I'm not sure. Favian is off on a mission for Father right now so I can't leave until he returns anyways, but I believe Mother wants us to stay for the official ball for Prince Sebastian's return."

"How are you dealing with the new Prince?" Baldemar asked with a knowing look on his face.

Did everyone know how I felt about Favian?! "Fine," I responded softly.

"I cannot tell them apart yet. Have you figured out a way?" Baldemar asked.

I laughed bitterly. "Only their voice so far. Though I have considered smearing some juiceberries on one of them to stain them for a little while, but I don't think they would appreciate that."

Everyone laughed and Baldemar said, "Or you could cut one of them somewhere visible so you would see their bandage and know which was which."

That was actually a really good idea that I should have thought of myself.

"You cannot cut one of them," Alex said seriously to me.

"Oh, come on. I could just give one of them a little cut on their cheeks that could scar and then we would never have problems telling them apart again," I said with an evil grin.

Farrar and Fabron said, "Sounds like a good idea to me."

Alex shook his head. "You shouldn't encourage her."

We finished our bread and Baldemar asked to see my weapons. I followed him to his work bench and laid my swords and daggers out on the bench. He took one look at the daggers and groaned. "Boys, tend to these."

Farrar and Fabron each took three of my daggers and then went to their separate work benches to clean and sharpen them.

"You need to treat your weapons better, Marin," Baldemar chastised me.

"I clean them after a battle, but ogre blood is difficult to clean," I complained.

He examined my swords closely, but never touched the blades. "Would you be willing to leave these with me for a day?"

"Can you give me some loaners? I hate to be without swords."

Baldemar stood up and walked to the wall where he hung all of the weapons he had recently finished. "I think these might be adequate replacements for now," he said as he handed me two identical swords with shiny black pommels. "I should only need your weapons for one day. Come back tomorrow night and I will give them back."

"Thank you," I said sincerely as I put the swords in my sheaths on my belt. "And thank you for lunch as well."

"Thank the boys, I didn't make it."

"Thank you, Farrar and Fabron," I said with a little bow to them since it was difficult to give them a formal bow on crutches.

"Bye Marin," they called from their benches where they were vigorously cleaning my daggers.

Alex said goodbye to the family and then we headed back to the stables. "Do you need help with any other chores?" I asked him while he checked each horse to ensure they hadn't done anything to injure themselves while we were gone.

"I'm going to turn them out in the pastures in a minute and I had planned just to watch them play. I'd enjoy your company if you don't have anything else to do," he said with a smile.

I knew he was flirting and I realized that I was enjoying it. It had been a while since any males had flirted with me, aside from Sebastian. "I'd help you lead them to the pastures, but my crutches are burdensome for leading horses."

"Why don't you go wait at the pastures while I get them together and take them out there?" he suggested.

I would have rather tried to help, but knew I would most likely get in the way in my current condition. So, I took his advice and made my way to the pastures, sitting down against a tree which had a perfect view of the three pastures. Alex walked out of the stables with the horses all obediently following behind him in a straight line with no bridles or ropes at all. I used to believe he had magical powers or used a spell on the horses because whenever I tried to get more than one horse to listen to me at a time, they ran away. For Alex though, the horses walked quietly and slowly along and obeyed as he separated the mares into one pasture, the stallions into another and the foals into the third. Once all of the gates were securely shut, he sat beside me, pushing my shoulder over so he could lean against part of the tree as well.

"I swear you use a spell on them to get them to behave so well," I whispered as the horses started running up and down the pasture.

He laughed. "No. But thank you for the compliment."

"I wish I was as skilled with the horses as you are. I have always envied you for that," I admitted to him.

"I've always envied you for your fighting skills, so I guess we are even," he said with a sweet smile.

"How can you be envious of my fighting skills when you are better than me?" I asked curiously. I had seen him fight in the arena and he was almost as good as Favian.

"True, I am able to win against you in a fight, but I envy how much you enjoy fighting and how skilled you are for your lineage. I also envy your determination. I watched you many times when you would sneak off at night and practice with Favian. No matter how many times he knocked you down, you continued to get back up and practice."

I wasn't sure how to reply to that, so I chose silence and watched the horses. It was nice to sit and watch Fire playing with other horses. I felt bad that she was not with a herd most of the time, since horses were herd animals. Unfortunately, I could not do anything about that unless I gave her up, but then I would just have to take another horse and it would be the same thing all over again.

"Have you ever been hurt by a horse?" I asked Alex. Now seemed the best time to get to know him a little better. I felt bad for having known him most of my life and yet not knowing anything about him.

"Many times," he said with a nod of his head. "Once I had a mare bite me because I entered her stall with her newborn foal. She was just being protective, which is natural, but I spent many hours with her after that to ensure she understood that things like that were not okay when it came to elves. I've been stepped on, bitten, kicked and even bucked and reared off just like every other rider."

It was hard to imagine horses doing these things to him since I had only ever seen the horses obey his every wish. "Wow, I just never imagined the Horse Master would have those kinds of problems."

He shrugged. "Every horse is different and you have to witness their problems before you can begin to try to fix them."

"Where are your parents?" I asked since I had no idea who they were and had never met them, to my knowledge.

"My parents died when I was only five, about the time that you came here. The previous Horse Master took me in since he was friends with my parents and taught me everything that he knew. He died when I was twelve and I inherited the title and the responsibilities. At first Queen Amadis was opposed to the idea of me becoming Horse Master so young, but after witnessing me taming a wild mare, she changed her mind."

"I wish Mother would be proud of me in my job," I whispered.

"The Queen is very proud of you, Marin. I have heard her boast to others about your accomplishments."

I wasn't sure if I believed him, but it did make me feel better. "So, why haven't you begun courting females?" I asked him, no longer able to hide my curiosity.

He shrugged nonchalantly. "There are a few who draw my attention, but they are out of my league."

"Out of your league?" I asked. "How?"

He plucked a piece of grass and ripped it in half slowly. "I'm just a stable boy and I know my place. None of the ladies I fancy could ever want a man who smells of manure every day."

"I think you smell wonderful," I said before I could stop myself.

He laughed and kissed my cheek. "That's kind of you, but I am afraid you are the exception, not the rule."

"So, who is it that you fancy?"

He shook his head. "That is my secret and I shall not part with it."

Drat. I had hoped he would tell me so that I could try to set him up.

The sky began to darken as day shifted to night and the horses stopped playing, waiting by the gates so that they could go back to the barn to be fed. I was getting hungry as well, but didn't want to spoil the nice night that we were having. Luckily, he stood up and herded the horses into the barn to feed them. I followed behind, watching as he talked to the horses as though they were his children and fed them their dinners. How could such a kind, gentle, talented and amazing elf think he wasn't worthy of a female? It was the females who were not worthy of him.

CHAPTER FIVE

"Good evening, Marin," Sebastian said softly from behind me at the entrance of the stables.

I turned and smiled at him. "Hello, Sebastian."

He looked incredibly handsome in a full formal suit which was usually worn for balls and other fancy events. "Would you do me the honor of joining me for dinner?" he asked in a very princely tone.

I curtsied as best as I could with the crutches and broken foot and said, "I would be honored to." A wide smile split his face and I said, "Your lessons with Amadis are going well I take it?"

He nodded his head. "Yes, but there is much to learn and remember."

Alex approached us.

"Thank you for keeping me busy today so that I didn't go stir crazy with this broken foot," I said once he was close to us.

He smiled happily. "You're welcome. I enjoyed spending time with you. If you ever need some distraction, feel free to come help me clean tack again."

I laughed and nodded my head. "I'll do that."

He picked my hand up and kissed the back of it softly. "I had a great time today. Thank you."

Surprised by his gesture, I wasn't sure what to say at first, but finally managed to say. "I had fun as well."

"Shall we go to dinner?" Sebastian suggested. "We shouldn't keep the King and Queen waiting."

I nodded my head and followed behind him out of the stables, taking one last look back at Alex who was smiling as if he had been given a Pegasus. After a few minutes of silence Sebastian asked, "Did you have a nice time?"

"Yes," I answered, looking at him curiously. Was he jealous? No, he couldn't be jealous. Yet he had a strange tone to his voice that I had not heard before. "So, what did you learn today?"

"Proper greetings and etiquette that I already knew, but it was nice to have a refresher course since I will need to use them soon."

"Soon?" I asked. "Where are you going?"

"They're having the feast for my return once Favian has returned, remember?"

Actually, I had forgotten. "Of course, I didn't forget," I said with a smile.

He laughed. "You're a horrible liar."

"I am actually very skilled in deceit," I said in indignation.

"Most females are," he said with a wink and then opened the door to the castle for me.

"Males hide things instead of using deceit," I said as we walked down the hallway.

"I don't know what you're talking about," he said, but I could see a slight smile forming on his lips.

"Males especially hide their feelings, which is very frustrating."

"I do not hide my feelings," he said with a sideways glance at me.

"Really?" I asked. "Then why were you upset when we left the stables?"

He opened his mouth and then snapped it shut. "I don't know what you're talking about."

I laughed and opened the door to the ballroom. "That, my friend, just proved my point."

"Hello, Daughter," Mother said with a smile. "Did you have a nice day today?"

I sat down and leaned my crutches against the wall behind me. "I did."

"What did you do?" Father asked from his chair where he was slouching comfortably and watching me with an amused look on his face. He was hiding something, something he wanted to say or ask me, but hadn't yet. It worried me when he looked like that.

"I helped Alex with some chores and then we watched the horses play in the pastures." I stopped and then asked, "Do you think it's wrong of me to keep Fire from belonging to a herd?"

Father's amused look faded a little at my serious question. "I think Ice and she have their own little herd of two when you are out on missions."

"What would you do if it were wrong? Would you not use a horse?" Sebastian asked.

"I honestly do not know," I admitted. "I just worry that I should be doing something differently with her sometimes."

"Dinner is served," the chef said as he wheeled in a cart with our trays on it.

We ate in silence and despite my better judgment I asked, "Have you heard from Favian or Kato?"

Father shook his head. "Not yet, but I'm sure they are alright."

I hoped they were and knew that I should trust Kato to keep his word. Besides, if Kato couldn't protect Favian, then there was no way that I could.

After dinner Sebastian escorted me to my room and we resumed making paper animals. This time we made the opposing army and Sebastian learned the new animals quickly.

"You seem distracted," Sebastian whispered after a few minutes of silent paper folding.

"I'm sorry," I said sincerely. "I'm being rude."

He shrugged. "I'm just enjoying spending time with you, but if you would like to talk about whatever it is that is bothering you, I'm all ears."

"Have you ever met a demon?" I asked softly.

He stopped folding his jumping frog and met my eyes. "I met a demon once, when I was about six. Why?"

I folded my crane a couple more times and then asked, "Do I resemble one to you?" I had wanted to ask him since the day at the arena, but until now had been too embarrassed to.

"No. Why would you ask me that?"

"When you saw me fighting you..."

He interrupted me and picked my hands up in his. "I was a fool and said a cruel thing only because I was impressed by your skill."

Despite my attempts not to like it, I enjoyed him holding my hands in his and having his undivided attention on me. "Could it be possible that I am part demon?"

He studied me for several seconds and then released my hands to sit back. I resisted the urge to rub my now cold hands together and waited for his response. "It is possible for people to be possessed by demons, but I do not believe that you are possessed."

"What if my father was a demon and impregnated my mother?" I asked.

He shook his head. "You are a good person, Marin. Why would you think that you could be part demon?"

"I do not know *what* I am! That is the problem. I know that I am human and something else. My father is a mystery that I must unravel, but I have no idea where to start and no clue what to expect. What if my father is something evil and what if that makes me…"

"You could never be evil, Marin. Besides, it does not matter what your birth father is, but how your father, Cesar, raised you. It does not matter what you are, but who you are."

He was right, but I was still worried. I was tired of worrying about it so I decided to change the topic. "Why didn't you ever come to the Elven Kingdom before? You obviously knew you were an elf. Why not come here and find your parents?"

He resumed folding our paper army and said, "I thought about it a lot as a kid. I even planned out a trip to come here when I was ten."

"Why didn't you?" I asked softly.

"Generally, males try to hide their weaknesses from females."

"It helps if we know your weaknesses so that we can help you and try to assist you in your moments of weakness."

He set down his finished jumping frog and sighed. "I was afraid that they had sent me away because they did not want me. I did not want to return and be turned away instead of welcomed."

I was incredibly shocked by his confession. "How do you feel now?" I asked because I knew he had indeed been welcomed by Mother and Father.

He laughed. "Now I wish I had come years ago. Perhaps then I could have attended Macon Academy with you and Favian and been able to grow with you and know you. Now I must take as much time as you will give me to learn as much as I can about you."

"Why would you care to know about me?" I asked him with my heart in my throat.

He leaned closer to me and whispered, "I want to know about your past, your present, and what you want for your future. I want to know *you*."

I found myself mesmerized by his lips which were closer to me now. "Why me when you can have your choice of any female in these lands? Why do you care to know me?"

"Because you are beautiful, smart, funny, and one of the most intriguing beings I have ever met," he whispered as he moved even closer to me.

We were so close together now that I could feel his body heat as though I were next to a fire. I could not come to a decision about whether to kiss him or not despite the overwhelming urge to kiss him. Luckily, I was saved from making the decision when someone knocked on my door and pushed it open. I sprang away from Sebastian as though he were a poisonous snake and pretended that I was getting more paper for us to fold and trying my hardest to ignore my now throbbing broken foot which I had landed on.

"Marin, have you seen… Oh there you are," Mother said with a pleasant smile on her face. "Could you come with me Sebastian?"

He gathered his jumping frogs and set them on my dresser beside the rest of the paper army. "Of course." He stopped between me and the door and turned to me. "Good night, Marin."

"Night," I managed to say in a whisper before my throat constricted again. I could tell he wanted to say something, but with Mother there he had no option to.

"Good night, Daughter."

"Good night, Mother," I said as she closed the door behind her.

I threw myself onto my bed and screamed into the comforter. What was I doing? I had almost kissed him! How could I be stupid enough to do this?! I screamed again into my comforter and mentally kicked myself. I could not hurt Sebastian by making him think we could be together. I loved Favian and since I could not have him I could not have anyone. It was possible that the only reason I was even falling for him was because he looked like Favian. I tried my hardest to ignore the nagging voice in my head telling me that I knew that wasn't true since I knew very well that he was Sebastian and not Favian. I still could not take that chance. I refused to hurt him.

I really wanted to go kill something, but with the broken foot I wasn't able to do much, so that idea was out. I needed to do something productive though. I closed my eyes and focused on the flame within me that was my magic. Favian had taught me how to increase my power and I hoped that maybe if I did so now I could speed up my healing, or at least increase my magic. I concentrated on the flame, pulling it into my palms and then back into myself, picturing it as an even bigger flame. Unfortunately, I had not calculated for the newly opened power that lived within me or the possibility that both would mix together and as they did, I felt power like never before. I screamed in both pleasure and pain as the magic filled me up and instantly healed my body. I craved the death of ogres and before I had even consciously thought about it, I was dressed with my weapons strapped on and out in the stables.

Alex spoke to me, but I couldn't hear him with all of the power swirling around me and propelling me to find ogres. He must have felt it or seen it because he stayed away from me as I saddled Fire and rode out of the barn. The gates opened at my approach and I rode off into the night, searching for the twitchy feeling I got when ogres were near.

Time seemed to pass faster and yet there were moments missing from my memory. I tried as hard as I could to hold on to my consciousness and to stay who I was while this power filled me, but it was very difficult. After what must have been half a day

I felt a pull to the east and as I turned in that direction my body became taught with unspent energy and I knew I was heading the right way. Fire obeyed my every command as though she could sense my urgency and we maneuvered through the countryside easily.

I dismounted as we entered a cliffy area and ground tied her so that she wouldn't follow me. I didn't need her getting hurt because of my negligence. The night was dark and the moon was high above, allowing very little light to shine down so I had to use my senses to carefully sneak down the cliff towards the cave where I could see fire and smell blood.

"That girl must die," one of the ogres said.

"She is too strong. She killed over two hundred of us at once," another said.

I stopped moving so I could listen to their conversation, which was apparently about me. Not that I was conceited and thought everything was about me, but I hadn't heard of any other girls killing over a hundred ogres.

"We must gather all ogres together," the first one said.

"That will only help her and let her kill us all in one night,' the second said angrily. "You must be smart about this."

"You should listen to me," a third man's voice said. "I can help you defeat her."

"We do not want your help in ogre matters, shapeshifter," the first ogre said.

I felt a smile lift the corners of my mouth and I ran into the cave, decapitating the two ogres before they even knew I was there. I met the shapeshifter's eyes and asked, "What have I done to earn *your* hate?"

He stayed where he was, casually leaning back against the wall of the cave carving a piece of wood with a claw from one of his hands that was now a lion's paw, seemingly unperturbed by my presence and the fact that I had just killed both of his ogre companions. He said, "I have nothing personally against you, but I do have an issue with your elf boyfriend."

"First of all, he is not my boyfriend," I said irritably. "Now it seems that your issue with Favian has created an issue between you and I. How shall we resolve it?"

"You think you can beat me, girl?" he asked with a laugh as he dropped the carving on the ground. "You're a human."

"I might surprise you." Although as I said the words, I felt the energy dissipating within me.

"I know you are skilled at killing ogres, but you have no idea what you are up against when it comes to shapeshifters. We are stronger, faster, and able to shift into forms that can tear your skin apart in seconds," he said with a sneer.

"Then why are you still cowering in the back of this cave if you are so strong?" I asked as I pulled my throwing daggers from my belt.

He snarled, sounding like a lion, and leapt towards me. I threw my daggers into his throat and chest, but he simply yanked them out and dropped them as though they had been nothing more than mosquitoes. Maybe he was right, maybe I was outmatched by him. His other hand changed into the paw of a lion and I jumped backwards, narrowly avoiding the long claws. I pulled my swords and opened up several large wounds on his body, but he wasn't slowing down or even acting as if the wounds caused him pain. What kinds of beasts were shapeshifters!

I swung both swords at his head at the same time, but he caught the swords with one paw and yanked them from my hands. I backed away, trying not to get frightened and trying to keep my cool. I still had my other power opened up; I just had to figure out how to use it.

"It is going to bring a smile to my face when I hear his grieving wail across the valley when he finds your mutilated body on the front gate of the Elven Kingdom," the shapeshifter said with a smile. "I'll make your death quick, so you don't have to suffer needlessly."

"You're very cocky. Is that a common shapeshifter trait?" I asked him as I tensed my body in preparation of attacking him. I was bound to get cuts from his claws, but I needed to get in close to him so that I could disable him. I lunged forward and punched him and kicked him as quickly as I could and in as many damaging areas as I could. His claws opened several large wounds and the power I had was draining from me. Why couldn't I use it? Why couldn't I harness this energy now against the shapeshifter when it was so easy to use against ogres?

"I can see why Favian likes you," he said as he grabbed me around the throat. "You are very feisty. It's very sexy." He stabbed his claws into my stomach and I screamed in pain despite my attempt not to. He growled happily at my scream and sliced downwards, opening the cuts deeper and further.

"Marin!" Sebastian yelled as he charged inside. I wanted to yell at him to stay back, but I could hardly breathe with the shapeshifter's hand clenching my throat.

The shapeshifter hissed and said, "If you want her to live, you'll stop right there."

Sebastian stopped moving and glared at him. "I'll spare your life if you release her now. If you continue to harm her, I *will* kill you."

"I'm making the rules around here!" the shapeshifter yelled. "Take off your weapons, slowly, and toss them out of the cave.

"No," I gasped out. "Run."

"Stop choking her and I will do as you ask," Sebastian said.

The shapeshifter set me down on my feet, but kept his claws against my neck. "There."

Sebastian tossed his belt with weapons out of the cave and spread his arms. "Now I'm unarmed. Release her."

"Run," I whispered as I drew in long draughts of air against my sore throat.

"Why do you smell differently?" the shapeshifter asked. "You look like Favian, but you do not smell like him."

"That's because I'm Sebastian, his twin," he said angrily. "Now release her or I'll kill you."

The shapeshifter tightened his claws into my neck, drawing blood. I grunted in pain and then the shapeshifter licked the blood from my neck. "She tastes incredible," he whispered around a growl. "What are you girl? Your blood tastes different than any I've ever tasted before."

Sebastian charged forward as the shapeshifter drew his head back to let it change into a lion's so that he could bite me. I spun out of his hold, but his claws still tore into my throat as I did so. I stumbled out of the cave and dropped to my knees on the ground. The blood was pumping out over my hand and if I didn't put a compress on it soon I would not live. I tore a piece of material from my shirt and pressed it against my neck as hard as I could and then tore another piece to tie around my neck to hold it in place. Sebastian and the shapeshifter were fighting in a battle that truly frightened me, but I couldn't move much. I had to do something though. I had to help Sebastian somehow.

Sebastian groaned in pain as the shapeshifter opened a cut on his arm. I looked around for something to throw at the shapeshifter and saw Sebastian's sword just a foot away from me on my left. I grabbed the sword and tossed it towards Sebastian when he stepped back for a breather from the fight. He caught it and in a spinning motion that I envied, sliced the shapeshifter's head off.

I was trying to breathe shallow breaths so as not to aggravate my neck wound, but it wasn't helping. I needed a healer and fast.

"Marin!" Favian's voice yelled from behind me.

"Favian," I whispered as I turned and found him and Kato running down the cliff side towards me.

"What have you done!" Favian accused Sebastian. Favian

pulled his sword and moved towards him. "What did you do to her!"

"I saved her life!" Sebastian yelled back.

"Shape. Shifter," I whispered to Kato. "Cave."

Favian looked in the cave and cursed. "Why are you two out here?" he asked Sebastian.

"She ran off and I followed her," he said. "I wasn't sure where she was going, but she looked like she was going through bloodlust. I wanted to make sure that she was alright."

"She's obviously not alright!" Favian yelled.

"Princes, we must get her to the castle and to a healer immediately," Kato said as he inspected my injury. "If we do not she will die."

"You say the sweetest things," I rasped slowly.

Favian sheathed his sword, but glared at Sebastian again, obviously still not believing him. "Kato, I want a full investigation and I want him questioned thoroughly. I want to know exactly what happened."

"You could just ask her after she's better," Sebastian said bitterly.

Favian picked me up and walked away. "I will." I opened my mouth to speak, but Favian gave me *the look,* so I stopped talking. He mounted Ice as easily as if he weren't carrying me and called Fire's name to follow. The two horses set off at a fast gallop back towards the castle. "Why can't you stay out of trouble for one week?" he asked trying to sound angry, but sounding more worried than anything else. "If he had something to do with your injury, I'll kill him," he whispered. I gripped his arm and looked up into his eyes. I wanted to say something, but if I talked the blood pumped faster. He looked down into my eyes and whispered, "He had better pray he wasn't lying."

I had never seen him so fierce before. It was incredibly sexy and yet frightening since his anger was aimed at Sebastian who was innocent. We made it to the castle and he carried me while he ran into the healer's room.

"You again?" she asked. "Wasn't a broken foot enough to deal with?"

"Broken foot?" Favian asked. "How'd she get a broken foot?"

The healer ignored him as she examined my throat and stomach wounds. "These are bad, but I'll be able to stitch them up easily. Favian, grab the brown bottle with the liquid to knock her out. She is not going to want to be awake for this."

I tried to protest, but Favian pressed the rag over my face and whispered into my ear, "I'll be right beside you."

I groaned and then the vapors of the liquid put me to sleep.

CHAPTER SIX

I woke up feeling warm and my throat feeling very sore and stiff. I reached up to touch it, but a hand grabbed mine before I could reach it.

"You shouldn't touch the stitches yet," Favian's voice said quietly.

I opened my eyes and found his face above mine. "Where Sebastian?" I asked softly.

Favian's face darkened and he said, "He's in Father's war room."

"He saved me," I whispered.

"Hardly," Favian said angrily. "The healer is the one who saved you."

"Tried," I whispered. "I would have been eaten by the shapeshifter had he not interfered."

"Stop talking," Favian ordered. "Your stitches are fresh and you need to rest while the skin knits itself back together."

"I'm sorry I got myself into trouble again," I whispered, ignoring his order. "I was healing my broken foot by using that technique you taught me to increase my powers and it ended up merging with the other power in me. After it merged I needed to expend energy and I needed to kill ogres. Unfortunately, that shapeshifter was there as well and I couldn't defeat him."

"Stop talking," Favian ordered again. "We can discuss it later."

"Don't mad at him." I knew I was hardly making sense, but my throat hurt too much to talk in full sentences.

Favian sighed. "Okay, now will you please stop talking?"

I smiled and closed my eyes. "Yes."

"How is she?" Sebastian asked.

"Awake," I whispered as I opened my eyes again.

"You're still talking," Favian said angrily.

Sebastian sat down on my other side and I felt like I was going crazy with a Favian-looking person on either side of me. "I'm sorry that he hurt you," Sebastian whispered as he brushed the back of his hand down my cheek.

"Stop touching her," Favian said angrily.

Sebastian looked up at him. "I'm sorry, are you courting her? She told me that you two were only partners."

"No, I am not courting her," Favian said with gritted teeth.

"Then why does it bother you that I am touching her?" Sebastian asked with a strange look in his eyes.

"I think you and I need to talk outside," Favian said as he stood up angrily.

I grabbed Favian's hand, but he pulled out of my hold and walked out of the healer's room. "I'll be back shortly," Sebastian said with a smile at me.

I tried to grab them, but they both left too quickly. Why must Elves be so stubborn!

I started to sit up, but Father came in and pushed me back down. "Easy, you can't get up yet."

"Favian, Sebastian, fighting outside," I whispered.

Father shrugged. "They must work out their differences."

"Fighting. Over me. Being injured," I whispered back.

His eyes widened and he stood up. "Why didn't you say so before?" He picked me up and ran out of the castle faster than I had ever been carried. How could he be faster than the younger elves? Did you gain speed with power?

We found the twins facing off in the fighting arena with swords drawn. "Put your swords down," Father said commandingly.

"He has insulted my honor," Favian said.

"Only after you insulted mine," Sebastian said back.

I jumped out of Father's arms and walked to the center of the ring. Instantly both sheathed their swords to reach out for me as I stumbled from the pain of the stitches in my stomach. "You shouldn't be moving," Favian said angrily.

"She wouldn't be if you weren't…" Sebastian began, but I put a hand over both of their mouths.

"Stop fighting," I whispered. Father moved towards me and I held up my hand towards him. "I need. Talk Sebastian," I said quickly.

"What about?" Favian asked.

I glared at him. "Go."

"Come on Favian, let's leave them to talk," Father said as he put an arm around Favian and basically drug him away.

"Please. No fighting," I whispered to Sebastian. "You. Need. Be friends."

"Stop talking, Marin. You're going to rip your stitches. Come on, we need to get you back inside and lying down," he said.

I needed to tell him that he couldn't fight over me because I couldn't ever court anyone, but I was in a lot of pain and I really did not want to have the conversation anyways. "Fine," I whispered as I hobbled back towards the castle. "Just promise no more fighting."

"I promise I won't start it, but if he attacks me, I will defend myself," he said as he held open the door for me.

"Be nice," I scolded.

He winked at me. "I'm always nice."

I pushed him away from me playfully and pointed at my throat and then held up a clenched fist to Favian who was waiting for us just inside the doorway. Pointing to a wounded area then holding up a clenched fist was our way to tell each other that we were in pain when we couldn't speak. Favian picked me up and started carrying me down the hallway. "You should be in bed."

I wanted to argue or force him to put me down, but I quite enjoyed being carried by Favian. "Watch out, she doesn't like being carried. She has a wicked elbow."

"I'm well aware of her likes and dislikes," Favian said as we walked into the healer's room.

"There you are!" She yelled. "Why aren't you in bed? Favian, you know she needs to rest."

"Father carried her out and I'm bringing her in," he said as he laid me down. He looked in my eyes and said, "I'll chain you to the bed if you try to get up again."

I stuck my tongue out at him and then sucked it back in my mouth before he could grab it. It was a dumb game that we had played since we were toddlers.

"I'll take my leave," Sebastian said as he walked to me and kissed my cheek. "I'm glad that you are alright."

Favian watched him leave with a fierce look in his eyes and then sat down in a chair beside my bed. "I tried to tell Father that it was a bad idea to leave you behind, but he thought you would stay out of trouble."

I rolled my eyes at him. He was such a brat.

"I told him that I needed to keep you in my sight, but he refused to let you go because he knew the shapeshifter was too strong. He was right, of course, but you ended up finding him anyways since he was traveling with ogres. Sometimes your keen sense of ogres is troublesome."

He was preaching to the choir on that one. I really wished I could figure out how to use my power against any one that was trying to hurt me, not just ogres.

"Mother is planning a big ball to welcome Sebastian into the family in the next couple of days. Every elf is supposed to attend. I'm not really looking forward to it. I guess I haven't really given him a chance though. Is he a good person?"

I nodded my head.

"Well I guess if he meets your standards then I should go make nice with him, but I'll wait and do it tomorrow."

I was surprised that he was talking so much, but as expected he left shortly after that.

I had spent too much time being a girl and being in the Kingdom. I needed to get out and fight. The only problem was that the ball was happening soon and I was still recovering from my *newest* injuries. I relaxed on the bed and thought of all of my options. I finally made up my mind and though I was happy with my decision, I did not feel happy inside. Truthfully, I felt frightened and nervous at the prospect.

Favian and Sebastian visited me frequently, but most of the time they just sat quietly with me and seemed to be deep in thought about something.

Each day I used the power increasing technique to help heal my injuries, but was sure not to combine my powers or imagine it building much more than a small amount each time. After two days of lying in the bed doing nothing, the healer released me to walk around, but made me swear not to do any fighting.

I walked through the tall grasses of the fields towards the forest on my last girly mission. After today I would no longer have an interest in males and would become a single Mercenary with no emotional ties to anyone beyond friendship. Or at least that was what I hoped to do. Mother always said that I was too kind a being to ever hate anyone or deny myself affection from others, but I had to hope.

The brothers had noticed my standoffish attitude, but neither had commented on it, rather they had continued to show their friendship to me and loyalty. I stepped into the forest and a chill settled over me. It was not due to fear, but rather nervousness. I was doing something forbidden and I was not sure what the outcome would be. I walked confidently through the forest, ignoring the various sets of eyes from the forest animals as I made my way. I was incredibly happy that my wounds were completely healed and hoped if I were punished for what I was doing that it wouldn't be too severe. The forest was only about ten miles across in this spot as it grew out a little from the rest of the forest. My nerves built as I neared the edge of the forest and stood at the farthest point which I had ever traveled this way.

I took a deep breath and picked my foot up to walk out, but a voice in my head whispered, *"Stop."*

I put my foot back down and looked around. "Who's there?"

"You aren't supposed to be here, Marin."

I finally recognized the voice as Silvermist, the Queen of the Pegasus herd which lived here. "I am not here for myself," I answered strongly.

"I am aware of your reasons for being here, child, but if you step foot onto this land your father will have no option, but to punish you."

I was afraid she would say that. "I need only a minute of your time," I asked humbly. "Please, Queen Silvermist."

The Pegasus Queen stepped out from behind a tree to my left and I gaped at her magnificence as she walked. She shimmered like silver and her mane and tail floated as she moved. I had only been allowed to *speak* to her when I was younger, but I had no doubt that she had the smoothest gait of any four-legged being. She nudged me backwards with her head, pushing me back farther into the forest. *"You are lucky I was nearby and heard your thoughts."*

"Then you know what I've come to ask for?" I asked softly.

She bobbed her head and her eyes sparkled with humor. *"If it were for anything else I would nip you in reprimand, but your heart and intentions are pure and I am willing to give you this gift as long as you promise me one thing."*

"What thing?" I asked suspiciously.

"That you never enter our realm unless there is an emergency which I, or the King, have summoned you for."

I didn't want to agree to it, but I knew she was being extremely reasonable considering I had almost broken one of the only laws I had in this Kingdom. "I swear it," I said with a bow.

She nickered in approval and turned her body sideways towards me. *"Hop on and I will take you to a spot most suitable for this type of work."*

I didn't waste any time because I rarely got the opportunity to ride a Pegasus and hopped up onto her back, trying to be as gentle as possible. "Thank you."

She trotted out of the forest and then took to the sky, flapping her wings hard as she ascended. I held on tightly with my legs to keep from falling and enjoyed the feel of the wind on my face as she flew. We leveled out over the top of the forest as she glided over the trees and I couldn't keep the smile off of my face. She was magnificent and even if I never rode a Pegasus again, I would always remember this moment. It was truly an honor to ride the Queen.

She took me deep into the forest, passed all of the small streams and up and over the waterfall to the fast rapids and an open, sandy shore. She folded her wings in against her body and landed lightly on her hooves, hardly jarring me at all. *"If you search the shallow parts of the sand just in the water you will find blue shells, which are rarely seen or used. Collect forty of them and then I will help you with the next steps."* I looked at her in shock a moment and she lifted her top lip in a smile. *"I watched you making the necklace for Prince Favian and have watched your struggles with all things feminine. I will help you with this task to ensure it is as beautiful as your intentions for it to be are."*

Stunned and immensely grateful didn't begin to cover how she was making me feel at the moment. I resisted the urge to hug her and stepped in to the water as I began searching for the shells. I had to dig deeper than I thought I would need to, but I finally found where the shells were buried. I pulled one out and stared at it in complete shock. They were a deep blue with a shine that made them look to be gemstones. It was by far the most beautiful shell I had ever seen.

Silvermist folded her legs beneath her, laid down and dozed on the beach while I searched. She looked as regal as ever, even in sleep.

It took me an hour to collect forty of them, but I finally had them all in a pile on the beach. "Done," I said softly.

She opened her eyes and looked at the pile. *"Good. Now take out one of your daggers and I will instruct you on where to cut the hair from."*

I pulled my dagger and approached her nervously. I did not want to screw up or upset her so I had to be extremely careful. As careful as if she were a baby I did not want to hurt.

"Stop worrying, Marin. Now, from the underside of my tail cut four strands at the base and hold them in your hand. This is going to be difficult because you will have to continue to hold the hairs while you continue cutting, but if you set them down anywhere they will be blown away. You understand?"

I nodded my head and approached her rump where she was holding her tail up for me to reach the underside. I separated four strands out and cut them gently. I held them in my hand and then turned to her face.

"Good. Now continue that process all the way around the outer part of my tail. Once you've done that you will come to the top of my mane and I will instruct you on that."

I worked slowly and efficiently, being sure never to take more than four strands and never to prick her tail with my dagger. "Why can't I visit the Pegasus herd?" I asked her as I approached her head to begin on her mane.

"We are a proud race and though many of us have watched you grow up with the elves and are fond of you, there are some who view you as what you are. You are human and some detest the presence of humans. Some would view it as a crime punishable by death if a human found their way to our herd's sleeping area."

"I'm not completely human," I reminder her.

She snorted. *"Yes, we are aware of your father. Which reminds me, why haven't you uncovered your father's identity yet?"*

I sighed. "I don't have any clues except his swords and that medallion. Plus, I haven't had time to search him out yet."

"You should search him out soon. It is good to know who your father is."

"Why don't you tell me?" I asked.

"Because you must take the journey just as the others did. You must find out on your own who you are. It is part of the process of maturing and coming into your powers."

"This bites," I whispered.

"Everyone must find their place in the world. Your journey is just a little more complicated," she said with a laughing neigh.

We resumed the task so that we would not be out in the dark. I listened to her directions and then began to slowly cut strands of her mane and added them to the growing pile in my hand. After I finished she had me sit down and arrange the hair into three equal piles and place a medium sized rock on top of them to hold them down. Then I had to sort through the small blue shells that I'd found until I found three that were small enough to look nice on a bracelet and yet big enough to fit the end of the tied, braided horse hair through. She explained that the shells would be the clasp for the bracelet and that she had made me pick so many shells to be able to find three suitable ones.

Plus, she suggested that I make two bracelets from the shells for mother and father as gifts.

I looked at her curiously and she whispered, *"I can sense your urgency to escape. Remember that I can hear your thoughts and I know what truly lies within your heart. That is the only reason I am helping you."*

I did not have a response to that so I did as she asked, sorting through the shells for at least an hour until I found three that were perfect.

After laying the hairs out side by side and then tying a knot into each of the three sets I started braiding. It took a long time and my fingers had burns from the hairs as I worked slowly to make the most beautiful braid possible. Finally, three braided strands were done. I tied a knot in each of the ends and then measured out how much I actually needed for the bracelets, undid the braids to there and retied a knot and then cut the extra off. Getting the knotted part into the center of the shell and then to the outer edge in the inside was difficult, but I managed and was overly pleased when I had three perfect Pegasus hair bracelets in my hands.

"They're beautiful," I whispered as I looked at the shiny silver hair.

"Surprised that you could create it?" she asked knowingly.

"Yes," I said even though I knew she already knew the answer.

"Good. Now let's work on the bracelets for the King, Queen and Kato."

The day was coming to a close and the ball was to begin that night only three hours after sunset. I tried not to rush myself to ensure that the bracelets would be beautiful and with Silvermist's help I was able to finish just an hour after sunset.

"Now place all six of the bracelets in between your palms and hold them out. I want you to picture your Mother, Father, Kato, the two Princes, and yourself. Hold the image of them in your mind and be completely still."

I wasn't sure what she was up to, but I did as she asked, standing in front of her as I held out my hands with the bracelets between them. I closed my eyes and pictured the six of us and relaxed. I was beginning to wonder what she was up to when she sneezed on my hands. Irritation started to boil, but then I felt magic working between me and the bracelets. I kept my mouth closed and kept the image of the six of us at the front of my mind. The magic built and then disintegrated with an audible pop.

I opened my eyes and hands and stared at the slightly glowing bracelets. "What was that?" I asked softly.

"That was a spell which will allow you to communicate with the wearers of the bracelet no matter distance. Once you all are wearing them, you only need to think their name and conjure up an image of them and then you will be connected. You can block it by picturing darkness if you are in a spot where you do not want to communicate."

"I do not know what to say," I whispered. "I am greatly honored."

She nickered happily and stood up. *"It is time to return you to the castle so that you can get ready for the ball."*

I put the bracelets inside my coin pouch which was attached to my belt and hopped up onto her back. "I will never forget what you have done for me today."

"You're welcome." She replied and then took to the sky. My heart beat faster as I went over the plan in my head again. I had everything set up and I was ready to begin my journey.

Silvermist dropped me off at the back side of the castle and then flew off to rejoin her herd. I rushed into the castle and up the stairs to my room, blowing passed Sebastian and Favian and ignoring their calls as I shut and locked my door. I had two hours to get ready, but I needed all of that time. I rushed through a sponge bath, brushed out my hair and then picked the most beautiful dress I had and laid it on the bed. Two hours was normally a long time, but tonight it seemed like a short amount as I worked on my hair and face and prepared myself to look my most beautiful.

I double checked that the clothes I would change into were laid out on the bed and that everything else was packed and then took my money pouch with the bracelets as I walked down the staircase towards the ballroom. Mother was waiting for me at the bottom and her eyes sparkled and a smile split her face as soon as she saw me. "We were worried that you had run off when you were away all day."

"I wouldn't miss an Elven Ball," I said with a smile as I kissed her cheek.

"You look beautiful," she whispered. "I love that dress."

I curtsied to her and then we walked with linked arms to the doors of the ballroom. "After we eat, I would like to gather you, Father, Kato and the Princes together for a private family moment, if that would be alright?"

"Of course," she said happily.

She stepped into the ballroom and I waited as she was announced and the applause died down. I smoothed down my dress and took a deep, calming breath before stepping into the ballroom with a wide smile on my face, trying my hardest to imitate Mother.

The crowd clapped as I walked inside and headed to the head table where the royal family ate. Favian looked at me in shock and Sebastian had a pleasant smile on his face as I sat down beside Mother on the other side of Father from them.

Father raised his hands and everyone sat down at their tables. "I am pleased to announce the return of our stolen prince, Sebastian!" Some of the crowd who had just arrived gasped in shock while the rest clapped happily. "Let us eat and celebrate this joyous occasion."

We ate our food and as soon as I was done, I made my way to the other tables, making pleasant conversation with everyone I knew. When I made it to Alex he whispered, "Fire is ready." Then he turned away from me. I hoped he was not mad at me for asking him to help me sneak away, but I did not have the time to stop and ask him.

I whispered thank you back and continued around the room, playing host as Mother had always asked me to. The dinner finished and the dancing began with the Princes having to dance with every single female elf present. I walked to Kato who was talking with some of the soldiers and curtsied. "Good evenin', Kato."

He smiled at me and bowed. "Good evening, Marin. What brings you to my side this evening?"

"I was hoping you would honor me with a dance?" I asked sweetly.

"You promise not to step on my toes?" he asked.

I laughed. "I promise to try."

He picked my hand up and twirled me around before leading me to the dance floor. "You were missed today," he whispered as he led me through a slow dance despite the fast tempo of the music playing.

"I was with Queen Silvermist," I whispered back.

He pulled back and stared at me in shock. "Please tell me that you did not go find the Pegasus herd."

"I did not," I said with a smile. "I never set foot in their territory."

He exhaled and spun me around in a small circle. "You had me worried."

"Would you meet me at the head of the room in ten minutes? I would like to gather the entire family for a moment," I said.

He nodded his head and then bowed to me, kissing the back of my hand as the song ended. "I would be delighted."

I curtsied to him and then kissed his cheek. "Thank you for the dance."

I was preparing to move off of the floor, but was swept back onto it by Father. "So, you will dance with Kato, but not your own Father?" he asked, feigning hurt.

"I would save my Father's toes from pain," I said with a smile as he led me around the room.

He grimaced as I stepped on his toes and then smiled. "A few hurt toes are nothing compared to the joy of dancing with you."

I relaxed in his presence and over the next ten minutes danced with Father, Favian and Sebastian before I finally had them all gathered at the front of the room. My throat was dry, but I ignored it to get this moment over with. "I gathered you all here to give you presents," I said with a sweet smile.

"Presents?" Favian asked in shock. "What for?"

I pulled out the bracelets and handed the shelled bracelets to Mother, Father and Kato and then two of the three braided Pegasus hair bracelets to Favian and Sebastian. "I was with Silvermist today and she helped me make this and spelled them for me. These are so that we can always communicate to each other, no matter the distance. That way, if one of us were to be stolen we could find each other," I explained as I slipped my own bracelet on.

"They're beautiful," Mother said happily. "Thank you."

I curtsied to her and then grabbed Alex's hand as he tried to sneak passed us and pulled him out on to the dance floor. His shock was obvious, but then it was quickly replaced with happiness as he danced with me. Although I did enjoy dancing with him the true reason I had grabbed him was to allow me to move away from the family and to the side of the room where I could make my escape. I kissed Alex's cheek and thanked him again.

"Anytime, Marin," he whispered before heading off towards his friends.

The family was still talking together as I inched towards the back door and then squeezed out of it. I ran to my room and changed as quickly as possible, leaving my dress on the bed with the note I'd written the previous day explaining that I had to set out on my own to find my true father.

I grabbed my bag and climbed out of my window and down the rope I had secured to my bed. The night air bit into my skin, through my cloak as I made my way around the castle and to the stables. Fire nickered a greeting to me as I walked inside and opened her stall. "Hey pretty girl. Ready for a trip?"

She bobbed her head as she followed me out of the stable and I was extremely grateful that Alex had her saddled for me. I swung up onto her back and clucked my tongue to urge her forward. She moved into an easy canter and we headed away from the castle and out the front gates. I let Fire decide the pace and relaxed as we headed down the familiar path. I wasn't sure where I needed to go to begin my search for my Father, but I decided to start at the town my human parents had come from.

As Fire slowed to a walk I pulled my bracelet out and looked at its glowing beauty. I was hesitant to put it on because as soon as I did the others would be able to communicate with me and I wanted to be far enough away that I wouldn't have to worry about Favian or Sebastian catching up to me.

The stars twinkled above and the moon cast enough light for me to see down the road as I continued on my first solo mission. Despite the nervousness that thrummed through my body I also felt excited. I was on my own for the first time and I was searching for my father's identity. I had no idea what I would find and yet the possibilities were narrowing down. I hoped I could find a mercenary job in the next couple of days. I needed to increase the number of missions I'd completed so that I could reach my goal of becoming a Protector sooner rather than later.

As night turned into day, I dismounted from Fire's back and made camp. I needed to sleep for at least a few hours before continuing or I would become reckless and could get in to trouble. I didn't bother making a true camp, just threw out my bedroll and took off Fire's bridle, leaving her saddle on in case I had to leave quickly. She stood beside me and dozed as I lay down and fell asleep.

CHAPTER SEVEN

I slept in a little later than usual before starting off again, but as I made my way down the forest road I heard another rider approaching quickly. I stopped Fire and prepared myself in case I needed to protect myself, but once I was able to see the rider a smile split my face.

"Micah!" I called happily.

He stopped his horse just in front of mine and smiled back. "Marin. I was on my way to the Elven Kingdom to find you and Favian."

"What's up?" I asked him.

"I was sent to give you two a mission."

Magic to my ears! "Really? What type of mission?"

"Where's Favian?" he asked instead of answering my questions.

"He's back at the kingdom dealing with Prince duties. Now, about this mission..." I prompted.

He frowned. "You and Favian always do your missions together."

"I need to do a mission, please," I pleaded with him. "I can't wait for Favian to be available. I am just as capable without him as I am with him."

Micah didn't look like he believed me. "I am sure you and I can handle it by ourselves. We don't need Favian do we?" I asked hopefully. I really wanted to spend this time away from them all.

Micah looked at me suspiciously a moment and then laughed. "Alright, I was supposed to head back to Macon, but I'll go with you instead. He won't mind if I'm a couple of days late."

My face stretched as far as it could as I smiled at him. "Thank you."

"You owe me," he said with a somewhat serious face.

I laughed. "Alright, I'll owe you one."

He turned his horse around and we headed back the way he had come. "So, how have you been?"

I shrugged. "Good. I did a couple missions with Favian and then we were summoned home. Then I discovered that he has a twin brother and that brother was found and now he is being transitioned into the family and the Elven way of life."

"Wait, he wasn't with the elves before?" Micah asked.

I shook my head. "Apparently he was kidnapped right after they were born and he was raised by humans."

"So you were raised by elves and he was raised by humans?" he asked with a smirk.

I laughed. "Yeah, it is sort of funny."

"Is he nice?"

I nodded my head and felt a pang of sadness. I shoved the feelings down and said, "He is great, exactly what a prince should be and he looks *exactly* like Favian."

"Really? Like identical twins?" he asked. I nodded my head. "Wow. That must be confusing for you."

I shrugged. "I finally figured out how to tell them apart so it's not so bad now."

"I meant emotionally."

I turned and looked at him in shock. "What? Why?"

He laughed. "Come on Marin, it's obvious that you are in love with Favian."

Dammit. How could he have figured it out? "Well it doesn't matter."

"Because he's the Prince?" he asked. I nodded my head and he sighed. "I am going to pull my nose out of your business now, but I really do not think it is that big of an issue."

"So, how far are we going?" I asked to change the subject.

"Grundio," he said with a grimace. "It's not the nicest place. The people are a little rough, but they have good drink and food. It is a day and a half ride."

"What information do you have?"

"The only information we have is that the villagers are being picked off slowly and even though they are a tough lot, they can't defeat these silent killers, which they claim are ogres."

"Silent killers? That doesn't sound like ogres," I said skeptically. Ogres were noisy and smelly and preferred to bellow as they chopped off your head.

"That's what I said, but one of the villagers swears they saw ogres taking off with one of the villagers."

It sounded highly questionable to me. Could it be an ogre working with someone else? I had certainly witnessed that recently. We rode in silence as I absorbed what he had told me and I felt my excitement building as we rode closer and closer to our destination. We had to stop to sleep and let the horses rest for a few hours and as soon as my bed roll was down, I slipped on the bracelet and prepared myself for my family's thoughts.

As soon as the bracelet touched my wrist I heard a chorus of *"Marin!"* in five different voices.

"I'm on a mission with Micah. I'm safe and I just wanted to let you know."

"Where are you? I'll come meet up with you," Favian said in an irritated tone.

"We'll be fine by ourselves," I replied testily.

"Are you sure you can handle it with only a human as your back-up?" Sebastian asked.

Unfortunately, I knew he was right to question that, but I didn't want Favian rushing to my side. I needed to prove that I could do this on my own. I needed to prove myself to become a Protector.

"I'll contact you all when I'm finished with the mission."

"Stay safe," Father said.

"Yes, I need to scold you for leaving a ball early when you are done with your mission," Mother said in a chastising tone.

"Love you all," I said with a laugh.

"Marin," Favian said. *"Tell me where you're going."*

"I'm going on a mission," I responded and then took the bracelet off. I put the bracelet back in my pocket and sighed.

"What were you doing?" Micah asked me curiously.

"I was talking with my family."

"You were what?" he asked disbelievingly.

"The Queen of the Pegasus helped me make items which allow us to communicate telepathically," I explained.

"Magic is a magnificent thing," he said with a smile.

It was common for humans with no magical abilities to fear magic. Micah on the other hand craved magic and he possessed quite a bit of it. He was always looking for more ways to increase his magic and expand his spell casting knowledge. I laid down to keep his eyes off of me because I knew a spell that would increase his magic exponentially, but it was an Elf-only spell and I couldn't tell him. He may have been one of the few friends I had while in the Academy, but he wasn't an Elf and I couldn't tell him.

"Let's try to leave early. I'd like to get there as soon as possible," I said as I closed my eyes.

"Agreed."

As we neared Grundio, I felt a twitchiness that I only had when ogres were near. "There are definitely ogres here," I whispered to Micah as we walked our horses into the town.

The town, if it could be called that, only had a couple of buildings and those buildings looked in need of desperate repair. All of the townspeople stared at me with stern faces and I gave them blank looks back. They were a hard-looking group of people with thick beards and clothes made of animal hides. If I had seen a group of them riding together I would have assumed they were bandits. Could a group of bandits make a town? Was that what this town was?

Micah led the way to the last building and dismounted his horse. "We'll speak to the petitioner and try to get as much information from them as we can."

I dismounted, tied Fire to the hitching post and looked at the building in front of us. Loud piano music played from inside and I could hear the clanking of glass. "A bar?" I asked.

He shrugged. "This is where I was instructed to meet the petitioner." He looked around the town and then said, "There really aren't that many options anyways."

I sighed and untied my cape, draping it across Fire's saddle. I wanted to have quick access to my swords and daggers if the men inside decided to try to cop a feel, which often happened to me when I was in a bar.

Micah smiled, knowing why I was doing it and said, "It might make this trip more interesting if you left the cape on."

I made a face at him and stepped up onto the porch of the bar. "Let's get this over with so I can go out and locate the ogres."

"Don't be so feisty, men take it as a challenge."

I sighed. "I will punch you."

He laughed and pushed open the door and waved his hand. "Ladies first."

I stepped into the bar and all conversation stopped. The patrons in the bar looked even meaner than the ones we had passed by in town and every single one was male. There were approximately ten wooden tables with four chairs each in the bar. A piano sat in the farthest corner with a young boy playing on it, or at least he had been until I'd walked in. There were no decorations and no barmaids.

I walked passed their staring faces up to the bar counter and leaned my elbows on top of it. "Two mugs of beer," I said in my stern voice.

The barkeep continued to stare at me as he wiped down the bar top on the other end, not moving towards the mugs. "You're a little young," he said in a gruff voice.

I whipped my dagger from my belt and stabbed his rag to the bar top faster than he could blink. "I'm older than I look," I said with a pleasant smile.

A man in the back of the room laughed and said, "Give her a mug, Tom."

I pulled my dagger from the wood and put it back in the sheathe on my belt. The barkeep left his rag where it was and got two mugs from the stack to fill them. Micah sat on a stool next to me and whispered, "You've done this before I take it?"

I shrugged. "Similar type of town, though this one is a bit tougher." And Favian wasn't with me this time.

The man who had spoken walked to us and held out his hand to me. He was tall, well over six and a half feet, with arms as thick as my waist and a face as soft as Favian's. He was muscled and the scar across his cheek helped him to fit into the town, but I knew he had to have caught hell growing up with that sweet face. "Murdock McCreery," he said with a smile that no doubt made girls swoon.

I shook his hand and gave him my business face. "Marin."

Micah held out his hand and Murdock shook it, but his eyes never left mine. "You're a Mercenary?"

I nodded my head. "I am."

"But you're a woman."

"Did the boobs give it away?" I asked with a smirk.

"What can you tell us about the recent events?" Micah asked to bring things back on topic.

Murdock looked at me a moment longer and then turned to Micah and said, "They've been happening once every three nights. So far they have taken two men in their sixties and one ten-year-old boy."

"Where were the people taken from?" I asked.

"They were taken from their homes as far as we can tell, but we don't know if they were inside or outside," he answered with a scowl.

"They all lived alone?" I asked in shock. Why would a young boy live alone?

"We are a poor town. None of us could afford to take care of an additional boy so he took care of himself," Murdock answered my unspoken question.

"Has anyone seen the attackers?" I asked. The barkeep set the two mugs of beer on the bar top and scowled at me. Apparently, he and I weren't going to be friends.

Murdock nodded his head. "I saw the boy taken. It was two ogres and they made absolutely no sound. I'd never seen ogres do that. I tried to catch up to them, but they disappeared into the forest."

"Have you tried sending out parties in search of them?" I asked.

He scowled at me. "Of course we did. We aren't cowards."

"What did they find?" Micah asked.

"Nothing."

"Nothing?" I asked in shock.

Murdock nodded his head. "Nothing. There were no footprints, no scents, nothing. It was as if it hadn't happened."

This was getting extremely weird. As far as I knew the only way to accomplish that was with a magic spell and ogres have no magical abilities. Who was helping them and why?

"When was the last attack?" Micah asked.

"Two nights ago," Murdock said.

"So, if they're going to keep to their pattern, they're going to take someone tonight," I said with a smirk. I drank my mug of beer and headed out the door to Fire.

"Why was she smiling?" I heard Murdock ask.

"She has a feud against ogres. She tends to get excited when the opportunity to kill them presents itself," Micah answered as he stepped out of the bar and headed towards his horse with Murdock following.

"I'm going to scout the forest," I said. "You scout the homes."

"Meet back in an hour," Micah said seriously.

I mounted Fire and tied my cape on. "Yes, sir." Fire cantered off with no urging and I felt my blood churning. I was finally going to get to kill more ogres and I was going to kill whoever was helping them as well. And I would be able to complete a mission *without* Favian. I calmed myself with a deep breath and focused on my surroundings as we neared the forest. There had to be a trail they took often, or some sign that they had been there.

I moved towards the forest and felt my twitchiness increase and my heart beat faster. Ogres were definitely near, but how close? I stopped at the entrance to the forest and hopped down from Fire's back to survey the ground. There were no wards and no charred lines to indicate a spell. I squatted and looked at the forest floor to inspect the animal trails. Strangely there were none. Even if these people over hunted and dwindled the large animal population, there would still be rabbit or squirrel tracks here. I walked into the forest and continued my search, still coming up with nothing. Had these people killed off their entire animal population by over hunting? Including squirrels? They were a poor town, but they didn't seem *that* poor.

Finally, about a mile into the forest I came across a few trails, but they hadn't been used recently. I walked back to Fire and looked around, feeling like I was being watched. What was going on that Murdock hadn't told us? He was withholding something from us.

Fire trotted back to town and I looked around at the people. They were scared, something that I had not noticed when I had first come. The town of large, frightening people was scared. Micah trotted up to me a few minutes later and whispered, "There's something they are not telling us."

I nodded my head. "There weren't any animals within a mile of the forest entrance. The trails are cold," I whispered.

"And the town is frightened. What could be so scary that these people would ask for our help?"

"Magic user," I whispered. "If they don't have any in their town and they haven't experienced it, they could be frightened of one, especially if he was using ogres for muscle."

Micah sighed and ran a hand through his hair. "We need to decide our strategy for tonight. We can't be at everyone's house at the same time."

"We need to ask Murdock for a map and mark where the kidnappings happened and see if there's a pattern."

"You think there will be?"

I shook my head. "No, I think we're going to need to wait at the edge of the forest and follow the ogres into it and hope we can see through the spell. How much have you improved?"

"I'll see through it, don't worry."

I stared into his eyes. "Don't let those ogres escape."

He smiled. "I won't deprive you of your kills."

I nodded my head and dismounted. "Let's eat. We only have a couple hours until dark."

We dismounted and walked into the bar. This time only a few people stopped talking when I walked in. I sat at an empty table and Micah sat down with me. The more I looked at the people, the more I noticed their unease, which made me more uneasy. Micah sat still for a moment longer and then walked up to the bar to order our food since there were apparently no barmaids at this bar.

Were they upset because I was here and this was a male-only place? I could certainly understand why that would upset them, but I had no intention of leaving especially since this was the only place we could get food.

Micah came back and sighed. "Apparently we have to fend for ourselves."

"What?" I asked in shock.

"They don't serve food here, just alcohol."

Scratch me being here then. "Alright, let's go." I stood up and headed out the door without any other prompting. I didn't want to make these men anymore uncomfortable than they already were. We mounted our horses and headed out of town towards the forest. "We should camp just outside the forest so we don't get caught in the magic users trap if they use the perimeter of the forest as their guide."

Micah nodded his head in agreement. "You set up camp and I'll catch us some food."

Micah continued into the forest as I stopped in the field just before it. I dismounted and started clearing sticks and stones from a patch that would serve as our sleeping area. Once I was satisfied with my work I unsaddled Fire and set my belongings in my sleeping spot and then grabbed large rocks and began making a fire circle. The sun lowered close to the horizon as I started the fire with firewood I had collected and Micah finally came back with two dead rabbits.

"You're right that the animals are unusually far away. I'm sure it's because of the ogres," he said as he dismounted, tossed me the rabbits and then began unsaddling his horse.

I set the rabbits down and pulled a dagger from my belt to start skinning them. "This situation bothers me," I whispered to him.

He sat down next to me and started on the second rabbit. "It bothers me as well. I think we should have enlisted more help."

I ground my teeth together and said, "We can handle it."

He smiled. "Easy girl. I wasn't saying we couldn't handle it, just that I would feel a little better if Favian were here."

"We should split up tonight to cover more area," I whispered again. For some reason, I felt whispering was necessary. I felt like I was being watched and I didn't like it. "I do not want them to get another person from this village."

"Agreed," he whispered back.

We stopped talking after that and cleaned, cooked and ate the rabbits. As the sun went down a chill swept over me and my body began tingling all over. Ogres were approaching. I looked at Micah and whispered, "They're on the move."

He stood up and put out our fire, not to hide our position, but simply to keep it contained and not catch the rest of the forest on fire if it somehow spread. I stood and checked all of my gear before saddling and mounting Fire. I closed my eyes as I sat upon her back and inhaled deeply, the scents of the forest were the first to greet me and then I smelled the foul reek that hung around ogres like a mist of poison. My blood began pumping harder and I felt my other power awakening the closer the ogres moved towards me. Micah set off at a canter to the other side of the forest, closer to the homes. Now all I had to do was wait.

Fire cocked a back leg, bored with the situation. I opened my eyes and surveyed my surroundings, but found nothing out of the usual. Where were the ogres? I could feel them near, but they weren't anywhere to be seen. Had I been wrong to separate Micah from me? Should we have stayed together?

Someone screamed on the other side of the forest and then I heard Micah's telltale whistle, two octaves higher than anything I could accomplish. I made a kissing noise and squeezed my legs together and Fire instantly responded, charging forward into a gallop and racing along the outside of the forest as quickly as she could.

It seemed like hours, but minutes later we made it to the other side where Micah was off his horse, fighting with a man wielding a staff while three ogres headed towards the forest with an older man in their arms. I leapt from Fire's back and pulled my swords before I'd hit the ground, charging after them.

"Stop!" I yelled at the ogres who had turned towards me with creepy, evil smiles on their faces as they ran towards the forest. I caught up to the ogres and sliced my sword along the back of one of the ogres who bellowed in pain. He didn't slow down or turn to engage me and as I raised my swords for another move, a blast of hot air hit me in the back of the head and knocked me to the ground.

"Marin!" Micah yelled.

I leapt up, ignoring the dizziness and pain in my head and lopped off the nearest ogre's leg. The ogre fell to his knees, but the other two continued on with the man in their arms, ignoring their fallen comrade. The ogre I'd hurt turned and slapped me with the back of his hand across my face, sending me flying backwards. I hit the ground on my back and slid a few feet before coming to rest. My head buzzed with pain and confusion, but I couldn't let them get away. I stood up and opened up more of my power, using it to mask my pain and ran back to the fleeing ogres, swords raised to attack.

My sword fell on emptiness as the ogres before me disappeared. "NO!" I screamed as I spun around in search of the magic user and Micah. Micah lay on the ground, either dead or unconscious, but I couldn't take time to check. I attacked the magic user, but I was not protected and he used a spell which knocked my legs out from under me. I landed on my face, unable to move my arms to catch myself.

He leaned down next to me and whispered, "Today I let you live, but tomorrow I will come back for my last person and I will take your magic, Little Death Bringer."

How did he know who I was? "I will kill you," I snarled.

He laughed. "See you tomorrow."

A bright light flashed and then silence filled the area. How had he beaten us? How? My body finally loosened and I was able to move. I stood up and took inventory of my body, which was thankfully fine, minus the bruising from the ogre smacking me. I ran to Micah and turned him over gently. His eyes opened and he cursed a very inventive string of names. "I can't believe that bastard used a sleeping spell on me."

I stared at him in shock. "You got caught by a cheap beginner's spell?"

He glared at me. "I didn't think he would use something as juvenile as that." He looked towards the forest and ground his teeth together. "He got away."

I nodded my head. "Yes, but he's coming back tomorrow."

"What?" he asked in shock.

I explained what had happened and what had been said and then rubbed my nose gently. Getting hit by the ogre and then falling on my face had made it swell, but thankfully it wasn't broken. Hopefully I wouldn't have a black eye from it either.

"Can you beat him?" I asked Micah quietly.

He glared at me. "Of course I can. I've got something special in mind for him when he returns."

"What is he doing with these people?" I asked angrily. Part of me didn't want to know. Part of me was scared to know.

"There are several rituals he could be performing, but I don't think that's what he is doing," Micah said as he looked at the ogre leg lying on the ground several feet from us.

"What do you think he is doing then?"

"I think this was a trap for you," he whispered.

I closed my eyes and sighed. Not this again. "Why me? What could he want with me?"

"You possess an incredible amount of magic for a human. So much that he could suck out half of it, leave you alive and he would be incredibly more powerful while you would still be alive."

"So why kidnap these people then?" I asked. "Why not just find me on a mission?"

"You're not that easy to track down unless you are at the Elven Kingdom and going there to attack you would be suicide on his part. He must have heard about your disdain for ogres and devised this plan to draw you here. He would need at least two sacrifices to complete the spell necessary for stealing your magic, but since you hadn't come yet he must have just continued to steal more. I think we should contact..."

I opened my eyes and glared at him. "I am not contacting Favian. We can handle this."

Micah sighed. "Alright, but I want it noted that I objected and tried to get you to contact him. I don't want to get beaten by him if you get injured."

"Then you will just have to use all of your magic to stop the magic user while I kill the ogres," I said with a smile.

The moon rose above us, glittering brightly and looking sad. Was it a bad sign? Or was I just worried? "We had better get to sleep. I need to gather some items for tomorrow night."

We gathered our horses and then headed to our camp for the night. Tomorrow, I would kill the ogres. Tomorrow, I would kill that magic user. Or, I might not live to see the next tomorrow.

* * *

THE TOWNSPEOPLE WOULD NOT LOOK at us as we walked through town. I had expected them to be angry that I had not stopped another person from being stolen, but instead they seemed afraid of meeting my eyes. Why?

I grabbed an older man and pushed him up against the side of the building. "What aren't you telling us?" I asked him with steel in my voice.

"What are you doing?" Micah asked in shock.

"Just let him take you!" the man screamed at me. "Let him take you so that he will leave us alone!"

His eyes were wide with fear and his breath stank of alcohol. I pushed away from him and turned towards Micah. "You better catch him with your spell, so I can slide a blade through his heart." No man should be able to cause such fear in an entire village, especially a village like this.

Micah nodded his head in understanding and we continued on our way. It took Micah most of the day to gather his materials and combine them in accordance with the spell, but as the sun began to set we were finally ready.

I stood with my hands resting on my sword's pommels, waiting for the feeling I always got when ogres were nearby. "Are you sure that you are ready?" I asked Micah.

He nodded his head. "Yes. As long as you take care of the ogres, I will take care of the magic user."

The ogres would be easy. The magic user was the one I was very worried about. Should I have contacted Favian? What if this was the last time I ever got to talk to him?

I was about to reach into my pocket to get the bracelet when I felt the ogres. "They're coming," I said as I headed into the forest, towards them. I drew my swords and waited, taking deep breaths to keep calm.

The forest took a deep breath and then ten ogres appeared ten feet in front of me. I spun into action, letting the other part of myself, the one that relished in killing ogres, take over.

My blade bit into ogre flesh again and again, decapitating, mutilating and killing. I could hear Micah chanting and sense magic being used, but I still had three more ogres to kill before I could go assist him.

The ogres that were left began circling me, trying to come up with a plan to attack me. "It's no use," I told them. "I will kill you."

"Little girl talks a lot," one of them said. "I will shut you up!" He charged at me and I ducked his punch, sliding my right sword up into his stomach and then sliced off his head as his body fell.

"Who's next?" I asked the other two.

They looked at each other and then started running towards the magic user and Micah. I ran after them, refusing to let any ogres live.

Micah yelled something and the other magic user flew backwards, slamming into the ground on his back. Yes! I threw one of my swords into the back of one of the ogre's heads, killing him instantly. I grabbed my sword out of his skull as I ran past and then tackled the ogre trying to engage Micah.

The magic user tried to use fire against me, but Micah countered the spell, saving me from being burned alive. I decapitated the ogre and thought I could relax when the magic user spoke a word that instantly knocked out Micah. He was preparing to use fire so I ran forward, jumping in front of Micah just as the word was spoken. Flames engulfed me and I screamed in pain. I rolled on the ground, but the flames would not go out. I screamed for Micah, but I passed out from the pain.

Chapter Eight

"I'm surprised that you are so willing to die for your comrade," the magic user said from nearby me. "He is pretty useless."

I tried to open my mouth, but every part of me hurt. I could smell my burnt skin and hair and even though I was thankful I was alive, I was not thankful for the burns covering my entire body.

"You're lucky that I need you alive for this spell, otherwise I would have let you die."

I opened my eyes slowly, moaning from the pain that opening my eyelids caused. We were in the middle of the forest, next to a small house made of logs. A large wooden table was to my right and lying face up on it, bound at the wrists and ankles was an older man with a piece of cloth tied around his mouth. His face was turned away from me, but his chest was moving up and down as he breathed which meant he was at least alive. On the porch, hanging by his hands was a little boy. He looked at me with pleading eyes and tears leaking down the sides of his face. His wrists were bleeding from the ropes cutting into his skin.

I tried to move, to stand, but the burns were too much. I screamed, which stretched my face and mouth and made it hurt even more, making me scream longer and louder.

The magic user laughed happily. "It's so wonderful that I can hurt you without even touching you. I should have thought of this myself. Well, you live and learn." He walked over to the old man and slapped him across the face and then turned the man's face so that I could see it. "Let her watch as you die."

I moved my hand slowly into my pocket, ignoring the pain it was causing me and grasping with my fingers, desperately reaching for the bracelet. I knew he would not be able to rescue me, but I at least wanted to say goodbye to them.

The magic user began chanting as he held a dagger up over his head with both hands, poised to stab the old man. I reached deeper into my pocket, closing my eyes as I bared with the pain. My burned skin peeled back as I pushed my hand into my pocket and the air felt like a thousand ants biting me. I opened my eyes and took shallow breaths through my nose.

The magic user's voice began to slowly increase in volume and then he thrust the dagger straight down into the old man's heart. I watched with despair as the old man stared at me accusingly.

My fingers finally grasped the bracelet. I closed my eyes and the minds of Cesar, Amadis, Kato, Sebastian and Favian linked with mine. *"I'm sorry. I love you all,"* I said to them, hoping they would all understand.

"Hold on Marin. We're coming," Favian said. *"Hold on."*

The magic user slapped me forcing me to open my eyes again and making me drop the bracelet from my fingertips due to the pain. "Don't die on me yet, girl. I need you to live long enough to drain every last ounce of magic from you. Your kind are hard to find."

I wanted to say something sarcastic to him. I wanted to hit him, but I could only lie there like a pathetic wimp. I needed to heal these wounds quickly. I needed to use the trick Favian had taught me to open up my magic and speed the healing process.

The magic user untied the old man and pushed his dead body off of the table. "I was told that no more of you existed, but I knew it had to be a rumor. Probably a rumor started by your own kind. Of course you still existed! The God and Goddess still exist so therefore, your kind must as well. I searched high and low, listening for legends of incredibly strong men and their outlandish stories. Many of the stories were preposterous and outlandish as word of mouth can lead things to be. I had heard your story from one man but thought he was insane. No girl could possibly have killed so many ogres by herself."

He grabbed the rope holding the little boy up and cut it with his knife, letting the boy fall to the ground in a small heap. The boy did not even cry out in pain. I focused on my magic, deep inside of me and willed it to speed up the healing of my skin. My fingertips tingled as the old skin began to fall off and new skin began to grow. Every hair follicle tingled as the hair grew again, helping push the dead skin off.

"I traveled closer and closer to your school and the stories about you became even greater," he said as he dragged the boy along the ground towards the table. "I knew I had to set a trap and find a way to make you prove your lineage. So, I went to the market and set up a booth as a jewelry salesman. As I predicted, you came to my booth and you were drawn to the amulet. Unfortunately for you, you had no idea that you were drawn to it like a moth to fire. It assisted with your capture by those idiots who were focused on the fact that a girl had become a Mercenary." He laughed. "If only they had known what you are, they would have simply killed you where you stood."

He picked the boy up and tossed him on top of the table, untying his wrists from the single rope and retying him by both wrists and ankles. "I knew you would escape them, but I had no idea that you would be saved by that Elf. That was when I realized I needed to think out my plan very well. I could not have you rescued by him."

The skin from my fingertips to my elbows was healed and I could almost move enough to get my swords and kill him.

"I knew you would come if I baited you with ogres. The only problem I had was keeping them in line and keeping them from killing and eating these two humans. I could have stolen more of them, but the ogres seemed pleased with eating the two older men I let them capture first."

I flexed my fingers and then my wrist to ensure that they were healed enough to handle the sword. Why had the idiot left my swords on me? Did he really think I could not heal myself enough to use them? How arrogant.

He finished tying the boy and picked up the knife he had just used to kill the old man. "Tomorrow, I will be the strongest human alive thanks to your power. I will take over the humans and then, eventually, the world!"

I stood up, pulling my sword from my sheath and said, "I don't think so."

He turned around, absolute shock on his face and asked, "How?"

I tried to stab him, but he blocked me with his staff, which he produced from thin air. "Elf tricks," I said through gritted teeth. I should have made my legs heal as well because they were hurting worse than anything else as I moved.

He started to cast a spell so I punched him in the mouth as hard as I could, cracking a couple of his teeth. Why hadn't I thought of that earlier! He howled in pain and I used the distraction to thrust my blade into his stomach. He yelled in pain and tried to get away, but I stabbed him again. I wanted to talk, to tell him I was killing him for those people. To tell him that he would never have my magic, but all I could do was stab him again and again.

His lifeless body lay on the ground, but I had to be sure he could not get back up so I cut off his head. I walked to the boy, satisfied that we were safe now and cut the ropes binding him to the table. He pulled the cloth from his mouth and whispered, "Thank you."

I would have responded, but my legs chose that moment to give out. I landed on my knees and careened sideways, lying on my side as my head swam with dizziness.

"I'll get help," the boy said. "Please, don't die."

Even if I died now, which I would not, it would be worth it. The boy was safe and the magic user was dead, unable to steal my magic from me. I relaxed on the ground, trying to regain my energy and heal. I had come too close to death too many times these past few years. I needed a vacation.

I heard yelling and felt wind on me, but I stayed where I was. If someone else wanted to kill me, then this was the perfect opportunity.

"Marin!" Favian yelled.

I smiled and then regretted it, hissing in pain from the still unhealed, burned skin. I realized that I probably looked like a monster and really did not want Favian to see me like this, but I could do nothing about it at the moment.

"Is she alive?" Sebastian asked as people moved closer to me.

"She's breathing," Favian said. "That man's not though."

"No, it would be difficult to breathe without your head," Sebastian said.

I stifled my laugh, not wanting to hurt any more than I already was. "Go away," I whispered, trying to move my lips as little as possible.

"She smells terrible," Sebastian said.

"No worse than usual," Favian responded. "You haven't spent two months in the forest on missions with her."

Mother sat down in front of me, her hand over her mouth as she spoke. "Hello, Daughter. You are quite the mess."

"She isn't talking," Favian told her. "We insulted her several times and she is still ignoring us."

"Favian!" Mother scolded. "Come look at her and it will explain everything!"

Favian walked around me and gasped. "Marin! I'm sorry. I could not tell from the back that..." He looked at his mother. "Will she be alright?"

"Marin, can you talk?" she asked.

"Hurts," I whispered, moving my lips slowly.

"How did this happen?" Sebastian asked.

"The magic user set her on fire," Micah said. "He was aiming for me and she leapt in front, saving me."

Favian moved to touch me and Mother smacked his arm. "Do not touch her. Any movement will jar the dead skin and hurt just as bad as being on fire."

She was right about that.

"How did she kill the magic user?" Sebastian asked.

"She healed her forearms and attacked him," the little boy said. "She saved my life."

"I'm going to heal you, but it is going to hurt. You understand?" Mother whispered to me. I met her eyes and she smiled. "It will be alright. I will heal you fully, even your hair. You won't have a burn scar on you when I'm done."

I hoped so. I really did not want to walk around with permanent burns on my body. Not that I would not have walked around proudly with them, but if they could be healed, then I wanted them to be.

"Make sure you don't heal her other scars," Favian said. "She is very proud of those ones."

He knew me so well.

"And you might leave one burn mark as a reminder for her," Micah said.

"Where is she?" Murdock asked from somewhere behind me. "Is she alive?"

Favian stepped over me, intercepting him. "She is alive. No thanks to you and your village."

"We could not help," he said with shame in his voice. "The ogres alone were too strong for us."

"Pathetic," Sebastian said. "You are so pathetic that you would not even *attempt* to assist her."

"We summoned Mercenaries for a reason," he said.

"Boys," Father chastised. "Leave the human alone."

"I'm so sorry this happened, Marin," Micah whispered. "It is all my fault. I thought I could handle him, but he proved to be too strong. Will you forgive me?"

I just stared at him. Did he really think I was going to talk to him right now?

"Heal her mouth last," Favian suggested. "That way we will continue to have this peace and quiet a bit longer."

I closed my eyes and used my own magic to assist mother in healing me. I healed my mouth and said, "You are a spoiled, egotistical, self-righteous, Elf. I would expect this if you had saved me, but you did not. I saved myself. So, I would appreciate it if you would shut up and let Mother heal me."

Favian squatted down in front of me and rested his hand on newly healed skin on my cheek. "There's my Marin. I thought you were playing dead when you did not automatically respond to the first taunt, but I had no idea how badly injured you were. Are you sure you're alright?"

Why was his concern making me tear up? "I am in pain, but mother is healing me rather quickly."

"Will her hair grow back?" Sebastian asked.

Mother nodded her head. "She will have a full head of luscious hair again once I am done."

"Good, she looks like a boy bald," Favian said.

I reached forward and pinched his leg, startling him because he did not know that I could move. "I know where you sleep," I reminded him.

He smiled at me and then stepped over me to talk to Father.

"He was very worried about you," Queen Silvermist said as she dropped her head down enough for me to see her nose.

"Why are you here?" I asked in shock.

"We provide the quickest transportation, so we were the best option to bring your family to you."

"Thank you," I whispered.

Sebastian sat down next to me and laced his fingers through mine. "Is the pain bearable?" he asked.

"Yes," I said, feeling tingly from him holding my hand.

"You should have asked for assistance. What if we had not been able to get to you in time?" he chastised me.

"Don't reprimand me, please. I get that enough from Favian."

"Apparently not, since you continue to put yourself in terrible situations," Favian said, glaring at Sebastian and my joined hands.

"I could not let that little boy die because of me," I said defensively.

"What do you mean because of you?" Father asked.

I could not see him. "Can you let Father sit here, Sebastian? I can't see him."

He nodded his head, standing up and letting Father sit in front of me where I could see him. I told him word for word what the magic user had said. He listened intently, his eyes widening incredibly. He glanced behind me and asked, "Do you think he was right?"

"It would make sense," Kato said.

"Care to enlighten the rest of us?" I asked them.

"There have been people, humans, with extraordinary powers.

Most believed they were magic users or shape shifters or even humans with something in their lineage that contributed to it, but some claimed that they were the offspring of the God or Goddess themselves."

"That's ridiculous!" Sebastian said.

I closed my eyes and thought about it. Was it possible? Could my father be the God of everything? Could I be a half-god? I laughed and said, "I highly doubt that I am a half god or goddess or whatever. I am hardly godly."

No one answered me.

It took Mother two more hours to finish healing me and then she and I both had to rest for the night to regain all of the magic we had used. Favian and I were lying on the grass looking up at the stars while the others were preparing dinner. It was the first time we had been alone since our last mission.

"I'm mad at you for leaving me behind while you went on a mission," Favian said softly, anger clearly evident in his tone.

"I won't apologize," I said. "I have to learn to do missions on my own. Soon you will be running the Kingdom and won't have time for missions with me."

"What are you talking about?" he asked, sitting up and looking down at me.

I sat up and said, "You are supposed to start courting females and running the Kingdom alongside Father so that you can learn to do it. Then you will be married and your wife will not want you out running around in the forest killing ogres with me."

"My wife?" Favian asked in shock. "What?"

I stood up and clenched my fists angrily. "I think it's time that we separate ourselves."

"What are you saying?" Favin asked, standing up and meeting my eyes.

"Dinner is ready!" Mother called.

"We will talk more later," I said. "But you know what I am saying."

I started to walk away, but Favian grabbed my arm, making me look back at him. "Is this because of Sebastian? Are you breaking our partnership for him?"

"Of course not," I said angrily. "This has nothing to do with him. He isn't even a Mercenary, so why would I break our partnership because of him?"

"Then why are you doing this? Why are you trying to leave me?" he asked.

The way he said it sounded very much like he thought we were breaking up. Or was that just how I wanted to hear it? "I already told you. You are not going to have time for me once you start courting the females."

"I will always make time for you," he said. "You're my best friend."

"Marin. Favian. Come eat," Father called.

"We're busy," Favian called back angrily.

I had never heard him speak to Father so disrespectfully before. Apparently, Father was just as shocked because he just stared at us.

"Favian, apologize to Father," I whispered.

"You and I are perfect partners. Why do you want to find another partner?" he asked me.

"I don't want another partner," I said honestly. "I won't find another."

"So, you want to be solo?" he asked.

I jerked my arm away from him and yelled, "I don't *want* any of it! I want to live in the fantasyland where I get everything that I want, but that won't ever happen!"

"Tell me what you want," he whispered as he moved closer to me. "And I will give it to you."

I blinked in shock and disbelief. He had no idea what he was saying. "You can't give me what I want," I whispered back.

"Who do you want?" he asked, anger building in his eyes. He stood upright, his spine tight and his fists clenched. "Who is it?"

"There is no one," I said through clenched teeth. "I swear on Fire that what I have told you already is true."

"We can work something out," he said.

I laughed and shook my head. "You have always been the optimist."

"Favian, we need to talk," Father said from beside us. I hadn't noticed his approach.

"Please, Father. We are in the middle of an important discussion," he said.

I shook my head and walked away. "No, we are done." I would die for Favian and I would die seeing him with another female, but I could not do nothing about that.

"Don't walk away from me," Favian called. "We are not through talking."

I ignored him and continued walking towards the bar where we were going to eat with everyone else.

"I command you as Prince to stop walking and talk to me!" he yelled.

"Favian," Father chastised.

I stopped walking and stood in shock. Had he really used his title on me? Did he really think that I would listen to him if he threw that at me? What had gotten in to him?

I turned around slowly and said, "I am not an elf and therefore I could give a rat's ass whose Prince you are. Go talk to Amile. I'm sure she would fall to her knees at your requests."

"Marin. Favian. You both need to stop. Whatever is going on between the two of you can be figured out another day. You are both stressed and exhausted from this ordeal."

"Don't do this, Marin. Do not do this to me," he pleaded.

I walked away, heading over to Fire and mounting her instead of heading to the bar. I could not stay here. I could not see his face anymore. If he cornered me I would give in. I would give up because I truly did not want to end our partnership. I wanted our partnership to last fifty more years!

Fire galloped away and then slowed to a walk two miles away. She walked the rest of the way home, not stopping even after an entire day had passed. We reached the Elven Kingdom's gates and Favian stood before them with his arms crossed waiting for me.

I cursed under my breath and tried to walk past him. He grabbed Fire's reins and looked up at me. "I will not allow you to dissolve our partnership. Tomorrow we will head out on our next mission and we will do so as partners. You and I have been partners since you came to live here and I will not allow you to try to dissolve our partnership just because you think you are endangering me."

How did he know? I hadn't even said…

"I know you Marin," he said as he stared into my eyes. "And I will not let you kill yourself by working alone just because you are worried that I might get hurt like you did. I know it was hard to see that man killed, but that won't happen to me. I am not as easily killed as an old human man."

"I could not live with myself if you are killed protecting me because of how weak I am," I whispered.

He tugged on Fire's reins and she lay down so that I was eye level with Favian now. He stared straight into my eyes and said, "I will follow you wherever you go. I will follow you to the ends of the earth and back."

Every ounce of my body wanted to leap for joy at his words and to kiss him, but I could not. "You know what I said was true," I whispered.

"That time will come, but not for a while. Don't you want to enjoy what time we have left?" he asked.

I climbed off of Fire and let her stand up so that she was not uncomfortable. "Favian, I…"

He grabbed my arms and stared into my eyes with fear in his own. It was a fear I had not seen before and it frightened me. "Please, Marin. Please let me enjoy these last years of mercenary work with you. Do not force me to retire so soon after we graduated."

I had been afraid of this, which is why I had left. Dammit, why did I always give into his eyes! "Promise that you will try harder to stay safe," I whispered.

"Only if you promise to stop trying to throw yourself into every dangerous situation," he said with a smirk. "It's not my fault if I'm in danger because you lead me there."

I smiled and then he hugged me. "I'm sorry," I whispered.

"Soon we will go on another mission and you will get to kill something and all of this will behind us like a bad dream."

"Promise?" I asked.

He laughed and said, "Yes."

I walked around him, leading Fire towards the stables and felt defeated and yet happy at the same time.

"Hello, Marin," Alex said cheerily.

I smiled at him despite everything spinning in my head. "Hello."

He took Fire and helped me unsaddle her. "You look even more worried than you had when you left."

I groaned, sat down on the straw in Fire's stall and buried my face in my knees. "Why does life have to be so complicated?"

Alex sat down beside me and put his arm around my shoulders. "It will all work out. I know you can handle anything that is thrown at you."

"You haven't heard about my recent mission, have you?" I asked, peeking up at him from under my eyelashes.

"That you were fried to a crisp? Yes, we have all heard."

I groaned. Why did elves have to gossip so much?

"We also heard that you saved a little boy and your partner's life and even when you were so close to death, you killed the man responsible. That sounds like a positive end to me."

"My family had to save me again," I whispered.

"True, but you did complete the mission without Favian."

He was right. I had. Even though I would have died had mother not shown up, I had completed a mission without Favian! I sat up and kissed his cheek. "Thank you, Alex."

He stared at me blankly and mumbled, "Sure."

I kissed Fire's nose and then headed out of the stable. I had some research to do.

I ran into the castle and straight to the library. The library was an acre big with shelves that went from the floor all the way to the twenty-foot ceiling. Several rolling ladders were set up and yet it still seemed like quite the task just to get to the books at the top. Momo, the very old librarian smiled warmly at me. "Princess Marin, it is good to see you."

"Momo, do you have any books that talk about half-gods or beings who were thought to be the offspring of the God or Goddess?"

Momo nodded his head. "Yes, right this way." He led me deep into the shelves and stopped at a bookshelf which had five books on it. "Here you go. The demigod section."

I took the first book and blew the dust off of it. Obviously, I was the first one to use these books in a long time. I sat down and opened the book, only to find out it was written in old Elvish. I grabbed the other books and headed out to find Favian. "I'll bring them back as soon as I am finished," I called.

"Don't burn them," Momo called after me.

I groaned. You accidentally set fire to one child's book and you're forever damned by the librarian. "I will protect them," I called back.

I started to head to Favian's room, but decided it would be better if I went to someone else. Father and Kato would not have arrived yet. Who else knew old Elvish?

"Marin, what are you doing walking around? You should be resting," Sebastian said behind me.

I turned around and smiled at him. "I was just looking for you."

"For me?" he asked unbelievingly. "What for?"

I held up the books and said, "I need a translator."

"Ah, so you wish to use me for my brain."

Why did it sound bad when he said it like that? "Well, I suppose. I just need someone to help me."

"Why aren't you seeking out Favian?" he asked. "Are you two still quarreling?"

"If it is such a bother, then I won't waste your time," I said angrily. I turned around and started to storm off to my room.

Sebastian placed a hand on my arm and said, "I'm sorry. I shouldn't have been so rude."

"Apology accepted," I said and started walking again.

"Do you still want my help?" he asked.

"Perhaps after you've rested and are in a better mood, you can come find me," I said angrily.

"You can't accept someone's apology and then still be angry with them."

I ignored him and continued up to my room. I could do whatever the hell I wanted. Just let them wait and see.

CHAPTER NINE

I ended up sleeping for an entire day and when I finally woke up there was a small paper Pegasus sitting on the table beside my bed. I smiled, knowing that Sebastian had made it for me and put it with the other animals we had made. My body was stiff, but I did not feel any pain from the burns I had had yesterday.

Mother had left one burn mark on my wrist as requested and it was good to have as a reminder. I hurried down and bathed before heading to the dining hall. When I entered, I was glad to see that everyone was home again. I sat across from Sebastian and took the lid off of my plate to begin eating. "Thank you for the gift," I said to Sebastian.

He smiled, pleased with my thanks. "You're welcome."

"How are you feeling?" Mother asked.

"A little sore, but otherwise I feel very well. Thank you."

Favian glanced at me a few times while I ate, but I kept my eyes on the plate of food in front of me. I felt a little awkward after our interaction yesterday, but knew it would fade soon.

"Do you still want my help today?" Sebastian asked.

Favian looked at me and I felt his eyes burning a hole into me. I stood up and started heading towards the door. "Yes, if you have time."

Sebastian followed me and said, "I always have time for you."

I went to my room and grabbed the books and then we went outside to get some fresh air while he translated for me. I let him read the books in silence for a while and then he relayed the information to me. Most of it was unimportant, some of it tales of men with extraordinary strength, but so far nothing helpful.

How did one determine if they were a demigod? Could I talk to my father?

I laughed and Sebastian glanced at me curiously. "You think if I tried talking to him that he would respond?"

He shrugged. "You never know unless you try."

Maybe, but I was not going to try right now.

After three hours, we still hadn't found anything except hungry stomachs. We returned the books to the library and then stretched in the hallway. After sitting for three hours stretching felt wonderful.

"I'm sorry those books weren't much help," Sebastian said.

"It's not your fault," I said. "I appreciate you reading them and helping me."

"I'd do almost anything to spend time with you," he said, picking up my hand and kissing the back of it. "Why don't we go on a mission together?" he asked me. "Just you and me. You can show me the ropes."

Before I could register what happened, Sebastian was against the wall with Favian's arm pressed against his throat.

"Favian!" I yelled. "What the hell are you doing?"

"If you're going to attack me at least take this outside," Sebastian said with a sneer.

"Gladly," Favian said, pushing off of Sebastian and heading towards the door.

I grabbed Favian's arm. "Stop this. Why are you trying to fight him?! He didn't do anything wrong!"

"He and I have boundaries to discuss. For now, why don't you go see Mother in the dining hall," Favian said angrily, jerking his arm away from me.

Sebastian smiled and said, "Don't worry, Marin this will be over with quickly."

"I'm glad you realize that you're weaker than me," Favian said. "Perhaps you should stop flirting with Marin now that you realize that you are not her equal."

"Favian!" I said in shock. I hadn't heard him speak so cruelly to someone in a long time. What had gotten in to him?

"Are you going to keep talking or are we going to settle this?" Sebastian asked angrily.

Favian and he marched down the hallway and I felt torn. Should I go outside and stop them? Or was this something that they needed to do?

I groaned in frustration and hurried to the dining hall. Mother and Kato were whispering to each other conspiratorially, but stopped when I walked in. "What's wrong?" Kato asked me.

"They're fighting again," I said. "I think Favian's mad at me and taking it out on Sebastian."

Kato stood and patted my shoulder. "I'll make sure they don't permanently harm each other. Boys fight, it's natural."

I plopped down in the chair beside Mother and sighed. "I don't understand what's angering Favian so much."

"What was Sebastian doing before Favian incited the fight?" Mother asked.

"He was flirting with me and asked if I would take him on a

mission. I didn't even get a chance to respond and Favian came in there."

"Why would that upset Favian so much?" Mother asked.

"Because I tried to end our partnership yesterday," I said honestly.

Mother's eyes widened in shock. "Why would you do that?" she asked. "You fought us for years to allow you to go to mercenary school so you could be partners. You only recently graduated."

"It's complicated," I mumbled.

"Tell me," she ordered.

"Favian is going to start courting females and will soon take over here. So, I said we should just separate now before his wife tells him to stop going on missions with me."

Mother smiled softly and laughed. "Oh, Marin."

I stood up angrily, knocking over my chair. "I'm glad my pain amuses you."

I started to leave, but Father entered the room and said, "Sit down." I picked up my chair and obeyed. "Kato is keeping an eye on them, but Favian is furious. What happened?"

"He's afraid that she might leave him for Sebastian," Mother answered.

"You say that as though we are a couple," I grumbled. "We're only partners and we all knew that eventually our partnership would end so he could take over the realm and become a King."

Father sat back in his chair and sighed. "I see."

"Can I go?" I asked.

"Why do you think Favian is so upset about the thought of you leaving with Sebastian on a mission?" Father asked.

"Because he doesn't fully trust Sebastian and is over protective of me."

Mother laid her hand on Father's arm and he smiled at me. "Things will work out, Marin."

That settled it. "I'm leaving tomorrow to continue on my path of becoming a Protector," I said angrily.

"Marin, you need to calm down and think rationally," Father said. "I understand that you're upset, but leaving won't solve anything."

"Don't you understand?" I asked him with tears brewing in my eyes. "There is no true happiness for me except in my work."

I ignored whatever they said behind me and walked out of the dining hall despite my grumbling stomach. I climbed up the stairs and packed my bag for tomorrow's departure. I shouldn't have come back here at all. I should have just gone to Macon after the mission.

I finished packing and went out to see how Favian and Sebastian were faring. Kato was leaning against the fence focused on the twins. I started sneaking towards him and he said, "You still stomp around like a crazed boar."

I climbed up onto the fence and sat down on it. Favian and Sebastian were both breathing heavily and sweating. They were also bleeding from various small cuts on their arms. "They're stupid," I told Kato. "This fight will solve nothing."

"It might unite them," Kato said. "Your father and I fought several times before becoming friends."

I spoke louder so that the twins would hear. "Favian is only mad because he thinks I'm going to stop being his partner to be Sebastian's. Perhaps you should have let me answer for myself first."

They had paused in their fighting to look at me and to catch their breath.

"I'm just as good of a fighter as he is," Sebastian said, walking towards me. "Why won't you let me be your partner?"

"Favian has been my partner since I was four. When I don't have him as a partner, I will just go solo," I said.

"You can't go solo," the twins said at the same time.

"I can do whatever I want," I said defensively.

"You've been hiding something from me for a while now and it's not just that you're worried that me being around you will endanger me. What is it?" Favian asked.

I shook my head and walked away from them all. "You don't understand and you never will."

"Try explaining it to me," Favian said from in front of me.

I had seen him move quickly before, but this was ridiculous.

"No," I said, avoiding his eyes and continuing walking.

"You're running away from your problems again!" he yelled.

I stopped and turned to face him. "You have no idea what I'm doing!"

"Then tell me!" he said.

"I can't," I whispered, looking down at the ground.

He yelled angrily and stormed into the castle.

"I'll make sure he doesn't break anything," Kato whispered as he walked by.

"Marin," Sebastian began.

"I cannot court you," I said to him. "You're wonderful, but…"

"You're in love with Favian," Sebastian said. I grimaced, but nodded my head. "So why aren't you with him then? It is obvious you both have feelings for each other."

"He's going to be King and he will need an Elf female as his Queen. I cannot let him find out my feelings for him. I cannot lose him as a friend," I said as I leaned against the wall of the castle, my energy on very low reserve. "That's why I'm hiding it from him."

"Why couldn't you be Queen? You're the King and Queen's daughter," he said.

I shook my head. "He is going to start courting females next year and I can't interfere. The only thing that would happen if I told him I loved him would be that it would ruin our friendship."

"Then why can't I court you?" he asked as he moved closer to me.

"Because I love Favian."

"And?" he asked. "That doesn't mean that you couldn't love me in time."

I shook my head. "I could not do that to you."

He stepped closer to me and stared into my eyes. "You want Favian? Then pretend I'm Favian." I stared at him in shock, not knowing what to say to that and then he kissed me. I felt like all the bones had disappeared from my body and I was mud. I kissed him back and reached up to rest my hand on the base of his throat.

That was when I realized that he had no necklace. He was Sebastian, not Favian and I did not love him.

I stepped back from him and shook my head as tears fell. "I'm sorry. I cannot be with you if I do not love you. It would be cruel to you and would only cause us both heartache."

"In time, you would think differently," he said confidently.

He might have been right, but I couldn't do it. Could I? I shook my head.

"Are you going to stay single the rest of your life, not telling Favian how you feel and not allowing yourself to feel for others?"

He was right, but I did not have an answer for him that he would like. It was better if I went away from everyone and lived a solitary life so that no one would be in danger of dying like my human family had.

"At least I got a kiss from you," he whispered with a wicked grin. "Now I can die happy."

I laughed and wiped the stupid tears off of my face. "I'm sorry."

He hugged me and then put his arm around my shoulders as we walked back into the castle. "Don't apologize for your feelings. I'm glad that you think so much of me."

"You're going to flirt with me still in front of Favian, aren't you?" I asked with a smirk.

He smiled. "Of course! Besides, it's not like he is going to have you and a woman as beautiful as you are deserves to be flirted with. Plus, I have heard what a terrible flirt you are when Favian isn't around."

"Rumors travel fast in the Elven Kingdom," I mumbled.

Favian turned the corner and stopped in front of us. He looked at Sebastian's arm around my shoulders to the tear tracks on my face and asked, "What were you crying about?"

"Truly it was me who was crying," Sebastian said as he released his arm from around me. "My heart is broken."

"Can I talk to you?" Favian asked.

"I think we have talked enough," I said as I walked towards my room to grab my bag.

"Marin, please let me talk this out with you," he asked.

"There is nothing to talk out."

"You're being stubborn and hiding yourself from me," he said.

He was right.

"Marin," Kato called. "You have received a summons to Macon."

I nodded my head and said, "I was already on my way."

"I will come with you," Favian said.

"He did not summon you," I reminded him.

"And I do not leave your side unless you run away in the dark of night," he said angrily. "We are a team and I will go with you to Macon."

"Fine, I will meet you at the stables," I said resignedly. I was happy and yet part of me knew I should have truly ended our partnership already.

I hurried to Baldemar and retrieved my weapons from him, giving him back the loaners. "Those blades are special," he told me. "Be careful with them."

"Thank you," I said with a bow.

"Stay safe," he said as I walked out. "Come home to see us soon."

Alex was standing in front of Fire's stall when I came in and did not turn around when I walked inside the stable. "You're leaving, aren't you?" he asked.

"Yes, I was summoned by Macon," I said as I grabbed my tack.

"You would have left anyways," he said knowingly.

"It is time for me to go," I whispered.

He turned around and said, "You are always welcome here, Marin. I know you don't need to hear that from the stable boy, but no matter what you think or feel, I will always welcome you here and in my house. Some of us look forward to your returns."

It was one of the nicest things I had heard from an Elf other than my family in a long time and I appreciated it. I hugged him and then kissed his cheek. "You will make some female very lucky. I value your friendship."

He hugged me again and whispered, "Please stay safe."

"I will try."

Favian entered the stable and got Ice ready, waiting for me as I got Fire ready.

I put the gear on Fire and then mounted her and we set off at a gallop out of the barn. The journey to Macon took half a day and as I entered the Academy grounds I felt a little better. This had been my second home and I really enjoyed being here. I walked into the office and found him sitting at his desk with his fingers steepled. He saw me and smiled. "Marin. I am glad to see that you are no worse for wear after that last mission."

I sat in the chair in front of his desk and smiled, "Elves are amazing healers."

He looked at Favian and said, "You were not summoned."

Favian said, "No, but she is my partner and we rarely separate. Would you like me to stand outside?"

"You may stay."

Favian sat in the chair next to me and I felt the pressures of our royal life slip away being in the Academy and in front of Macon.

"So, do you know why I brought you here?" he asked me. That

was part of why I liked him, he was straight to business with no fluff.

"I am guessing that you're sending me out on another mission," I said.

He nodded his head, "Yes, but first thing is first. Please stand up."

I stood and he walked around the desk. "Follow me." I obeyed and followed him outside and towards the arena where there were several mercenaries and the Council, a group of five Protectors and five Mercenaries who essentially ran us and decided who promoted.

Macon made me stand in front of them in the arena as he went to stand with them, being the Chairman of the Council.

"Marin, your recent mission along with your many others have been brought to our attention for our consideration," one of the other members said. If I remembered correctly his name was Octavius and he was one of the few humans capable of taking down rogue shapeshifters.

"After careful consideration, we have decided to award you the title of Protector. It is not a title to be taken lightly and it is not given lightly. Your power and passion and the desire to protect the people of this land with your own life are the reason you are being given this title. We have all heard how you saved your partner and the child from the magic user in Grundio and are very impressed," Octavius said. "Congratulations and may you use your title with honor."

Protector. I was a Protector. I wanted to shout for joy, but instead bowed and said, "I humbly accept the title and will ensure I do not tarnish it."

"We are sure that you will not," Macon said with a smile.

"We have a mission for you and Favian," Octavius said.

Favian stepped up next to me and we waited to be given our mission instructions.

"Our spies learned that there is a group of rogues gathering ogres and others to use in an attack against the human King. We need them eradicated before they can start the war. If you can kill them before then you will save hundreds of human lives," Octavius said.

I nodded my head. "I understand."

"Macon will give you a map of the location. We look forward to tale of your victory," he said with a smile.

I bowed and smiled at him. "I look forward to finishing this mission."

"Congratulations," Favian said.

"Are you mad?" I asked him softly so the Council members and Macon who was walking in front of us would not hear us.

"No, why would I be mad?" he asked me, looking genuinely confused.

"Because you might have become a Protector too if you had come on that mission like you were supposed to," I said.

He shrugged. "It was always your goal to become a Protector. I am fine with just being a Mercenary."

Probably because he would have to quit soon anyways.

Macon gave us the map and dismissed us. We would stay the night at the Academy and leave early in the morning tomorrow. We had a very long trip south before we reached our foes.

We bowed to him and left to the dining hall to eat. I was very hungry. I opened the door and most of the people inside were students, but a few were familiar faces from when I had attended the Academy. I went up to the cook who smiled happily at me. "Marin! I did not expect to see you here so soon! Congrats on becoming a Protector!"

"Thank you," I said with a wide smile.

He gave me my tray of food and I sat down at an empty table to eat. The students whispered loudly around me and it pleased me to be so infamous among them already.

"How does it feel to be the first female Mercenary and the

first female Protector?" Doug asked me as he sat down across from me.

He had attended the Academy with me and Favian, but had not really interacted much with me. "I'm shocked and pleased," I said honestly. And I really had not thought about being the first female Protector!

"You deserve it," he said honestly. "We have all heard about your missions. You're quite an amazing woman." He finally turned to Favian to acknowledge him. "Favian," Doug greeted him with a handshake. "How's it going?"

"Good."

"So now that you're a Protector, what are you going to do?" Doug asked, turning back to me.

"Go on missions like usual," I said with a shrug. "Not much will change except my title and probably the difficulty of the missions."

"We should get some rest," Favian said. Clearly, he was uncomfortable, but I wasn't sure why. He had just said he did not care about not being a Protector.

I nodded my head without looking at him and then grabbed a bread roll and left the room. I walked to the stables and tossed an apple into Fire's food bucket. "Eat up, girl. We are going to be riding very far tomorrow."

"Are you sure you want to do this mission?" he asked me softly.

"Yes."

He looked away from me and exhaled. "Mother is very upset that you left without saying good bye."

"I'll send her an apology note when we finish the mission," I said.

"Sebastian almost followed me here," he said.

"Did you tie him up?" I asked only half joking.

"He told me that you refused to court him," Favian said softly. "But he would not tell me why you refused him."

"I don't need to give a reason," I said as I waited to find out where he was going with this.

"Alex seemed very distraught when we were leaving," he noted.

I cringed. "He is a more emotional Elf than most, but I'm sure he will be fine."

"So, what is your plan?" he asked me.

"Find the rogues and ogres and slay them all."

"Not for the mission, for your life," he said.

I sighed. "I don't know," I answered honestly. "I'm already a Protector, so I guess I can focus on finding out who my Father is for a while. I know you have to help Father with the Festival next month."

"Are you planning on going alone?" he asked me.

"Yes," I answered simply.

"Whatever it is that you're hiding from me, you can tell me," he whispered. "No matter what it is, you know that you are my best friend and nothing could come between us."

I said nothing because there was nothing I could say to him. I could not tell him that I loved him and that this distance and this coldness between us was killing me.

"Amile has been following Sebastian around," he said with a laugh.

"Does that upset you?" I asked him.

He frowned. "Why would that upset me?"

"She used to follow you around all the time and now she is following him."

He shook his head. "I don't care about her. I'm glad that she has found someone else to flirt with and bat her eyelashes at."

I wasn't sure if I believed him or not, but I did not press him on the matter. "At least he seems to be fitting in nicely," I said.

He nodded his head and opened his mouth, but then closed it again. I was curious what he was going to say, but he stood up and said, "Let's go get some rest."

CHAPTER TEN

The next day we packed our supplies and headed south. We barely spoke, just checking to make sure the other was ready and then brief comments. It was weird and I could feel our friendship straining. I needed to fix this, to keep our friendship intact. Maybe I should try to talk to him about females.

"So, how was your night at the ball?" I asked him with a smile.

He glanced at me and shrugged. "It was okay until I realized that you had run away."

I'd forgotten about that. "Did you have fun with the females? Was it less painful getting to split the duties with Sebastian?"

"The females were much different this time," he admitted. "In fact it seemed like they were more enthusiastic than usual to dance with us."

"Well there were two of you this time," I reminded him.

"Does it bother you?" he asked me.

"What?" I asked him, unsure what he was specifically asking me about.

"That he looks like me."

"Very much," I told him honestly.

"Is that why you turned down his courtship? Because of how similar we look?"

"No," I answered honestly. It wasn't *just* how they looked, but that they weren't the same.

"You know that you can be honest with me," he said. "I won't hate you if you do like him."

"I do not *like* him in that way," I said. "And that is why I turned down his courtship."

"Jovian said he saw Sebastian kiss you," Favian whispered.

Crap. Why had I brought this up again? "He did."

"Did you punch him?" he asked with a smirk.

"No, but I told him I could not court him right after he kissed me."

"So, he didn't even ask to court you? You just refused him?"

"I guess," I whispered. "Why are you so worried about me courting him or not?" I asked him.

"I just don't want to see you get hurt," he replied, but looked away from me. "I still don't fully trust him."

"You never will," I said. Even if he wouldn't admit it, he would always distrust Sebastian. There was nothing that Sebastian could do to earn his trust either.

"So, are you and Alex courting?" he asked me.

"I'm not courting anyone," I answered through gritted teeth. Why was he suddenly so interested? Usually you did not start courting until eighteen and that was still two years away.

"I know there are many who want to court you," he said. "I saw the way they looked at you at the ball."

"None of them will court me," I said. "And besides, I won't court any of them."

"Elven men not good enough for you?" he asked a bit angrily.

"It has nothing to do with that!" I yelled in shock. "You are well aware that I prefer Elves to humans."

"Then why?"

"I don't want any of *them*!" I yelled and then turned away. Dammit.

"Who do you want?"

"Who do *you* want?" I asked him back.

"You answer me first," he said.

"What I want doesn't matter anyways. I am going to be a Protector and spend my days hunting ogres so I won't have time for a domesticated female life."

"You can't do this when you're old," he said.

"Watch me."

"Don't you want children?" he asked. "I've seen you teaching the young ones when you think no one is watching."

"The thought has crossed my mind, but until I found out my true patronage I won't subject that upon my children."

"I take it Sebastian wasn't able to help you with those books?" he asked.

"No...wait? How did you know about that?" I asked him suspiciously. He pretended to scout the trees around us, avoiding looking at me. "Were you spying on me?"

"Jovian seems fond of you," he said to try to change the subject.

"He likes sparring with me. Now, why were you spying on me?"

"I was worried about you. You spent a lot of alone time with him and you stopped talking to me about stuff. You've been hiding things from me since we left the Academy."

"I'm sorry," I answered him honestly.

"What can be so terrible that you won't tell me about it?" he asked.

"There are some things that you are just better off not knowing," I answered him honestly.

"That's not fair," he said. "You should give me the information and let me deal with it myself. I am more level headed than you."

I ignored the dig at me and stayed quiet.

"Will you ever be able to tell me?" he asked me.

I shook my head. "Nope."

"Why not?"

"Because I can't tell you," I said.

"Did you kill someone?" he asked.

"You know about everyone or thing I have ever killed," I said.

"Are you pregnant?" he asked me with a disapproving look.

"Favian!" I yelled. "How dare you insult my honor! I have never lain with a man!"

"Just checking," he said. "It would explain your mood swings."

"Rude."

"Did you do something against Elven laws?" he asked.

"Almost, but no that's not what it is about." I really did not like this twenty questions game.

"Almost?" he asked.

"I went to see Queen Silvermist that day to make the bracelets, but she stopped me before I set foot in their land."

"You were going to enter the Pegasus lands!" he asked in shock.

"I had a good reason," I mumbled.

"You're lucky she stopped you! I can't imagine what Father would have done if you had entered their lands."

"Calm down, I didn't enter their lands so there's no reason to get so worked up," I said with a roll of my eyes.

"What else could it be?" he asked me. "What else could you think that I would possibly care about that you are hiding it from me?"

I said nothing. I could not tell him the truth.

We rode in silence and now he seemed even more agitated. I

was glad that our ride south did not involve us riding over mountains and into the cold. We made camp off of the rode and ate our dinner in silence. I could tell he was in deep thought and so I let him be. He would probably just ask me more questions that I could not answer for him. Part of me wanted to tell him and to be honest with him, but the other more dominant part of me did not want to hear his reaction and know our friendship was over because he did not love me or think I was pretty. He had said I looked beautiful when I had come to breakfast in my dress, but he could have meant that I had looked good for me since I rarely dressed womanly.

I climbed into my sleeping bag and hoped I could kill something tomorrow and take my mind off of this ridiculous relationship quandary. I turned away from Favian and closed my eyes, but sleep came much later and I was continually roused from sleep despite knowing what woke me. It wasn't until the third time that I finally heard something while awake.

I opened my eyes and staying very still scanned the area in front of me, but only saw Ice and Fire dozing together. I rolled over with my eyes closed, pretending that I was trying to get comfortable and once I was on my side again I opened my eyes. Ten feet behind Favian I saw a flash of a weapon. They were moving quietly, but apparently, they were not quiet enough. I glanced at Favian and met his opened eyes. I jerked my chin in the direction behind him and grabbed my dagger from the ground in front of me. The attackers leapt out of the dark and grabbed for Favian, but he dodged them and tossed them to the ground. I leapt up and out of my sleeping bag and readied myself for another attack, but none came.

One of the attackers ran off and the second was immobilized due to Favian sitting on top of him. "Why did you attack us?" he asked.

I looked at his torn clothes and dull blade and said, "He's a beggar."

"We just wanted your clothes and food," he said. "Money if you had it. We didn't realize that you are Mercenaries."

Favian stood up and gave him a roll of bread. "Perhaps next time you should ask. Others will kill you before asking and I don't think you would prefer dying."

"Thank you," the man mumbled and then ran out into the woods after his friend.

"That was unusually nice of you," I said as I lay down again.

"He was all bones and skin. One roll won't matter to me, but it does to him."

I closed my eyes and was almost asleep when Favian asked, "Can't we go back to how things were when we were in the Academy?"

"What do you mean?" I asked him.

"This awkwardness that is between us is troublesome and I don't like it," he said. "Can't we just pretend for this mission that we are just fresh out of the Academy and none of the other things matter?"

"I will try," I said softly. I did not like this awkwardness any more than he did. I wished it could go back and I would not know of my love for him as well.

I stood up and strapped my weapons on. There was no way that I was going back to sleep tonight. Fire walked over to me and I saddled her quickly, getting on her back and heading towards the rode. "I will scout ahead. I need a minute to clear my head."

I heard him say something, but Fire was galloping away and the wind was too loud for me to hear it. I rode for a while and then the sun rose and with it the smell of cooking meat and loud voices. I left the road and scouted ahead slowly. It was an army encampment of at least ten human soldiers. Ogres were nearby, but at least a mile or so away still. I dismounted and continued forward on foot to get close enough to hear their conversation. I hid up in the canopy of a tree right next to their camp and held very still as I listened.

"Which Mercenaries do you think Macon will end up sending to try to fight us?" one asked.

"Probably that Elf, Favian, since Macon thinks he is one of the strongest," another said.

I looked at them closer trying to figure out if I knew them, but they did not look familiar. I knew that we were well known, especially since Favian was Prince of the Elves, but why were these men talking like they knew Macon and our Academy?

"They'll definitely send Marin to fight the ogres, but I heard she and the Elf had had a falling out," said another.

"A falling out? Over what?" asked the first who had spoken.

Why the hell were they gossiping about us like women?

"Well she took that one job in Grundio without him. She took it with a human man, a sorcerer."

"Perhaps Elf men aren't as good in the sack as so many say," one said with a sneer.

The men laughed and I felt my cheeks redden. I knew people assumed things about Favian and me, but hearing it like this was very embarrassing.

"Well, Marin will take out the ogres, but she doesn't like fighting men so we should be safe. That leaves Favian to fight us, but they could send more. They might send the sorcerer."

"No, he quit after almost getting Marin killed," one of them said.

He had quit? I would have to talk to him. What had happened had been out of his control. No one could have known how strong he was.

"They would have to send more to fight us. There's no way that the two of them could take out our entire army," one of them said.

"I wouldn't be so sure about that," Favian said as he stepped into their camp.

That idiot! What was he doing?

The humans stood up and pulled their swords. "If you are here than that means the Death Bringer is as well, right?" one asked.

"You should be less worried about the Death Bringer's whereabouts and more worried about your life," Favian snarled. He was angry, so angry that his fists were clenched and shaking.

"So, we were right about you two having a falling out," one sneered.

"You know nothing about us and should not speak about things your small human minds can't comprehend."

The comment stung even me. Just because we were human did not mean we were stupid.

"Enough talk, kill him," one of the humans said.

Favian leapt into battle, wounding each man quickly and disarming them. He did not kill them though. What was he planning?

"Where are you getting your information from?" he asked them as they lay on the ground writhing in pain.

"As if we will tell you!" one snarled.

Favian stabbed the man in the chest, ending his life and turned to another man. "Where are you getting your information from?"

"We knew about you from our leader, who used to work at the Academy," he said quickly. "And everyone knows about you and Marin. The stories of her battles with the ogres are becomes legends already. Her name Death Bringer is spreading across the land and becoming bedtime stories for children to feel safe with."

"If I let you live, will you return to your home or report to your leader?" Favian asked.

"We would never betray the rebellion!" they all shouted.

Before I could get out of the tree, Favian killed them all. I knew it was necessary, but they had been right, I tried not to take human lives if I could help it.

"Are you done hiding in the tree now?" Favian asked without turning around.

"I was listening to their conversation to find out helpful information," I said defensively. "I was not hiding out of cowardice."

"Are there ogres nearby?" he asked me as he walked to Ice.

"A mile or so away," I answered him, mounting Fire.

"Lead the way."

He was obviously angry about what the men had been saying, but that was no reason to take it out on me. I led the way back to the road and we continued down it. The ogres seemed to be directly south. Half a mile down the road suddenly ended in a huge boulder. My skin itched like crazy and I could sense ogres in almost every direction. "I think we are surrounded by ogres," I whispered.

"That must mean that their base is nearby," he whispered back. He took the lead and we slowly and quietly made our way around the boulder.

Unfortunately, what lay around the boulder was a huge open space filled with tents and where an army stood waiting for us. Over two hundred ogres roared at the sight of me and the humans moved out of their way. I dismounted from Fire and pulled my swords from their sheaths and was about to attack the ogres, but Favian stepped in front of me.

"You are in violation of the treaty. If you do not disband immediately we will be forced to disband you ourselves," he said authoritatively.

A man stepped forward and I felt my heart sink. It was Triston, one of the men who had trained us at the Academy. "It's good to see you two again. Congratulations on becoming a Protector, Marin," he said with a smile.

"Why are you doing this?" I asked him.

"You're both young so you do not understand. The human king is old and does not know how to take care of the land. He needs to be replaced," he said as though lecturing us in class.

"Your attack will kill hundreds of innocents, not just the King and his guard," Favian said. "Why not assassinate him instead of this all-out war?"

"The people need to be made to understand that I am the rightful ruler. Assassinating him would only make me a bad person in their eyes. If I take it by force they will see me as being the stronger and rightful king."

"Or as the man who aligned himself with ogres to take over a human throne," I said angrily.

He smiled and said, "I was worried that you would come to slay my ogres, but I doubt that you will be able to defeat them once I use my trump card."

I did not like the sound of that at all. "I will kill every ogre who raises its hand against a human in this land."

"Will you do so, if it means Favian's dies?" he asked me.

I glanced at Favian, but he was still standing next to me, uninjured and looking as confused as I felt.

"We came here knowing the chances we had. And I think you will find that I am not as easy to kill as you would like," Favian said.

"You both have one weakness in common," he said. "And that is your feelings towards each other."

Did everyone know that I loved him!

I heard the distinct twang of a bow as it released an arrow and my heart sank. I had a feeling it was going to be aimed at Favian and I was right. Thankfully, Favian had heard it as well and stepped to the side, avoiding it. "Pathetic," Favian said.

Several more bows released arrows and then Favian was darting around and using his blade to block them.

Ogres ran towards him and I released the hold on my power. Energy swelled inside me and I screamed to release some of it as I ran at the ogres. This was more power than I had felt yet and I knew it was because Favian's life was in danger. I attacked the ogres, cutting them down like cattle in a pen and then began defending Favian from the humans who joined in to attack him. For once my power did not ebb as I attacked non-ogres. Favian cried out in pain and I turned to see an arrow shaft sticking out of his chest. He fell to the ground and stopped moving. "FAVIAN!" I screamed in panic. He did not move.

I moved closer to his body, cutting down men and ogres as they attempted to harm Favian in his immobile state. I had to protect him. I could not let him die! I knew that he could be dead already, but I refused to believe that. Favian was strong and fast and one arrow could not kill him. It had to be a potion or spell or something else.

I wanted to stop fighting and check on him, but that would only give my opponents an opening to kill me.

Father, I don't know if you can hear me and I don't know if you even exist, but please help me keep Favian safe. I prayed.

"You only had to ask and I would reveal myself," a man's voice whispered in my ear. "There are many who think you must make a journey to discover me, but you only need to ask and I would respond."

Help me. I pleaded. *Is he dead?*

"Kill them all and I will keep him safe," he whispered.

I had yet to see what my father looked like, but knowing he could speak to me was enough. It in fact fueled me even more and I could feel the ground growing ever more slippery with blood as I killed the army around me.

"You cannot win!" Triston said. "Even if you kill these men I will just gather more."

"Then you shall die," I said in the voice of power that I had when in this state. I wondered if it was because I was a half-god, but now was not the time for thinking. Now was the time for killing. I sliced and diced and punched and stabbed my way through the entire army. I could feel wounds on my body, but it did not matter. I was finally down to just Triston.

I walked towards him and he asked, "What are you?"

"Your executioner," I whispered.

He tried to fight me, but he was no match thanks to my power staying activated. I decapitated him and turned away. What a shame. I closed off my power and rushed to Favian. "Favian," I whispered. "Favian wake up."

"Pull the arrow from his chest and bind the wound," my father whispered in my ear.

"Why can't I see you?" I asked him.

"Soon enough. There is someone you must see first. A trip you must make before I fully reveal myself to you. You need to learn about your past so that you will make a better choice for your future. Once you make your decision there, then I will come see you."

"What name do you go by?" I asked him. It sounded strange to ask, but he could be a magical being who was not in fact *god* or he could be something that our little mortals brains could not understand.

"You must go on your journey first, my daughter, but you should focus on Favian for now."

I did as he asked, pulling the arrow out and then binding the wound. Bright white light radiated from the wound and then Favian opened his eyes. "What happened?"

"You got shot in the chest by an arrow that was coated in a sleeping spell of some kind," I whispered.

He lifted his head and surveyed the carnage around us. I was trying to avoid looking at it myself. "You killed them all?"

I nodded my head and then realized I was crying. "They were trying to kill you," I whispered.

He dropped his back to the ground and pulled me down so that I was pressing my face into the crook of his neck. "You did what you had to."

I knew he was right and hearing him say it made me feel better. "I spoke to my father," I whispered. "He healed you just now."

Favian sat up and looked around. "Where is he?"

"I'm here, but not visible yet," the voice said so that Favian could hear him.

Favian's eyes widened and he looked at me. "So, you are half-god."

"I wouldn't say that," I mumbled.

"You are a demi-god, daughter."

"Can you stand up?" I asked Favian.

He stood up and then removed the bandage I had put on. There was no sign of him ever having been injured. "I'm fine, but I should treat your wounds," he said as he looked at the cuts on my arms.

I sat down and let him clean and bandage my wounds. There were several and as he worked on them, I felt very tired. "Where am I supposed to go for this journey you talked about?" I asked my father.

"To where it all began," he said. "To your mother's home town."

"What'd he say?" Favian asked.

I was actually glad Favian could not hear him. I would prefer to go on this journey alone. "He's telling me where to go," I answered Favian.

"And where is that?" he asked.

"Many questions about your past can be answered there," my father said.

"What name can I call you?" I asked. "So I don't confuse you with my other father."

"You may call me father, I can tell which one you are talking about."

"So, the sooner I do this journey the better?" I asked.

"Yes."

"You're not an evil god, are you?" I asked him.

He laughed and it sounded heavenly. "No, you do not need to

worry about being evil. Even those nearest you can see your pure heart whether you believe it or not."

"Thank you for your assistance," I said. "I guess I will speak to you more after the journey."

"Yes, I am looking forward to it, Marin."

"Where do I find out the name of the village?" I asked him.

"You will find more information from a box Cesar has kept for you. Ask him for the box and keep an open mind," he said. That did not sound good. "Stay safe."

I wasn't sure how, but I could tell that he had left, or at least wasn't right with me anymore. It was strange. Very strange.

"We should head to Macon and report," Favian said as he stood up.

"Yes, and I need to speak with our Father about this journey my true father wants me to go on," I said.

"Are you going to try to ditch me for that journey?" he asked me. "Are you trying to slink off into the night like the human thieves in the towns?"

"This has nothing to do with me being human!" I yelled at him. "But then again it could be since we humans have such small inferior brains!"

He blinked and opened his mouth and then closed it. "I wasn't referring to you when I was talking to them."

I mounted Fire and headed down the road. "Oh, so you meant the other type of humans."

"I was angry about their gossiping, so I said cruel things. I did not mean that humans have inferior brains to Elves," he said as he caught up to me. "Besides you are not full human anyways."

I wasn't truly angry with him, but all of the emotions I had just gone through seeing him injured and bleeding had thoroughly confused me.

We reported to Macon who seemed a little shocked that we returned so quickly, but he did not make a comment to us about it. We took our payment and I debated traveling to Carn which was a half a day's ride from the Academy, and a town Favian and I had rarely visited, to purchase a home for myself. It was time that I started looking for a home outside of the Kingdom now that I was a Protector and I had quite a bit of money saved up from missions. I would have to do it when Favian wasn't around though, so it would prove difficult.

We returned to the Kingdom and I received a lecture from Mother and Father. I asked Father for the box and he took me into the private keep where all of the most precious items to them were kept. The keep was shelves and chests of items they prized and there was a section for each child, including me. He lifted a plain brown box that had a lock on the front of it and handed it to me. "This was one of the items we saved for you from the items your parents had been carrying with them in the cart when we found you and you killed those ogres," he said softly. "We never opened it since it did not belong to us, but kept it for when you were ready. We don't have a key for it though."

"Will Baldemar be able to open it?" I asked as I examined the box. There were no markings on the outside except for scratches which most likely occurred when the ogres attacked us. From what I had learned, my parents had been moving to another town.

"Yes, would you like me to come?" he asked.

I shook my head and said, "I should do this myself."

"We are here if you need us," he whispered.

I followed him out of the keep and to Baldemar's workshop. "Baldemar," I called. "I need a favor."

He walked out of the back and smiled. "You've returned already!"

"Yes, the mission was easier than we expected," I said softly. Or it had become easier since I'd killed an entire army by myself.

"That's good. You should stay home more often," he said.

I held up the box. "Can you get this lock off without damaging the box?" I asked him to change the subject.

He examined it and nodded his head. "It does not appear to be spelled so I could be able to just cut it off." He disappeared for a moment and the twins came out.

"Marin!" they said at the same time. I smiled at them and they handed me a bag of rolls. "We just made these. Will you take some to Alex for us?"

"Of course," I said. "Thank you."

Baldemar returned and asked, "Do you want the lock or shall I melt it?"

"Melt it, but can you make me another lock to use that has a key?" I asked him.

He walked to the wall where he kept baskets of items and returned with a lock and key. "Here you go."

I bowed to him. "Thank you."

"Anytime, Death Bringer."

I smiled and hurried to Alex to give him the rolls. I actually wanted to open the box in private so I would just give him the rolls and leave. I hurried to the stables where he was cleaning stalls. "The twins asked me to bring you rolls," I said as I hung the bag on a hook by the tack room.

"Oh, thank you."

I took a roll and smiled at him when I took a bite. "I'll see you later."

"Marin," he called after me. "Congrats on becoming a Protector."

"Thank you!" I called back as I hurried to my hiding spot. Sebastian and Favian were nowhere to be seen, so I sat down and after taking a deep breath I opened the box. It had several letters, a picture of a man, woman and baby, some money and a pretty sapphire. I examined the picture and realized it was my family, my birth family. I knew the man had been my mother's husband and not my father, but it did not matter to me who he was if he had been loyal to my mother. I gingerly set the picture to the side and opened the first letter. It was a letter from a relative to my mother asking her to come live with them. It seemed the relative was getting older and needed help around their farm. That was probably why my family had been moving when we had been attacked by the ogres. There were several more from the same relative, but I skipped over them to open a folded-up stack of papers. It was thick and heavy as I pulled it out.

It was a contract between my mother's husband and the mayor of a town called Aralia. I had heard of Aralia, but had never been there. The contract was for a large sum of money and listed my name. I stopped skimming the contract and really started reading it.

"Oh no," I whispered in shock. The contract was a marriage arrangement between me and the mayor's son. It said that at eighteen we would be married in Aralia. Oh, this was bad. This was terrible! I couldn't marry someone I didn't know! How could he have done this!

Was this where my true father wanted me to go? Aralia?

"Yes," he whispered. "You are to go there and seek out the mayor's son."

"I can't marry someone I don't know," I almost screamed.

"Keep an open mind and when you are eighteen you will need to travel there," my father said and then left.

"Marin?" Favian called. "Are you alright?"

"Yeah," I called back despite the horror I felt. I was fine for two more years at least and then I would have to travel to Aralia and end this arrangement. I put the items back into the box and locked it. I could not tell Favian. I would have to hide this from him as well.

Favian entered our secret area and smiled at me. "Mother wants us to join them for dinner," he said.

I stood up and smiled. "Okay."

He looked at the box and asked, "What did you find?"

"Just letters and some stuff of my mother's," I answered vaguely.

"So, do you know where this journey you are supposed to go is?" he asked me.

I nodded my head. "Yes, but I'm not supposed to go until I turn eighteen."

"Oh," he said in shock.

I smiled. "So, it looks like you are stuck with me until then."

"So, does that mean we can go out on another mission soon?" he asked hopefully.

Even though I knew breaking our partnership would be the right thing, I was being selfish and I wanted to spend these last two years with him. "We should pack our bags tonight," I said with a wide smile.

He hugged me and then started running towards the castle. "Race you to dinner!"

"You cheater!" I yelled after him.

Chapter Eleven

2 years later

I made my way to Carn while Favian was on a trip with Father on Elven matters. Sebastian had tried to tag along with me, but I had snuck away and made my way here. My birthday was in two days and I was getting a lot of attention. Over the last two years the Elves had grown even more fond of me and the fear that had been there before was now gone. I believed it was because we finally knew what the other half of my lineage was, but I never asked anyone to confirm that.

I purchased a house from the mayor of Carn who was more than pleased to sell the Death Bringer a house in his area. I knew I would probably get quite a few summons from him for aid, but that was fine with me. Mother had been upset when I told her that I was going to purchase my own house, but she said she did understand my need for independence.

It took me a ten-minute ride to reach my house, which had apparently been a former Mercenary's who had been killed in action a few months ago. I did not know his name, but then again, I rarely hung out with the other Mercenaries anymore. Favian had been training much more frequently with Father to learn to do his kingly duties, which meant that I had been doing very little. Despite Favian's adamant refusal, I had taken Sebastian on an easy Mercenary job and he had done very well. Macon had agreed to letting Sebastian train and become a Mercenary despite his age and so, he would start training next month.

I stopped at the entrance to my property and looked at the little archway that was built. It was cute and welcoming, something I would have to change. The house was in good condition, just dirty. There was no barn so I would have to build one before winter, but there was a creek nearby and plenty of trees for cover. I made a temporary corral for Fire, fed her, and went to work cleaning the house. Cleaning gave me a distraction from thinking about Favian. Our relationship was still stressful for me since I was still head over heels in love with him, but I had learned to deal with it a little better over the years. It helped that he had yet to start courting females. I knew mother was hounding him though.

It took almost an entire night to clean the house and clear it of spiders and rats, but it was finally done and I was pleased with my new place. I laid my sleeping bag on the ground and slept until the morning light came into my window. Drapes, I needed drapes so I could sleep in the next day.

I ate a small breakfast, released Fire to wander around and graze and went to gather material to make some items I needed, such as a bucket for water for Fire and to chop firewood for the fireplace. I also needed to find some rabbits or squirrels for dinner for myself.

"If you're planning to stop being friends with Favian once you move away from the Kingdom, then why not tell him how you feel?" my father whispered to me.

I sighed since I had already thought of that. "I do not want to hear him tell me that he could never love me like that. I would rather not know."

"What if he loves you?" he asked.

I laughed. "He does not."

"What will you do next?" he asked.

"I will spend one month isolating myself here and then I will inquire as to another job," I said.

"Shutting out love is not the answer," he chastised me.

"It is for me," I said angrily.

"I shall let you make your own decisions, but I do not like the idea of seeing my daughter constantly sad. Make your journey soon," he said before leaving me again.

He had spoken to me much more frequently and had helped me out of several rough spots. He told me that I would need to learn to take better care of myself and I knew he was right. When I lost Favian as a partner I would need to be more careful.

After Father left, I felt even more alone than ever before. I finished my chores, corralled Fire, and went into the house to get it ready for my departure. I did not know when I would be back again to sleep in it, but I felt better already owning this place.

Favian met me at the Academy and we accepted another job. First, we had to go speak to Karr, a man who had spies everywhere and who we weren't sure whether he was friend or foe.

"Where were you?" Favian asked me as we headed towards the bar that Karr frequented. Favian had grown taller and broader over the years and his hair was extremely long now. When on missions, he usually let his hair down and covered his ears which seemed strange. Why was he suddenly acting ashamed of his heritage? Almost everyone knew who we were anyways. We were legends already.

"I purchased a house," I told him since he would find out sooner or later.

"You did what!" he asked in shock.

"I purchased a house and went to clean it," I said.

"Where?"

"Somewhere," I said with a smirk.

"Are you going to try to hide it from me?" he asked angrily.

I laughed and shook my head. "Of course not, I purchased it in Carn. I'll show you it one of these days."

"Okay."

"You would just track me there if I tried to hide it," I said.

He smiled. "Right you are."

We stopped outside the bar and I said, "Let me go in and soften him up first. Why don't you go get supplies for our trip?"

He nodded his head. We had had several interactions with Karr and for someone reason Karr did not like Favian. "Be safe."

"Always."

I walked inside and within minutes Karr and I were arguing about something.

"Ogres are not the top assassins," I argued with Karr. He was a scummy man who spied on whoever he could in the world and used his knowledge to fill his coin purse. "They're too loud and too stupid to pull off a good assassination. You would have to send at least a hundred ogres to kill me while you would only need to send one or two Elves. Elves are the best assassins. Quick and silent."

"You only argue for elves because you favor one of their males," growled Karr.

I felt my cheeks burn as I pictured Favian. "My decision comes not from whom I am friends with, but who is better at the job."

"Better at the job of assassination or of love making?" asked Karr with a sneer.

I leaned across the table and punched him in the nose as hard as I could. The satisfying crunch of his bone and spray of blood let me know that I had broken it as intended. "Not that it's any of your business, but my chastity is still intact."

Karr held a napkin to his nose and snarled at me. "You would do well to keep your hands away from me."

I raised my hands in the air. "They are back at my side, as proper. You would do well to keep your rude assumptions to yourself."

Karr placed both of his hands on his nose and snapped it back into place. He inhaled and exhaled, checking his breathing. "That really hurt, you know?"

I shrugged. "You insulted my honor."

He stared at me in shock a moment and then said, "You insult my honor every time I see you."

"That is because you have no honor," said Favian as he sat down beside me. His long silver hair was held up by an ornate silver clip, letting his pointed ears show for the first time in months. Why would he suddenly go back to letting his ears show?

"Aw, we were speaking of you not but a moment ago, Elf," said Karr.

I rolled my eyes and put two gold pieces on the table. "What news have you from Avonlea?" I asked Karr, trying my best to avoid looking at Favian. I tried my hardest to hide my feelings because he and I could never be together since he was the Prince of the Elves and I was just a demigod who had been raised by them.

Karr picked up the gold pieces and slipped them into his pouch. "A band of ogres has been terrorizing a small village nearby. The King's men are too busy with the preparations of the annual celebration so nothing is being done about it."

"How fare the roads to Avonlea?" I asked as I stared at Karr, waiting for the thief and traitor to show his faults.

"Treacherous, full of bands of thieves and other nasties lurking about." His left eye twitched.

"Thieves associated to you?" I asked, already knowing the answer.

Karr pretended to look hurt. "I am no thief, ma'am."

"And I am no ma'am. Are the thieves looking for something or just pillaging?"

"I have not heard if they are seeking anything specific. There is no pattern to their attacks, so I believe they're just pillaging."

Favian stood. "Very well, we will make towards Avonlea."

I stood and half bowed to Karr. "Thank you for your time and information."

He smiled. "May the Gods protect you in your travels."

I smiled. "And may they continue to fill your purse," I said the phrase bitterly and felt sick to my stomach. Then again, every encounter with Karr made me feel that way.

Favian gripped me by the arm and led me away from the snake in man's clothing and out of the pub. He turned me around and stared into my eyes. "From now on I don't want you meeting with him alone, okay?"

He smelled of mint and pine and his body was entirely too warm for such a cold day. "I can take care of myself," I managed to say after enjoying his closeness a moment longer. "He was no threat to me."

Favian threw his hands up in the air and stormed away, towards our tethered horses. "No one is a threat according to you."

"Well, they aren't," I murmured as I followed him.

He spun around, sending a puff of dust up from his boots. "You aren't an eternal. You're a fragile human!"

I untied my horse and ran a hand along her silky soft neck. "A point you are sure to remind me of often these past two years."

He untied his horse and said, "Someone has to! You run around as though invincible and impervious to any dangers."

"You worry too much for me," I answered softly as I mounted my mare, Fire.

"And you worry too little for yourself."

I felt like screaming. Ever since we had begun discussing my eighteenth birthday a few months ago, he had been a great thorn in my side. I didn't understand it.

We road at a walk through the town to avoid trampling the townspeople, but I wished we could gallop off to Avonlea and the small town of Aralia near it. I debated whether to tell Favian about Aralia and my connection to it, but decided that it didn't matter. We were Protectors and our job was to protect all towns, no matter of personal feelings. Favian had become a Protector last year after saving a group of children from a chimera. The towns had seen a great increase in the amount of animals attacking towns and we weren't exactly sure why. The towns had changed and now most had guarded walls around the perimeters of them. It always made me feel claustrophobic.

"What are you thinking about so hard?" he asked as we exited the crowded main strip and headed towards the gate.

"You do not need to know everything that I'm thinking about," I said through gritted teeth.

He watched me a moment and then unclipped his hair, letting it fall down about his shoulders and obscure his ears. It had recently become a sign of anger and a way for him to shut me out. He had become much easier to anger since learning more about the kingly duties he was soon to take over. "I apologize for trying to be friendly," he said angrily.

I sighed and sagged forward, draping myself across Fire's neck. "Why are Elves so pissy?" I asked her.

She snorted in reply and stopped at the base of the gate.

One of the guards walked forward. "Where are you heading?"

I sat up and said, "We're off to a ball at the Elven Kingdom."

The guard frowned at me since he could hear the teasing in

my voice and Favian sighed. "We are going to Avonlea where there have been ogre attacks," Favian told him.

I shrugged. "I liked my story better."

The guard eyed us a moment longer and then saw the hilt of my twin swords, it's silver and black scrollwork unforgettable. "Death Bringer, I should have guessed. Be on your way."

I smiled and blew him a kiss, much to the amusement of his fellow guards. "Thank ye kind sir, for allowing us passage."

The guard's cheeks reddened and he shoved open the gate angrily. I rode by and waved once we had passed.

"You shouldn't tease men like that," said Favian angrily.

I shrugged my shoulders. "I do as I like."

"I am very aware of that. It has only gotten worse this past year."

I felt bad for upsetting Favian to the point where he had hidden his ears again, but I was too worried about Aralia to try to console him. The road before us was dusty and surrounded by trees, not much for sightseeing and incredibly boring. I leaned back in my saddle and closed my eyes. "Could you stop being angry with me all the time? Ever since Mother brought up my impending eighteenth birthday you've been constantly nagging at me."

"That's because you're a woman now and should be acting like one, not fighting and flirting like you have been."

I snorted like a pig to show my hatred of the idea. "I act as I have always acted. One more birthday should not mean I have to change who I am. A woman is just an older girl."

"Your flirtations before were tolerated and seen as cute, a girl with a crush, but now your flirtations will be taken seriously and men will begin trying to court you."

I looked at him in shock. "Court me?" He nodded his head and I smiled. "I would like to be courted. To have a man treat me as a woman instead of as Marin, the Death Bringer." I could just picture a man escorting me through town with my hand on his arm. The image of me in a dress however was not quite so clear. "Though I would not like to wear a dress every time I am with a man who is courting me. Can a woman be courted without wearing a dress? I know Mother would not approve, but I would prefer not to always be in dresses if I can help it." True I would like to be courted, but I knew it would never happen. The one I wanted could never court me.

Favian ignored my question, his eyes fixed on a horse and rider approaching from the west. The silver hair of the rider marked him as an Elf. "Today is getting better and better," Favian muttered as the rider stopped in the center of the road.

"Greetings, Prince Favian," said the Elf as he bowed his head.

Favian dipped his head. "Greetings, Balon."

Balon looked at me and smiled, a most charming smile. He moved his horse closer to me and picked my hand up, kissing the back of it. "It is an honor to meet you, Miss Marin."

He was a handsome Elf, with high cheekbones and a prominent jaw. I batted my eyelashes and said, "It is an honor to meet you, sir Balon." It was strange that I had not met him, but then again, there were *lots* of Elves and many who lived on the outskirts of the kingdom, some who I would never meet.

"Have you come to speak with me or did we just interrupt you on your way to town?" asked Favian with a bit of anger to his voice.

Balon released my hand and said, "I have come to give you an invitation to the Elven Kingdom for a royal ball for Marin's birthday in four days. The King and Queen request your attendance." Balon looked at me. "And the Death Bringer of course."

"Tell my parents I am unable to come due to a pressing Protector matter," said Favian as he moved his horse forward, trying to draw me out.

Balon looked shocked. "I will deliver the message." He looked me from head to toe and then met my eyes. "It is a shame that we won't see your beauty grace our dance floors, though."

"You surely jest, for if you had seen me on the dance floor you would know that the crowd often explodes in fits of laughter while watching me," I said. And hurt toes.

Balon smiled seductively, bringing a strange light to his eyes. "A woman as graceful as you are needs only the right man to lead her in dance. Were I given the chance, I could show you just how skilled a dancer any fighter like you can be."

"It is a shame that she won't be attending then," said Favian as he continued down the road. "Tell Mother she will have to postpone the Ball until we have finished our mission."

I bowed to Balon and trotted up next to Favian. "That was extremely rude behavior."

Favian's teeth ground together and he kept his eyes on the road ahead. "Your flirting was rude. There shall be rumors of this moment spread throughout the Elven Kingdom within days."

"Rumors of my flirting with an Elf? I have made no attempt to hide my liking of Elven men. I have been flirting with the Elves since I was ten."

"You keep forgetting that now you are a woman. Your flirtations were seen as cute by my people before, but now it will be seen as an insult against me."

"How on earth would it be an insult against you?!" I asked in shock.

Favian shook his head and sighed loudly. "You are as dense as a mountain."

"And you are as irritating as an ogre!" I yelled, kicking Fire and galloping ahead. I knew it was childish to ride away from him, but he was frustrating me beyond reason. I slowed Fire after a mile or so since it was a long journey and I didn't want to work her too hard. There was a possibility of an attack or ambush and she'd need to be rested for escape if need be.

Favian caught up to me and we rode in silence. I had known him so long that I knew that he was no longer upset, but worried about me. I could tell this because he kept glancing at me as we rode and tried to watch my movements to discern my mood. I relaxed in my saddle and closed my eyes. I had to think of a way to get us to the ball in four days. The ball she was planning to throw for me was supposed to be a huge event and I had been looking forward to it. I had attended many balls these past two years and I enjoyed the feast and flirtations of the male Elves. I wasn't sure why Favian thought me flirting with other Elves was suddenly inappropriate and looked bad on him. It didn't make any sense. I had told him that I would never court someone, so why was he acting this way now? Being eighteen did not change anything.

"Marin," he whispered. "I'm sorry I yelled at you."

I pulled Fire to a stop and looked at him in shock. He rarely apologized to me. "What?"

He looked into my eyes and said, "I said I'm sorry that I yelled at you. I had no right to be rude to you like that. You didn't deserve it."

"Thank you." I think? Was I supposed to apologize to him?

"Balon and I have been having issues this year and I am not fond of him," he explained.

"Oh, I see. Well then I'm sorry for flirting with him."

Favian's jaw clenched. "That isn't much of an apology."

I exhaled. "Could we not fight? Please." I knew I needed to discuss Aralia with him, but I was pushing it off. I definitely couldn't talk to him about it when he was in a foul mood.

"Alright. My apologies," he said as we started on again. We rode in awkward silence as I debated how to discuss Aralia with him. "What are you thinking about?" he asked softly. "Your face is scrunched as though you have a splinter in your foot."

I avoided looking at him and answered, "Nothing of import. Just wondering why the ogres and thieves are attacking Avonlea now. There's nothing going on and even though the King's armies are elsewhere, they know there are Protectors like us nearby. It just doesn't make sense."

"You're withholding something from me."

I turned my face away and took a deep breath. We were only a day away from Avonlea. Should I tell him now? Or wait?

I heard a whistling sound above us and didn't realize what it was until the arrow buried into my shoulder. The force threw me sideways and would have unseated me if Fire hadn't moved with me and kept me seated. The air filled with whistling as more arrows were shot at us. Favian galloped to me and grabbed Fire's reins as he led us into the forest and off the road. He stopped when we were thirty feet from the road and I watched as at least one hundred arrows buried their heads in the dirt where we had been.

"Marin!" Favian yelled.

I shook myself from the shock which was trying to set in and snapped the end of the arrow off. I put the arrow in my mouth and bit down as I shoved the rest of the shaft out of my shoulder. The bloodied arrow fell to the ground and I gripped the horn of my saddle to keep from fainting and falling off. Favian watched all around us for signs of our attackers while I bandaged myself as well as I could one handed. My head felt too woozy for this type of wound, which I had endured many times before. "Drugged," I whispered to Favian.

He leapt from his horse, Ice, to Fire, wrapping an arm around my waist to hold me steady as he inspected the injury. He sniffed my shoulder and then grumbled angrily before reaching inside his saddle bags for medicine Mother made and spread the medicine in my wound to remove the toxins. The toxins slowly leaked from my wound and dripped down my arm in a slimy black smear. He finished properly bandaging me and then spoke in Elvish to Ice. "Try to stay awake," he whispered.

"I'm not dead," I said angrily. "Just drugged, you silly Elf."

"It's probably best if you don't talk."

"You say that to me every day."

"I'm being serious now, Marin. Be quiet."

"Yes, Your Highness," I whispered as I leaned back against him. He tied the reins to the saddle horn and then squeezed his legs to get Fire to move. Ice followed obediently behind us as we moved parallel to the road in search of our attackers. I chewed on a piece of dried meat which had been in my pocket as I recuperated and let my body realize that I wasn't drugged anymore and not tired either.

Favian's grip on my waist tightened the closer we got to loud voices ahead. I reached down and laid my hand on his, squeezing softly in reassurance. He pulled his arm back and then stopped the horses. I stretched my arms, softly wincing at the injured one. I would have to hold one sword for the meantime.

We dismounted and crept towards the loud angry voices.

"They were on the road! I saw them!" yelled one.

"If they were there then our arrows would have pinned them to the ground, but the arrows landed harmlessly in the ground."

"Maybe it was an illusion."

"I know I hit her! I know that arrow got her."

"Or maybe they just moved off the road when the arrows came," Favian said angrily as he hopped over a log and decapitated the two nearest men. I sat down on the log and smiled at the fifteen human men looking at me and Favian angrily.

"Perhaps you were such bad aims that you missed us entirely," I said as I draped one leg over the other.

"Kill her!" the leader yelled as they rushed forward.

Favian's brow furrowed and he spun into a beautiful dance of death and protection. It always made my heart leap when he protected me and now was exceptional as he took his anger out on the poor, idiot humans who had dared try to hurt us.

In a matter of minutes fourteen more men died and one cowered on the ground in front of Favian. "Who hired you?" he asked angrily, pointing his sword at the man's throat.

"I don't know," the man whimpered.

Favian pressed the tip of his sword to the man's throat and growled, "Think harder."

"I don't know! I wasn't the one who took the hit. I just signed up because the purse was so large."

"Why did they want her dead?" he asked.

"I don't know!"

"Wrong answer," Favian said as he slid his blade through the man.

I stood up and brushed my butt off. "Well, now we know someone wants me dead, again."

Favian wiped his blade off on one of the dead men's shirt and glared at me. "Do not act nonchalant about this."

I rolled my eyes. "Do not overreact either. This is hardly the first time that I've had a bounty on my head."

He stopped in front of me, staring down into my eyes. "Does this have anything to do with your secret?" he asked.

I shook my head and swallowed nervously. How did he know? "No."

"You're sure?" he asked.

I nodded my head. "Yes."

"Why won't you tell me? I've never hidden anything from you."

"Can we get back on the road? The stench of their dead bodies is upsetting my stomach."

I turned to leave, but he grabbed my arm and turned me back around. "What is it, Marin? Why won't you tell me? Is it the same thing you've been hiding, or another? Why won't you tell me these things?!"

"Because I'm afraid it will upset you!" I yelled angrily. I ground my teeth together and exhaled. "I don't want to discuss it. I will take care of it as soon as we finish everything in Avonlea."

"Why would it upset me? What is it that you have to do? Are you putting yourself in danger?" he asked as he followed me back to the horses.

"Favian, please just leave it alone. I will tell you once I've completed my task."

"How can I protect you if you don't tell me what you're going to do?" he asked angrily.

I glared at him. "I don't need your protection. I can take care of myself."

"I see. Well then you can just go on your trip, while I deal with the Avonlea matter alone."

I stared at him in shock. "What?"

"You are a woman now and can take care of yourself, so I don't need to hold your hand anymore. It is obvious you are disregarding our partnership, so I will deal with the ogres in Avonlea while you go on your secret mission. Then you won't have to keep ignoring me and hiding it from me."

"Favian…" I began, but he just held up his hand.

"You will only slow me down with that wound anyways."

"Fine," I said angrily. "I'll just go to Aralia then."

Favian waved his hand towards the road. "On your way, then."

He was being incredibly cold to me. Never had he treated me so rude before and never before had he allowed me to go anywhere alone. When I first came to the Elves, he had vowed to protect me no matter what. Three years ago, I had been kidnapped and almost killed and he had told me then that he wouldn't let me out of his sight and had kept to that as well as he could. Why was he now letting me go alone? Why was he being so cold?

I squeezed my legs, urging my mare to a trot and made my way down the road, away from him. I didn't need him and felt humiliated at being struck by an arrow. He was right that I would only slow him down, but it still hurt. I squared my shoulders and lifted my chin up. I was a woman and I was the Death Bringer. I could take care of myself. I did not need the Elf Prince by my side. I only needed my swords.

I touched my pocket where the pouch was firmly tucked

inside and sighed. I only hoped this worked, otherwise I wouldn't be seeing Favian again.

As I rode towards Aralia I felt like a herd of cattle had stampeded over me. Sleep had evaded me due to my increased nervousness of being alone and having a bounty on my head. I had shivered all night and had done nothing but think about Favian and his coldness towards me. I had to find him as soon as I was done at Aralia and make amends. He was my best friend and I couldn't afford to lose him yet.

Finally, the town came into view after what felt like a month instead of a day. I urged Fire into a gallop and raced into town and to the Mayor of Aralia's house. An older male servant rushed down the steps and took my horse's reins. "What brings ye here?" he asked.

"I've come to speak to the Mayor," I answered as I headed up to the front door and knocked twice, not waiting for the servant to respond.

The door opened and I was staring into the chest of a very muscular man. He stepped back and I swallowed as the handsome face attached to the muscular chest smiled at me with piercing blue eyes. "Afternoon, Lady. How can I be of service?"

So many responses went through my head that I was sure my face must have contorted in a million ways. "I am here to speak to the Mayor," I finally answered.

"May I tell him who is here?" he asked as he looked me over.

"Marin," I answered.

"The Death Bringer?" he asked in shock, his eyes widening as he looked at me more closely. "I thought you would be bigger."

"Size is relative," I answered with a shrug. "Is the Mayor home?"

"He stepped out, but should return shortly. You can wait in his study for him."

I nodded my head. "Very well."

"I'm Alexandre," he said with a smile as he held out his hand.

I held my jaw from falling open and shook his hand. "Alexandre, the Mayor's son?"

He lifted my hand and kissed the back of it. "I think due to our circumstances that you can withhold the title."

I pulled my hand back and straightened. "That is precisely why I'm here," I said as he led me into a small room with a desk, couch and two bookcases filled with books and scrolls.

"So, you've finally turned eighteen and are here for our wedding?" he asked with a twinkle in his eye.

I sat on the couch and shook my head. "No."

The Mayor came in and stared at me in shock. "Marin! What are you doing here?"

I set the pouch on his desk and said, "Mr. Mayor…"

"Call me Leroy."

I cringed, but obliged. "Leroy, I'm here to reimburse you for my step-father's ill-conceived deal."

Leroy opened the pouch and gaped in shock. "I cannot take this."

"The diamonds are worth twice the dowry," I assured him.

Leroy shook his head. "The value is not the issue. Now that Alexandre and you are both eighteen, this is a matter which you two must work out." Leroy handed Alexandre the pouch. "I'll leave you two to talk alone."

I watched in dismay as the Mayor of Aralia left the room. Alexandre looked in the pouch and then looked up at me. "You wish to retract the marriage arrangement?"

I nodded my head. "It's nothing personal and has nothing to do with your family or this town. I'm just not ready to be in a marriage and I am definitely not fit to be a wife."

"I think you'd be a wonderful wife," he said with a smile. "You could go hunting with me and teach all of the children to fight."

"I'm a Protector and as such I'm required to travel and fight in dangerous battles, which would keep me away from home."

"You could quit," he said matter-of-factly.

I glared at him. "I will not quit being a Protector. I worked too hard to obtain my title and place."

He tossed the pouch to me. "I decline your offer. We will be married as originally planned."

I tossed the pouch back to him and turned away. "No. I will not marry you." I had just opened the door when he grabbed my shoulder. I spun around and twisted his arm up behind his back, or at least that was the plan, but somehow, he reversed the move and had both my hands pinned above my head with one of his. His body pressed against mine as he held me against the door. "Do not touch me," I said a bit in pain as my wounded shoulder burned.

"You are bound by our parents' contract to be my bride. I understand you have doubts, but I am not giving you up. I am a worthy mate for you."

"You're going to be dead if you do not release me," I answered through gritted teeth.

Alexandre released me and I winced as my arm fell back down and fresh blood oozed out of my wound.

"You're injured?" he said in shock as he moved towards me.

I spun around him and out the door. "I will take care of it and you will accept my offer."

"I admire your spunk, but you can see that you and I are a good match. In time, you will see that I am the best mate for you."

"Not going to happen," I said as I walked out of the house and to my horse.

"The wedding is in three days," Alexandre said from the doorway. "I'll have the seamstress meet you at the Inn."

"Don't waste her time. I won't marry you."

"Then you'll be locked up in prison for forfeiting a deal and stealing money."

"I have twice the money!" I yelled at him. "You're just being unreasonable."

"You're being childish," he answered with crossed arms.

I mounted my horse and trotted away from his house and to the Inn. What had I gotten myself into? The owner of the Inn showed me to a room and I collapsed onto the bed as soon as I entered. No one except the Elves had ever been able to pin me. And I'd never met a human man like Alexandre. There was something different about him, something that reminded me of myself.

I groaned. It didn't matter if he was attractive or strong or not. I couldn't marry him. I refused to be someone's prize or be forced to quit my job. I had worked too hard and been almost killed too many times to give it up.

Plus, I couldn't be without Favian. The thought of never seeing him again caused me physical pain and nausea. I wondered how he was faring or if he had found and killed the ogres yet. What if he got hurt and I was not there? I shook my head at the ridiculous thought. He would be fine. I on the other hand, was still bleeding and needed a healer. I changed clothes and walked down to the Inn keeper. "Can you please fetch your healer?" I asked.

He smiled. "The healer is waiting in the dining room for you. As is the seamstress."

I walked into the dining room and sat down at the table where two older women were talking quietly. "Who's the seamstress?" I asked.

The plumper of the two women stood. "That would be me."

"Your services are not needed, please leave."

She frowned. "I was giving instructions to measure you. I do not fail."

"You are not failing. You are simply leaving."

"I cannot leave."

"Tell Alexandre that I threatened to cut off your hand if you so much as held a measuring rope out."

"But you haven't threatened me," she said in shock.

I smiled. "I was hoping to avoid it, but I will not hesitate."

She stared at me in horror and shock a moment and then hurried from the Inn.

"You didn't have to scare her," the healer said.

I exhaled. "I am in an extremely foul mood and wish only to get out of this ridiculous arrangement and be on my way to the Elven Kingdom."

The healer pulled my shirt down and inspected my wound. "We've heard tales that you favor an Elf, but thought it idle gossip."

"I favor Elves in general," I answered truthfully. "Most human men are frightened of me."

"Alexandre is not," she said matter-of-factly.

I frowned and looked at the table as she began cleaning my wound. "No, he's not. I believe it may be due to a brain abnormality."

She laughed. "Or perhaps you have underestimated men." She finished bandaging me and smiled. "You should be fine by tomorrow."

"Thank you," I said as I waved at the Inn owner. "Food please."

"You might give Alexandre a chance. He is attractive, wealthy, and a very nice man. I don't think a marriage to him would be so bad."

I didn't say anything because she wasn't trying to be rude or nosey so she deserved no rudeness from me. The Inn owner set food down in front of me and I ate it all despite the fact that I had suddenly lost my appetite.

I finished my food and then sat in front of the fireplace. I was in a daze when someone sat in the chair next to me. "You threatened the seamstress?" he asked.

I turned and met Alexandre's eyes. It took me a minute to find my voice. "She wouldn't leave." He studied me a moment and then linked his fingers behind his head. I stared at his bulging biceps and then turned my attention to his face. "What do you want?"

"I want you to give me a chance."

"Why?" I asked. "You don't even know me."

He grimaced and dropped his arms. "I did know you when we were little. You and I used to play together."

I could only remember bits and pieces of my childhood here, but I did remember that we had played together. That did not mean he knew me though. "I'm not the same little girl you knew then. I don't even remember that."

He dropped his arms and leaned forward, peering at me with intense eyes. "Why are you so afraid to let me court you? Are you worried that you will realize I am actually a good guy and you could be happy with me?"

"Just take the diamonds so I can go. Please," I whispered.

"Give me two days to prove myself and if you still want to go then, I'll let you."

"I have a job I'm supposed to be at," I said angrily.

"Two days is all I am asking for. Two days and then you'll never have to see me again," he said with a bit of steel to his voice.

It was a good deal. I knew there was no way I would fall for him so I had nothing to lose except the time. I had always wanted to be courted and this was probably my only chance. "Fine, you have two days to court me."

Alexandre smiled happily and kissed my cheek before leaving. "See you in the morning."

I sat dumbfounded in my chair as I stared at the fire. After these two days, I would stay away from men for as long as possible, except for the Elves. Obviously Favian was right, and I needed to learn a few things about men before I flirted with them again. I made my way to my room and laid down on the bed. At least tonight I would be on a bed instead of the ground, though I still felt cold and slightly nervous without Favian with me. I knew I needed to get used to being alone to prepare myself for Favian inevitably leaving me to be King and choose a wife, but that thought had only made me crave his presence more and want to make the best of it.

I closed my eyes and pretended Favian was singing to me in Elvish like he did when I was sick or scared. I wrapped the blankets tightly around me and as I drifted off to sleep, I swore I could hear him singing from Avonlea to me.

Chapter Twelve

Two loud knocks woke me from my fitful sleep and then someone entered my room. I jumped up and held my swords out in front of me, leveled with my intruder's throat. Alexandre smiled pleasantly at me, apparently not worried that I had almost slit his throat open.

"Good morning," he said as he pushed my swords down with his fingertips.

"You should not startle me awake. I could have killed you," I said as I set my sword down on my bed and calmed my racing heart. I was also glad to learn that my shoulder did not hurt anymore. I was healing faster than normal lately.

"Breakfast will be ready in a few moments, so I'd appreciate it if you would wash up and get dressed so we can begin our day."

"What are we doing?" I asked as I looked at his muddy boots, short pants, and sleeveless shirt.

"I'm taking you on a short hike to the waterfalls."

"Waterfalls?" I asked in shock. "It's been years since I've seen waterfalls."

"Be sure to wear something you can swim in under your clothes," he said as he closed the door behind him and walked down the stairs.

My opinion of him rose slightly at his nonchalance at me nearly skewering him. I changed quickly due to my incessant grumbling stomach and brushed through my hair. I walked down the stairs and was pleased to see a smile on his face from my freshened appearance. Alexandre pulled a chair out for me and then scooted it in as I sat down. Even though I would never tell Mother, I did enjoy being treated like a lady now and then.

"Coffee or tea?" Alexandre asked as he poured himself a cup of coffee.

"Tea, please." He poured my cup and then the owner's wife brought out food for both of us. I laid my napkin on my lap and then took a sip from my cup. "Delicious," I said happily and in truth it was. Although nothing compared to the tea that Favian made.

I chastised myself silently for thinking of him and turned my attention back to Alexandre to give him a smile before eating my food. After our food was devoured, he led me through town and up the small hills that bordered the town. I felt a sense of familiarity with this range even though I hadn't been here since I was four.

"How was your breakfast?" Alexandre asked softly as we walked down a well-worn path.

"Very good," I answered.

"Do you not eat meat?" he asked. "I was under the impression that Elves ate meat, just not as much as humans and other species."

"I am not an Elf," I reminded him. "And they do not eat meat, but I do when I can."

"I am very aware that you are not an Elf, Marin."

The way he said my name sent a pleasant thrill through me. "Excuse me!" yelled a young voice. I stepped to the side and watched as two boys and one little girl sped down the path in front of us, cheering happily.

I smiled at the youngsters and then felt envy for them having a normal life. I had been like them until my parents had moved and then been killed. Alexandre held up a flower in front of me. "A beautiful flower for a beautiful woman." I stared dumbly at the flower. Alexandre reached out and slipped the flower on top of my ear in my hair. "I didn't think it was possible, but you are even more beautiful now."

I smiled politely back at him and said, "Thank you."

He continued down the path again and I gently brushed the flower. It was a beautiful flower.

The laughs and shrill yells of the kids announced the river just before I heard the pounding of the waterfalls. I walked faster and then stared in awe at the large waterfall. I watched in shock as a six-year-old child leapt from the top of the waterfall, plummeting down into the water below. "I am so doing that," I said excitedly and then heard Favian's voice in my head accusing me of trying anything possibly life threatening.

"Race you to the top," Alexandre said.

I stripped my swords and outer clothes off and then raced up the hill to the top of the waterfall. I peered over the edge and smiled in excitement. Alexandre came up behind me so I turned to him and I said, "It's so pretty, isn't it?"

He pushed loose strands of hair behind my ear and said, "You are the prettiest thing I have ever seen in this land." His body was layered with thick slabs of muscles that I wanted to touch. How could a human man be so muscular? Was he like me? Was he only part human?

He leaned down as if to kiss me and I panicked, flinging myself backwards off of the waterfall and twisting in the air to dive down towards the water. I screamed in joy and then plunged into the cold water. The current pushed down at me forcing me further under water. I kicked and surfaced a few yards away from the waterfall. The children smiled happily at me and I smiled back.

"Woohoo!" yelled Alexandre as he leapt from the top of the waterfall. I watched as he slid into the water almost silently in a perfect dive.

He surfaced near me and smiled happily. "Fun, isn't it?"

I nodded my head and kicked myself a little further away from him. "Yes."

One of the kids yelled a war cry and launched himself at Alexandre. I watched in surprise as Alexandre caught the child and tossed him up into the air. The child laughed happily as Alexandre caught him and then tossed him into the air again. The other children climbed onto Alexandre and he wrestled with the squirming children in the water.

"Throw me!" the girl yelled.

Alexandre picked her up and tossed her down the river. She squealed happily until she dropped into the water and then started swimming back. The other children began clamoring, "Me next! Me next!"

I was rarely around children, so I wasn't used to their rambunctiousness. I also wasn't used to seeing a man who was obviously a warrior playing with children and handling them delicately. Alexandre's smile never left his face as he played and tossed the children around. I faintly recalled my father tossing me in the air when I was little and felt a tear slide down my cheek. Cesar had been a wonderful father to me, but it was not the same. Alexandre's gaze caught mine and his smile disappeared. I swam some ways away from him and wiped at my face.

"What's wrong?" he asked softly as he swam to me.

"Nothing," I answered.

"Throw Marin!" the little girl yelled.

"Yea!" the boys said together.

Alexandre's smile returned and he grabbed me. I squirmed trying to get out of his hold. "No," I said, but without any real heat to it. Alexandre lifted me effortlessly over his head and then tossed me. I sailed through the air and then splashed into the water. I surfaced to hear the children laughing happily and see Alexandre's happy smile. Something in my heart sputtered and a distant part of me felt as though this is where I belonged. Was it possible that I could be happy living a normal life? A life where my greatest accomplishment would be teaching my child to ride a horse?

Alexandre splashed me with water and the war was on. The children ganged up on me with Alexandre at first, but after a little bit they came to my side and helped me drown him in tidal waves of water. He finally admitted defeat much to the pleasure of the children and I floated on my back in the river as I relaxed. I rarely had opportunities such as this in my regular life. Normally, I would be traveling through the province protecting towns from bandits and the nasty creatures of the world or at the Elven Kingdom training with the Elves to increase my skills.

"Marin," Alexandre called. I sat up and he waved his arm at me from near the base of the waterfall. "I want to show you something."

I swam to him and then followed him around the waterfall, having to kick extra hard to avoid the pull of the water. It was worth it though, to see the little cave behind the waterfall. I pulled myself from the water and walked around the cave, running my hands along the cave walls where townspeople had drawn and carved names, symbols, and initials into it. "Wow," I whispered.

"I thought you might like it," he said happily.

I stopped next to a carving in the wall of a heart which had

"Gwen + Marcus" inside it. I reached out slowly and laid my palm over the heart.

"Your mom and dad were the first to start the carvings when they were teenagers," he whispered from close behind me.

I was a warrior, the Death Bringer, one of the most feared people in the province, and yet as I stood here with my hand over the heart my parents had carved to preserve their love, tears streamed down my face. I missed them so much and yet I hardly remembered them. It pained me even more to know that the father who had been raising me was not my real father and I still had no idea who he was.

Alexandre wrapped his arms around me in a comforting hug. "I didn't mean to upset you. I thought you'd like to see it," he whispered.

I turned and kissed his cheek. "Thank you. I am very happy you brought me here."

He gently wiped the tears from my cheeks and asked, "What happened after you left here? I have heard rumors, but we never really knew what happened to you."

I stepped away from him and wrapped my arms around myself as I walked along the cave walls again, trying to hide my emotions from him. "My parents decided they wanted to move to Crentown to help a family member with their farm. Mom had been pregnant at the time." I personally didn't recall most of the story, but had apparently told it to Amadis and she had told it to me last year when I admitted that I could not remember parts of it. "We were halfway on our trip when a band of ogres attacked us. My father was brilliant with a sword, but there were six ogres and only my father was able to fight. He killed one before the last ones were able to take him down. My mother hid me in the back of our wagon to protect me, but after seeing my father killed, she climbed out only to meet her demise. Apparently, she was too pregnant to fight well. After seeing my father and then my mother killed, something inside of me snapped. I picked up my father's fallen sword and slaughtered the remaining ogres." I remembered nothing of that day, but father had seen me slaughter the last ogre.

"Why didn't you come back here?" he asked from across the cave where he was watching me.

"The King of the Elves watched me kill the last ogre and said I was covered in ogre blood. When he approached me, I began to cry and clung to him. Since my parents were dead and I could not stop crying or remember the name of the town we had come from or were going to, they took me to their land and the King and Queen raised me as if I were their own." I stopped talking and looked at the ground. Favian had been the first one there when I had woken up. He had taken my hand and told me that I was safe and he would protect me from any harm. It had been the beginning of our friendship, a friendship which could end in the next couple of months.

"My father would have taken care of you," Alexandre whispered from closer to me. "He would have raised you as if you were his own."

I looked up at him. "Or would he have looked at me in fear like all of the other humans did? I was only four when I slayed those ogres. Do you really think you would have wanted to play with me when you were playing on this waterfall and I was practicing with swords to kill more ogres?"

"I'm like you," he whispered. "I'm a demigod too."

I had sort of known it, but it still shocked me. "Your mom was the Goddess?" I asked.

He nodded his head. "That's why they wanted us to be married, they thought we would be able to handle this all together and we would make great children."

I was not at the point of wanting children yet. "I..."

"Did you know that we live longer than humans?" he asked. "We can live almost as long as eternals," he said.

"Really?" I asked in shock. That definitely meant I could not marry a human.

"So, the Elves raised you?" he asked, changing the subject slightly.

"Yes. They raised me just as though I were truly their child. I was trained by the Queen to be a proper lady, though it took a lot more training than normal, and the King and the males taught me to fight. When I was ten years old, the Prince and I went to the Academy and I finished the six years there to become a Mercenary." I closed my eyes as I remembered the first trip to the Academy with Favian. He had insisted that I ride behind him so that he could protect me better.

"Why didn't you ever come back?" he asked.

"At first, I couldn't remember the town's name or anything, but my father, my real one, recently told me about the box that the Elves had taken from my family's items and when I opened it I found the contract regarding our arranged marriage and this town. Also, I don't want your sympathy or for one of the townspeople to try to force me to stay here and take me from Fav...the elves."

"Who is Fav?" he asked, a bit of steel in his voice.

"Favian, the Prince of the Elves," I whispered, suddenly longing to be far from this town and with his overly protective and grouchy presence.

"Is this why you want to break off our arrangement?"

Yes. Mostly. "No. I simply want to be allowed to be a Protector and live my life as I want." That was mostly true.

He nodded his head, believing me. Thankfully. "We should head back for lunch."

I nodded my head and placed my hand one last time over my parents' carving. We dressed and began our walk back. The children had gone while we were in the cave, leaving us alone on our walk. The leaves rustled in the tree to our right. I spun, ready to attack whoever it was, but Alexandre had already caught the person and slammed them against the tree's trunk.

The teenage boy's eyes were wide with fear. "I'm sorry."

"Martin, this is not the time for these games," Alexandre said.

I put my sword away and asked, "Why did he try to attack us?"

"I've been training him," Alexandre said.

"Not very well," I commented.

"Who are you?" the boy asked angrily as he stepped around Alexandre towards me.

I pulled my sword and held it under his chin in a swift quick motion. "Do not try and intimidate me, boy."

He swallowed and stepped back slowly. Alexandre smiled wide. "Martin meet Marin the Death Bringer."

Martin's eyes widened and then he sneered. "You're the Death Bringer?" he asked sarcastically.

I sheathed my sword. "Yes, I know shocking." I was not in the mood to deal with this jerk.

I started walking away and heard Martin say, "You are such a liar. She is not the Death Bringer."

My anger got the better of me and I spun around and punched him in the face and then knocked his feet out from under him. He tried to kick my feet out from under me, but I simply jumped over his leg, pulled my sword while in the air and then dropped down to pin Martin's shoulder to the ground with my knees with my sword against his throat. "You should learn to keep your mouth shut; otherwise someone might cut it off for you."

Martin's eyes were three times their normal size. "Sorry."

I stood up off of him and walked away. "Sorry won't save you if you insult a person's honor who isn't as understanding as me."

"I told you," Alexandre whispered.

"Why in the name of the God and Goddess, would you want to marry that?" Martin asked.

I resisted the urge to skewer his stomach with my sword and

stepped into the Inn, slamming the door closed behind me so that I didn't have to hear Alexandre's reply. And he wondered why I preferred the company of elves over humans?

I ate my lunch in my room to avoid Alexandre and to be alone. I felt somewhat foolish for attacking Martin, but he needed to learn that you couldn't judge someone on their looks. I had really done him a service and possibly saved his life in the future. I sat on the bed and started cleaning my sword.

"Marin," Alexandre called softly as he knocked on my door.

"Come in," I said as I set my swords down on the bed next to me.

He smiled at me. "You can't hide in here from me. You agreed to two days."

I stood and sheathed my swords. "I apologize."

He led me out of the Inn and to the center of town where the town square was empty of its usual vendors. "Have you ever played ball before?"

"I've played the Elves version of ball, although it's probably different than yours," I said as a group of kids ranging from ten to fifteen came into the square. Two of the kids poured flour onto the ground in four spots. Another set long sticks on the ground next to one of the spots of flour while another stood in the center holding a ball.

"How about we watch them play for a minute, and then after you understand the game we can join in?" Alexandre offered.

The kids dispersed into what seemed to me as random positions around the flour spots. One picked up a stick and faced the kid with the ball in the center. He threw the ball and the other person hit the ball with the stick, sending it flying through the air. One of the kids in the back part ran back and picked the ball up from where it landed on the ground and then threw it to the kid at a flour spot where the hitter was running towards. The running kid touched the flour just before the kid caught the ball.

"Safe!" Alexandre called. He turned to me. "You understand it?"

"So, you try to hit the ball and then run to the flour spots?"

He nodded his head. "Yes."

"Sounds easy enough," I murmured as I walked and picked up a stick.

The kids all smiled at each other and the ball boy threw the ball. I swung and to my utter shock completely missed the ball.

"Strike!" Alexandre yelled. He walked to me and whispered, "Keep your eye on the ball while you swing." The kids moved closer to the flour spots and snickered to each other.

I nodded my head and tightened my grip on the stick. The boy threw the ball and I kept my eye on it as I swung the stick. The stick exploded from my swing and the ball flew over the heads of all of the kids and down the main street.

"Run!" Alexandre yelled.

I dropped the stick and ran to the first flour spot, the second, the third and then back to the beginning.

"Holy crap," one of the kids whispered.

"Did you see that?" another asked.

"Only Alexandre can hit it that far."

"That was great," Alexandre said.

"Thanks," I said with a smile on my face.

The game continued with three kids missing the balls three times. "Now we go out," Alexandre explained as the kids in the field walked towards the swinging line.

I walked out to the back and waited. Martin stepped forward and sneered at me, which made me decide that I should have hit him harder. The ball was thrown and Martin hit it as hard as he could with the stick. The ball went up into the air and sailed back, starting to go over my head. I refused to let him make it around the bases. I jumped up as high as I could go and caught the ball in my hand, much to everyone's surprise by the shocked wow's I heard.

Martin glared at me as he walked back to stand by the others waiting for their turn to hit the ball. I tossed the ball to the guy throwing and smiled at Alexandre who was smiling at me. "You're right, this is fun."

We played until the sun set and the kids started complaining they were hungry. Alexandre and a couple of the older kids went to get food for everyone. The rest of us sat around a small fire and I started telling them stories about my journeys and missions. Alexandre came back a little while later and divvied out food to the children. Adults started coming out and joined our circle as I told them about various missions. Everyone listened with rapt attention, but the more stories I told, the more I saw people scooting away from me. A few of the teenage boys stayed close to me, as well as Alexandre, but I could see the fear in the others' eyes. I stopped my tales and one of the eldest gathered began telling myths. I sat down and watched Alexandre playing with a few of the toddlers. It was heartwarming to see a man of his stature playing with children that were not his.

I yawned and said goodnight to the townspeople, heading back towards the Inn. Alexandre jogged to catch me and smiled down at me. "You've lived quite a life."

"Which is why I don't want to leave it," I said in irritation as I tried to hide my pain with anger.

"Why are you sad?" he asked, grabbing my arm and gently stopping me.

I didn't want to look at him so I stared at his chest instead since it was in my direct line of sight. "I told you they would be frightened of me."

"They are now, but after spending time with you they wouldn't be."

"Why aren't you frightened of me?" I asked as I looked up at him.

He smiled cockily. "Because I can hold my own against you."

"I highly doubt that," I said despite recalling him pinning me.

In a real fight, I had been trained by people much stronger than him.

"I need to go to sleep. Thank you for today. I…had fun," I admitted with a smile.

He wrapped an arm around my waist and a hand behind my head before I could react and kissed me deeply. I fought at first, more shocked than anything and then relaxed as my head swam with the passionate, yet tender kiss. He pulled back and whispered, "I shall be counting down the hours until I see you again."

I watched him walk away and then turned and walked into the Inn and collapsed onto my bed in the room. My stomach was fluttering with mixed emotions as my lips still tingled from the kiss. I had enjoyed today and the time playing in the river with the children, but could I do this every day? Could I sit idly by while others protected the realm?

I fell asleep replaying the kiss in my head only to be woken by screaming. I leapt from bed with my sword in my hand and ran out of the Inn towards the sound.

"Ar!" yelled an ogre behind me. I spun around and swung my sword, decapitating the ogre.

"Marin!" yelled the little girl who had played with us in the river. I picked up the ax the ogre had dropped and threw it right between the eyes of the ogre chasing the child who had yelled for me. I ran to the child and picked her up in my arms as I blocked a blade swinging down towards her. She clung to me tightly as I battled with the ogre and then I finally sliced off its head and ran the child to the Inn where the owner was gathering people inside.

I kicked an advancing ogre in the stomach, sending him flying backwards and successfully keeping him away from the townspeople. I jumped forward and buried my blade into his chest, right through his heart. I heard a man yell in pain and ran towards the square where I found Alexandre battling with three ogres. He decapitated one ogre and then one of the others sliced his arm. He knocked its ax away and stabbed it in the chest. I ran forward and blocked the third one's blade from Alexandre's back and sliced its throat open.

"There're at least eight more," Alexandre panted and then pointed towards the main street.

I flicked ogre blood off my blade and picked an ax up off the ground. "I'll take care of this," I said happily. "Go to the Inn."

He looked like he wanted to argue, but then neither of us got the chance because a second group of five ogres ran at us from the side of the village. Alexandre met the group of five head on, swinging his blade in a brilliant blur as I charged forward to meet the group of eight, slicing appendages off left and right with the sword and ax.

A fist slammed into my jaw, sending me stumbling backwards and really pissing me off. I sliced the ogre's hand off and then the rest of his arm. He howled in pain and fell backwards. I spun my sword and ax as I tried to keep the ogres from surrounding me, but they stayed back from my blades, moving into position. I watched as they looked at each other and then attacked as one. I leapt upwards like I'd done to catch the ball, much to the ogres' surprise, and decapitated two as I leapt over them and ran towards Alexandre who was losing his fight. I had just killed one when another stabbed him in the stomach. I screamed as he fell forward, blood foaming on his lips and the killing rage I experienced when around ogres finally kicked in.

My blade whirred through the air, invisible to the human eye as I sliced, diced and decapitated. Ogre blood soaked the ground and me as I took my anger out on those nearest me. An arrow buzzed through the air and imbedded itself into the ogre's head in front of me. I ignored the man who had apparently come to help fight the ogres and continued my killing rampage. The last ogre fell at the end of my blade, but my fury wasn't satiated. I screamed my rage and walked to the ogre who had killed Alexandre and proceeded to hack his body into smaller pieces.

"Marin," whispered a soft voice.

I stopped my destruction and dropped down next to Alexandre. "Alexandre," I whispered.

He gripped my hand in his. "I'm sorry."

"Don't be," I whispered as tear leaked down my face. "I'm the one who is sorry."

He pulled my hand to his lips and kissed it softly before closing his eyes.

"Don't die," I whispered. "Please, don't die."

The healer ran out and dropped down beside us. "Someone get me a stretcher!"

"You're the most beautiful and perfect woman I've ever seen," he whispered. "Especially in battle."

"Stop talking," The healer said angrily. Men from the town lifted Alexandre onto a stretcher and carried him away from me.

I let my hand drop to my lap and watched him go. Warm hands grabbed my shoulders and I spun around, ready to fight, but found Favian's eyes looking down into mine. "Marin," he whispered.

I collapsed into his arms and cried. He picked me up and carried me to the Inn, whispering reassurances to me in Elvish. I didn't remember making it to my room or falling asleep, but I woke up the next morning in the bed, under the blankets.

"How are you feeling?" the healer asked from a chair beside my bed.

I didn't respond, not yet able to fully comprehend everything or form logical thoughts. "Alexandre survived," she whispered. "And your Elf friend is downstairs."

I stayed staring up at the ceiling. It had almost happened again. I'd almost lost another to the ogres. "It isn't your fault that they attacked," the healer whispered.

She was wrong. The only reason they were here was because I was. I shouldn't have stayed for a stupid desire to be courted. I shouldn't have endangered all of these people. I should have tossed the bag of diamonds to Alexandre and left.

"He's been asking for you," the healer said.

I wasn't sure if she was talking about Favian or Alexandre, but decided it didn't matter. I needed to get up and use the restroom anyways. I used the restroom first and then walked to the dining room where I could hear Favian and Alexandre talking. I stepped into the room and both stopped talking to look at me. I couldn't look at Favian. I didn't want to see his disappointed face, so I walked silently passed him and sat in the chair beside Alexandre.

"Hello," he said with a smile. I looked at his pale face and bandaged arm. His stomach wasn't visible because he had a blanket pulled up to his chest, but I looked down at it anyways. "Just a flesh wound. I'll be fine in the next day or so." He picked up my hand from where they were clenched on my lap. "Are you alright?"

I nodded my head once and then pulled my hand back, taking the pouch from my pocket and setting it in his hand. A tear rolled down my cheek and he wiped it away with the tip of his finger in a small caress.

"I understand. I knew you couldn't keep to the arrangement anyways, but I still had to try."

I wanted to tell him I was sorry. I wanted to tell him that if things had been different I would have been more than happy to be his wife, but I couldn't speak at all.

"I'll always remember you, Marin."

"She doesn't mean to be rude," Favian said softly. "She's just having a bit of a breakdown, as I explained to you."

"Take care of her," Alexandre said seriously. "Or I promise I'll find you."

Favian bowed grandly. "I swear it. And thank you for discussing the other things with me. Once she is able, I will tell her everything."

"Good bye, Marin. I hope to see you again someday," Alexandre said.

I nodded numbly and walked out of the Inn. Fire and Ice were standing out front waiting for us with the little girl I'd saved yesterday holding their reins. I stopped just in front of her and she dropped the reins to hug my legs. "Thank you."

I stared down at her in shock and fought the tears which were trying to break free. She pulled back and then walked into the Inn. I started to sway and Favian grabbed me just before I fell. "It's alright, Marin."

I clung to him as I tried to keep myself composed in front of the townspeople who were watching from their houses, but knew it was too late. Favian helped me up into my saddle and then climbed on behind me, wrapping his arm around my waist and telling his horse in Elvish to follow us. Favian took the reins and we fled the town of my sorrow. As soon as the town was lost to our sight, the barrier I had created broke and I sobbed uncontrollably.

That had been my one chance at a human life and the ogres had come to take it away again. I had saved Alexandre, but scared everyone in the town into hiding from me. I knew then that I could never have a human life. I could never live in a quiet town and play ball with kids. The only place I could live was among eternals or alone where there would be no people to be frightened of me. I cried over the loss of my humanity and what could have been. I cried over the loss of my parents again.

Favian held me tightly against his chest as he guided Fire and whispered softly in Elvish to me. I hadn't fallen in love with Alexandre, but I could have and that hurt just as much. The tears finally stopped after what felt like an hour and I was able to breathe normally and think logically again.

"I'm sorry," I whispered to Favian. "I should have told you, but…"

"Don't apologize. You were right to keep it from me. I would have overreacted and we would have fought about it." He tucked my hair behind my ear and ran a finger along the curved outer part. "I'm sorry things didn't work out for you there."

I jerked and turned to face him. "You want me to…"

He put a finger to my lips. "I want you by my side as you have been my whole life, but I want you to be happy. You're my best friend and your happiness and health is my main priority."

"I'm happy," I argued and then frowned. "Well not right at the moment, but I usually am." I looked around at our surroundings and asked, "Where are we going?"

"To the Kingdom for your birthday," he said with a smile.

My eyes widened in shock and I asked, "Truly?"

He nodded his head. "We will make it in enough time, so of course we will go celebrate your eighteenth birthday."

I hugged him tightly. "Thank you."

"Are you alright to ride on your own?" he asked. I nodded my head despite my desire to keep him with me. He stopped the horses and then kissed my cheek. "I missed you."

I stared dumbly at him as he dismounted my horse to mount his. "Did you take care of the ogre problem in Avonlea?" I asked to change the subject.

He shook his head. "No, you did."

"What?" I asked in shock as we started on our journey again.

"The ogres ran from me. That's how I ended up in Aralia. I followed the ogres there."

"Someone really wants me dead," I mumbled as we started our ride again. "I wonder who it could be."

"We'll find out," he said seriously.

I didn't speak anymore as I tried to regulate my emotions. I had learned to shove my problems and emotions down, but sometimes it was difficult to do. I had just been too overwhelmed last night and this morning to shove them down properly. Now that we were away from the town and the people there I could pretend it never happened.

Favian rode silently beside me, but I could tell he wanted to talk to me by the way he kept looking at me. We stopped for the night and ate some Elven bread for dinner before laying out the bedrolls and lying down together.

Tonight, Favian must have thought I needed consoling because as I laid in the curve of his body he stroked my hair and sang to me. The return of his warmth and presence soothed me more than his song and I was almost asleep when he started whispering to me. "I missed you, Marin. I could hardly sleep because I was worried for you."

I wasn't sure why he was suddenly being so open with his feelings to me. Usually he kept quiet about whatever he was thinking or feeling. "I was the same way," I admitted.

He exhaled loudly, a rush of relief surging through him. "I was incredibly frightened when I saw you in Aralia with that man."

"Why?" I asked.

He tilted my chin up and I could barely see his features in the dying fire light. "Because I thought you had decided to stay there and I wouldn't be able to be with you anymore."

I rubbed my nose against his, something I used to do when we were younger as a sign of affection. "You'll always be my best friend."

A strange fire lit his eyes and he stared at me for a full minute before adjusting and whispering, "Good night."

I linked fingers with the hand which was curled around my stomach and whispered, "Good night, Favian."

Just before I fell asleep my father whispered, "Now you have made your choice here, but you will still need to make your choice when you arrive home and turn eighteen."

I wasn't sure why it mattered to him who I chose, but I knew he was right.

Two days later, we finally made it to the castle. The castle was magnificent to look at and its sight always amazed me. As soon as we were within the guards' sight, the gate opened. I looked at Favian, my sorrows shoved deep down within my chest and smiled. "Race you to the steps."

He smiled back and for a moment we were kids again. I squeezed my legs and Fire responded by leaping forward into a gallop. I lifted my butt from the saddle and stooped forward, lessening the strain on her back and urging her forward with soft words of encouragement. Ice edged forward until his nose was even with Fire's. Fire did not like to lose though and after swishing her tail in indignation she pushed herself even faster, inching away from Ice as we flew past the gate and into the entrance of the castle grounds. Fire slid to a step at the steps and I dismounted, patting her approvingly.

"It must be Marin, because none of the others would stir up so much dust," said a melodic female voice.

I turned and curtsied to Mother who looked as regal as ever in a flowing silver dress that made her hair shine like starlight. "Hello, Mother."

She smiled and then wrapped me up in a warm hug. "Happy Birthday, Daughter. You have been gone too long."

"Yes, she has," said a deep voice.

I turned from Amadis and was instantly enveloped in a much warmer and tighter hug. "Father," I whispered happily as I hugged the King of the Elves.

"I have missed you, Daughter," he whispered. "I was very close to ordering you brought here and your mission aborted when Balon reported back to us."

I smiled happily and pulled back from him. "I'm sorry. I will come more often to visit you two."

Mother hugged Favian and then Favian shook hands with his father. "The Death Bringer has returned!" yelled Maddock as he walked towards us. His silver hair was braided and hung down to his waist.

I pulled my swords and lunged at him as fast as I could, but he swerved away from me and stuck his foot out. I jumped over his foot and kicked him in the side. He grunted and we squared off. "You're getting slow," I commented.

"I'm simply trying to avoid harming the human," he said with a sneer.

I stopped moving and sheathed my sword, the play cancelled as his comment opened the recent wound of Aralia. "Then I shall take your leave and retire to my chambers," I said as I walked to my mare and began leading her towards the stables. Mercifully Favian, Mother, and Father allowed me to leave without trying to discuss the issue. I had just handed the reins over to Alex, when a hand gripped my shoulder and tugged me out of the stable and around the corner.

"What did I do?" he asked softly.

"Nothing, Maddock," I said.

He grabbed my chin softly and turned it from side to side as he examined my face for wounds and my eyes for signs of my emotions. "What happened? Did Favian do something?" He had become more open with me after the incident where his necklace had saved my life and we had begun to spar with each other every time I returned home.

I rolled my eyes at him and slapped his hand away from my face. "Of course Favian didn't do anything. How can you even ask?" I raised my hand, stopping him from answering. "Rhetorical question. I don't want to talk about it, okay?"

"You never want to talk about things with anyone but Favian and the Queen," he accused. "There are others who worry for you and care about you just as much as the Prince." I stared at Maddock in shock. I had known him as long as I had known Favian, but he and Favian were better friends than he and I were even with his newer interest in me. He smiled at me and brushed a loose hair behind my ear. "I had not thought you would be blind."

"Blind?" I asked after finally finding my voice.

He stroked my cheek softly with the back of his hand. "To the fact that many of us Elves fancy you."

"I know you are all friendly to me," I said softly, still unable to pull away from his caress or speak loudly.

He shook his head and laughed softly. "You truly are blind, Marin. I didn't not mean that we like you as a friend I meant that we wish to..."

"Marin!" Favian yelled.

I jerked away from Maddock as though I had been slapped. I

took a deep breath and then ran away from both males and towards the side of the castle. I burst through the door and right into an Elf. We tumbled head over heels a moment and then the Elf caught me and we stopped in a tangled pile on the carpet. "Sorry," I blurted as I untangled myself from the person.

Balon's face appeared from underneath my leg and he smiled at me. "Well, hello."

I climbed off of him and brushed myself off. "I'm sorry, Balon. I wasn't watching where I was going."

"Quite alright," he said as he stood up. "I'm always glad to assist a beautiful woman when she needs a man to fall on." I turned to go and he asked, "What brings you here?"

I turned back, wishing I could just hide in my room. "My birthday."

His eyes sparkled mischievously. "Really? I thought you weren't coming?"

"We finished our job in time," I answered.

"Marin!" Favian and Maddock yelled at the same time, but from different ends of the castle.

Balon watched as my eyes widened and I searched frantically for somewhere to go. "Do you require refuge?"

It took me a minute to understand his meaning. "Oh, no. Thank you for the offer, but I shouldn't hide anymore."

He walked to me and then snapped his fingers. A beautiful blue gemstone appeared in the air and he placed it in my palm before kissing my cheek. "I'll see you soon, beautiful."

I stood dumbfounded as I watched him walk away and then looked up to find Favian's furious face staring at the stone in my hand. He said a very bad phrase in Elvish and then yelled "My chambers, now!" He grabbed my arm and dragged me down the hallway.

"Favian, let go. I can walk on my own."

"Not without getting into trouble apparently," he said and then cursed in Elvish again when Mother stepped into our path.

"What's going on?" she asked, looking from Favian's vice-like grip on my arm and my shocked face due to Favian's strange behavior.

"I thought you were giving her lessons on all of our customs," Favian said softly as he tried to rein his anger in while talking to her.

"You are well aware that I have been," she answered.

"Did you give her lessons about courting and mating customs yet?" he asked as he kept his eyes on the ground.

Amadis stared at her son in shock and then looked at me. "What has happened?"

"Can we go to my chambers? I do not wish the entire Kingdom to know," he said as he started dragging me along again, this time up the stairs to the second floor.

"Please let me go," I said as I tugged at his arm.

"I'm not going to let you get into any more trouble."

"You're hurting me!" I shouted in both anger and pain.

Favian immediately released me and then turned and examined my arm. "I'm sorry, I wasn't trying to."

I pulled back from him. "I know that, but it doesn't change the fact that you did."

Mother linked arms with Favian and me. "Let's get out of the hallways and into the room."

Favian closed the door behind us and then started speaking in Elvish rapidly to his mother. I tried to follow the conversation, but he'd switched to the older dialect which I knew very little of, probably on purpose so that I wouldn't be able to understand what he was saying. Amadis listened to him a moment and then picked up the hand which was still holding the gemstone and opened it. She stared at it in silence and then said a very bad word, something the refined Queen never did. "Marin, you know that accepting gifts is a sign of accepting a courtship. I taught you that," Amadis said.

"He just handed it to me and walked away," I said defensively. "He didn't give me time to accept it or not!"

"For now, take it to your father and explain to him what happened. He will go speak with Balon," Mother said.

Favian took the stone and turned without looking at me. "I'll go speak with Father."

After Favian shut the door behind him she looked straight into my eyes. "There are more customs than just getting a gift, aren't there? You have a lot to tell me tonight, I'm sure. Let us go to the bathing room."

We hurried down the stairs and to the large room where a maiden filled tubs with hot water and helped bathe people. She and I usually bantered when I came in, but today she was dismissed by Mother as soon as we came in and I was left alone with the upset Queen. I undressed as Mother commanded because she was my mother and I never disobeyed her. Okay, except the time I had borrowed her horse without her approval and ridden it halfway across the country. She asked me for details about our trips since the last time I had been here. I told her everything that had happened starting from our departure from the castle last year until now. I told her every single detail and word I could remember because it was what she wanted and because she was the only one besides Favian that I could talk to.

I hadn't expected to tear up as I described my trip to Aralia, but as she washed my hair I felt the warm water slipping down my cheeks. She made no comment on my tears, just washed me silently as I talked. I finished with Favian hauling me down the hallway into her and exhaled loudly. "That's all of it."

She closed her eyes a moment and then sighed heavily. "Oh, Dear." I finished toweling off, waiting for her to elaborate, but she simply sat down in a chair, drumming the arm with her fingers as she thought. I put on a dress which was always here for me and then turned to her where she was now staring off into space. She shook her head and then motioned for me to follow her. We walked into my room and she said, "It is time to explain our customs to you. I am afraid that you will be dealing with a lot of them in the next few days."

"What do you mean?" I asked as I sat on my bed and folded my legs up next to me.

"You're no longer a child," she whispered and then laughed softly. "At least not in human standards and apparently the others have noticed." She turned to me and laid her hand gently on my cheek. "You have grown into quite the young woman, Marin, and it seems the others are now going to be expressing their interest."

"I'll have suitors?" I asked in question.

She nodded her head. "Yes, or so it seems. Though this is sort of a predicament because normally they would approach your parents' first, but since we aren't technically your parents they can approach you personally, as Balon did." She looked away and got a far-off expression on her face. "I'll start from the beginning."

A mind numbing two hours later, I fully understood all of the courting customs of Elves. I felt lightheaded and slightly nauseous. A servant knocked on the door and stuck her head inside. "The King requests your presence, Your Highness."

She nodded her head and stood up. "Take a nap, Marin. You look dreadful."

"Thank you," I muttered.

She smiled and kissed my forehead. "I am so glad to have you back."

I gave her a quick hug. "I'm glad I'm back too. At least mostly."

I watched her follow the servant down the stairs and then noticed Favian standing next to my door with a deep frown on his face. As soon as he saw me looking at him, he straightened and asked, "Did she explain everything?"

I nodded my head and opened the door. "Yes."

He followed me inside. "What are you doing?"

"Taking a nap as she ordered," I said as I face-planted into the bed and my luxuriously fluffy pillow.

"A nap?" he asked in shock and then sat down beside me. "Are you feeling alright?"

"Tired and dizzy," I admitted. "I've had a rough week."

He pushed the hair which was covering one side of my face away to look into my eyes. "I'm sorry I hurt your arm."

This was quite a week for me getting him to apologize. "It's alright. You didn't mean to."

"I was upset at seeing you with a gift from Balon and my anger overcame my common sense."

"I didn't accept it from him, Favian. He just dropped it in my hand and walked away."

He smiled. "I know. It was wonderful to see Balon's face when Father gave him the stone back."

"Was he mad?" I asked.

"Father was very upset."

I rolled my eyes. "Balon."

Favian glared down at me. "Why do you care if he was upset?"

"Because I do not need another enemy."

"Well if anyone is his enemy, it's me. He gave me quite the glare before slamming his door shut."

I rolled over and sighed. "Wonderful. Can you please leave so I can rest? My head feels as though a herd of ogres stampeded over it."

Favian bent over me and looked into my eyes. "You're really taking a nap?"

I closed my eyes. "Yes, now please go."

He laughed softly. "Alright, grumpy. I'll fetch you for lunch."

"Favian," I called as he was about to shut the door.

"Yes?"

"I understand Elf courting etiquette fully now."

He smiled. "Good."

He shut the door and I closed my eyes. Why couldn't I just flirt endlessly with as many Elves as I wanted and not have it mean anything? Life had been so much easier last year. I tried my hardest to sleep, but sadly sleep never came. With a nap out of the question, I decided it was best to go find Favian. I wandered around the halls, but didn't find him inside the castle, so I made my way out the back to the training grounds and then to the flower fields which towered a foot above my head beyond that. I had just entered the fields when I heard a female screech excitedly. "It's beautiful."

I turned around and found Favian holding a dagger with sapphires and emeralds all over the handle. The female Elf was gorgeous and also one of the few females I could actually stand, Emily. Emily turned seeing me and snapped her mouth closed. Favian followed her gaze and then tried to hide the dagger behind his back.

My brain finally put the pieces together and I realized he must be asking to court her. Instantly tears sprang to my eyes and I felt a physical pain in my chest and stomach. "I'm sorry I interrupted," I muttered before striding into the tall fields and disappearing from their sight.

"Marin!" Favian yelled. "Wait!"

"Marin, please come back!" Emily called.

I ignored them both and started running, heading towards the back of the fields where I knew a secret portal stood. The portal transported you to the stables and thus far away from them.

"Marin, please!" Favian yelled. "Let me explain!"

I didn't need him to explain. His mother had just explained Elf courting etiquette. I knew I had no right to be upset that he wanted to date the beautiful Elf, yet I felt betrayed and hurt. I smacked myself mentally for ever thinking an Elf could have wanted me, especially the freaking Prince of the Elves. Hadn't I been telling myself for two years that I would never have his love in return? So why did it hurt so bad to have that proven to me? I stepped into the portal and then appeared in the center of the stables right in front of Alex. He blinked and then smiled. "Marin, what brings you back?"

I looked at the King's stallion and said, "I'm borrowing him."

Alex bit his lip. "The King didn't say anything to me."

I grabbed the bridle from the stall door and looked into the stallion's eye. "I'm begging you to please take me from here for a few hours. I will groom you and not ask anything of you again for at least a year or more. Please."

The stallion met my gaze a moment and then bobbed his head.

I bridled him and then hopped up onto his back. "Thank you."

He trotted out of the stables just as Favian appeared inside. "Marin!"

"Now would be good," I whispered.

The stallion bobbed his head and then we were flying across the ground, his hooves only touching down long enough to propel us forward again. He was the fastest horse in the world, which is why I took him instead of Fire. I held on with my legs and had a fistful of mane and somehow managed to hang on as he galloped. He ran at a full gallop down the road and then dove into the forest on the side, hiding us from the guards' sight so Favian could not ask where we had gone.

The forest thinned and then we galloped into the center of the Elves' sacred meadow. I didn't understand why he had brought me here until he dumped me off of his back, right in front of Father. "Oh, Marin. I had thought we were past you stealing our steeds," Father said in a chastising tone.

I stood up and brushed myself off. "I didn't steal him, I borrowed him. I was only trying to disappear for a short while."

Father tugged my hand and forced me to sit down beside him in the meadow. Power like a warm wind filled me and eased my tension. "What has caused you to run away?" he asked as he watched me with half opened eyes.

"I…" I was going to say I didn't want to talk about it, but I knew I couldn't hide anything from father when he asked. "Favian is courting Emily," I blurted.

"And this upsets you," he said as a statement instead of a question.

"I know it shouldn't because I always knew he'd start looking for a mate, but…"

"But you love him."

I stared at him in disbelief. "No, I, uh…"

Father laughed and ruffled the hair on top of my head. "You and Favian may be blind, but Amadis and I are not. You've loved Favian since he vowed to always protect you when you were first brought here. It just took you a lot longer to figure it out."

He was right, but I knew it was pointless. "It doesn't matter how I feel," I muttered.

"And why not?" he asked.

"Because I can't have a family."

"You can't?"

"No! Alexandre tried and look where that got him! Everything I do is about killing and if I let anyone love me they will only end up dead!" I yelled.

"Am I dead?" he asked softly.

I looked into his kind eyes and frowned. "No."

"Is Amadis dead?"

"No."

He grabbed my chin and stared into my eyes. "Do you not love us?"

"Of course I love you, but…"

"Then why do you believe that anyone you love will die?" he asked as though it was the silliest question he had ever heard. And it might have been.

"My parents and Alexandre they were attacked…"

"They were humans my dear. What I'm saying is that you are destined for great things and as such you require a family of hardier stock than a human."

"So, you're saying I can never have a human mate?"

He shrugged. "Probably not, but do you really want a human mate?" No, but that wasn't the point. "Your life is centered around violence, but you have happiness and merry things happen as well. We have watched you dance at our balls and go an entire night without killing anything or anyone. You have spent the winter solstice with us and restrained from getting into any fights. You are not just the Death Bringer, Marin. You are a young woman who simply needs a more resilient mate."

"So, you're saying because I am so prone to violence that I need an eternal mate?"

He nodded his head. "Yes."

I guess that I had always known that.

He held out his hand and an apple appeared, which the stallion quickly took in his mouth and chewed on. "Have you figured out who your father is yet?"

"I know he is a god, but he has not shown himself to me. I am assuming he is *the* God."

"Did you talk to Alexandre about it at all?" he asked.

"A bit. He is a demigod as well, his mother was the Goddess, but he was not nearly as strong as me," I said.

"You were raised by very strong beings so it makes sense that you are tougher than he who was raised around humans."

"That's why he wasn't able to defeat the ogres?" I asked softly as I recalled the night he was stabbed. It felt like it had been so long and yet I knew it was only a few days.

"Because he was not trained as you are and because he is not as adept at fighting as you are."

This all made sense, but… "What does this have to do with why I came here?"

"You think you are not good enough for my son because he

should be with an Elf when it does not matter, since you are not completely human as you thought you were. And an eternal is better adept at staying alive and keeping you alive which would make him an ideal mate for you. Plus, you will live a much longer life. Honestly, we have no idea how long demigods live. You could live as long as Favian."

"He doesn't want me for a mate, Cesar."

"And you're going to give him up that easily? What happened to the girl who challenged Alice to a duel for a doll which had been stolen? You are one of the strongest women I know and yet you think you should cower and let another have him?"

"If he doesn't want me, why should I try to take him from her?" I asked as I angrily got to my feet.

Father sighed. "You've always been a stubborn girl."

"He needs to be happy and if another makes him happy, then so be it."

"What about your happiness?" Cesar asked.

I mounted the stallion and whispered, "My happiness is achieved when killing. After my birthday, I will have to start my life away from here and find happiness."

Father watched me go as the stallion returned to the stable. When we arrived, Alex exhaled in relief. "I was starting to get worried."

I returned the stallion to his stall and started brushing him. "Why? I was only gone an hour?"

"An hour?" Alex asked in shock. "Try four hours!"

I looked out the stable doors into darkness, having not paid attention when we had come this way. "Does time move differently in the Meadow?"

Alex nodded his head. "Yes."

"I was there speaking with Cesar. I hadn't really paid attention to my surroundings as we returned. I'm sorry that I worried you."

Alex wiped off the bridle with a soft cloth. "Thank you."

"Thank you," I said to the stallion who dipped his head in acknowledgment. I walked from the stables and wandered around the back of the castle. I knew it didn't make a difference, but talking with Father and hearing him say I needed an eternal made me feel a little better.

"There's my daughter," mother said from a short distance.

I turned and found her standing in the back doorway with Emily beside her. "I was speaking with Cesar in the Meadow," I said. "If you will excuse me, I need to get ready for the celebration and find a snack since I missed lunch."

"I can get you something," Emily said with a smile.

I smiled, but knew it wasn't pleasant. "I think you have enough."

Emily's mouth opened in shock and mother frowned at me, but I walked passed both of them and up to my room.

Favian stood beside my door. "Marin, where did you go? I looked everywhere."

"I was speaking with Father in the Meadow," I answered. "Now if you'll excuse me I have to get ready."

"Wait, let me explain." I ignored him and shut the door in his face, locking it in case he decided to storm in. "Marin, I'll just talk to you through the door," he said.

I ignored him, making loud noises as I opened and closed drawers and doors to get out the items I needed for the ball. I had just stripped out of my clothes when Favian popped into the bedroom using a magic stone that let you teleport to and from a specific location. "Did you really think..."

"Favian!" I screamed in shock as I tried to cover my body.

He stared at me a moment and then closed his eyes and turned away. "I didn't think you would actually be changing."

"Get out!" I yelled angrily. He squeezed his hand and disappeared, using the charm he'd made to bring himself to me to leave. I squatted down on the floor as my heart tried to slow.

How could a man seeing me naked be more frightening than a horde of ogres jumping me?

I finally managed to calm myself and stared at the dresses in my armoire. Mother always made sure I had the most beautiful dresses handy should I ever choose to wear them. I rarely wore dresses, which was why I had a billion I had never worn. I stared at a dark blue dress which would accentuate my black hair and yet highlight my blue eyes wonderfully since they were the same color as the dress. It had a plunging neckline that I hadn't dared to wear before, but suddenly felt the desire for.

After a few minutes of squirming and inventive curses, the dress finally hung on my body as it was supposed to. I stared in shock at my reflection as I saw myself as a woman for the first time. And a beautiful woman at that. My eyes did match the dress and yet they were so much more vivid than the dress that I looked stunning and I could actually see the blood other than human within me. I brushed my hair until it was tangle free and then slipped on high heels I'd only ever worn once.

I twirled in front of the mirror and smiled in satisfaction. Tonight, I was definitely going to turn a few heads. I opened my door, expecting to find Favian, but found the hallway empty. I would have had a horrible time walking if it hadn't been for the slit which went all the way to my knee and allowed me to walk almost freely. I held on to the railing as I walked down the stairs in case I decided to become a klutz, but I made it down without incident.

Mother stepped out of her chambers and smiled approvingly at me. "You look beautiful."

I curtsied. "You look stunning as always, Your Highness." And it was true. Mother wore a red silk dress that hugged her curves and made me look like a rag doll in comparison.

"We must hurry. Cesar is waiting on us since we are the last guests to arrive," she said as she tugged me along beside her. She stopped at the door to the ball room and smiled at the guard who prepared to open the door. "Stand up straight, Marin."

I adjusted my posture and took a deep breath. The guard opened the door for mother who walked inside looking every bit of the Elf Queen that she was. The guard closed the door behind her and smiled at me. "You look beautiful."

"Thank you, sir," I said with a curtsy.

He listened to the voices inside a moment and then opened the door for me. It was custom for the Queen and King to arrive alone so I had had to wait until she was at her throne before I could walk in. I stepped into the ballroom and every eye turned to look at me. I was thankfully used to that, so I strode forward confidently and sat at the table just beside the Royal table in a chair between an older male called Aaron and the oldest female, Mary. Father smiled happily at me and then raised his hands to quiet the murmuring which had started after I walked in. "Tonight, we celebrate Marin's eighteenth birthday! She has become a woman and in her short life span has been noticed by all, which earned her the titles Death Bringer and Protector. We are proud of the woman you have become, Marin and we love you. Happy Birthday!"

Everyone yelled "Happy Birthday!"

"Bring in the food!" he boomed.

Servants flowed into the room and opened the covered platters on the tables. I inhaled the wonderful smells and couldn't decide which I wanted to try first. I remembered my manners and stood up. "What would you like, Mary?" I asked so I could serve her food. She was a *very* old Elf who could barely get around anymore.

Mary frowned at me and pulled me down. "Sit down, girl. You don't serve."

I stared at her in shock. "What?"

She looked up and I realized someone was standing in front of our table. I looked up and Maddock smiled at me before looking at Mary. "What would you like this evening, Mary?" She pointed out the things she wanted and he gave her a small portion of each thing and then he turned to me. "What would you like this evening?"

I looked at Mary for help and she whispered, "It is customary for children and men to serve the women."

"But..."

"You're eighteen now," she said before I could continue. "So you no longer serve us."

"Marin, what would you like?" Maddock asked softly.

I looked up into his shining eyes and realized he was flirting with me. "A little of everything, please," I answered instead of flirting back. I would have, but I was in shock at the increasing changes in my life.

He piled my plate high and then continued down the row, serving everyone until he got to his seat at the end of the table and then served himself.

I looked up at Mother who smiled cheerfully at me before turning to speak to father. Favian was staring at me, but I ignored him and Emily who was sitting beside him and ate my food. As always, the food was delicious and as soon as everyone was finished, the servants cleared away the tables so everyone could dance. I carefully and discreetly made my way to the back of the room to avoid being pulled into the dances.

Aaron tsked at me. "You are supposed to be dancing, Little Death Bringer."

"You know I'm terrible at dancing," I reminded him.

"I'll make an exception since it's your birthday. Just don't expect a present."

"You could be nicer on my birthday than to say that!" I snapped. I exhaled and calmed myself. "I did not mean to snap at you. It is not your fault that I was ignorant of my bloodlines." I curtsied to him and smiled. "I'm sorry, Aaron."

He patted my hand and smiled back. "Not to worry. I am used to women yelling at me."

I laughed and his mate, Erin, walked over and smacked his arm. "I heard that."

I smiled at the couple and then felt a tap on my shoulder. I turned and found Maddock behind me. He bowed and extended a hand. "May I have this dance?"

I looked out towards the large dancing crowd and swallowed nervously.

"I will teach you," he said knowing what I was nervous about as he took my hand gently and led me through the standing crowd to the dancing Elves. "You look gorgeous," he whispered as he turned me to face him and clasped our hands in the proper dancing holds.

"Thank you," I said with a flirtatious smile. "You look handsome as always." A twirling couple caught my eye and I turned to realize it was Favian and Sarah, another beautiful Elf girl around our age. I knew he always danced with the females, but tonight it made me angry and hurt. Before I could pull away to leave though, Maddock was spinning us onto the dance floor.

He kept a hand firmly on my lower back and our other hands clasped together as he led me into the moves and surprisingly, I was able to stay with him. "See, I told you I could teach you."

I smiled up at him happily and started paying attention to the movements, memorizing the patterns as if it were a test at the Academy. After a minute, I had them memorized and moved with Maddock freely. He twirled me in a circle and I laughed merrily. The song ended and a finger tapped my shoulder.

I broke from Maddock's hold and turned to have Alex bow over my hand which he had picked up and kissed the back of softly. "May I have this dance?" he asked with a bit of nervousness. He smelled like hay, dirt and horses, which to me was wonderful.

"I would be honored to." I turned to Maddock and curtsied.

"Thank you for the dance, I hope to have the opportunity to dance with you again this night."

He picked my hand up and turned it over, kissing the bottom of it. "I will certainly dance with you again."

Alex spun me around and right into the dancing group of Elves. I giggled and stepped closer to him so he could lead. "I'm surprised you asked me, Alex," I admitted.

He spun us around Balon and Korteny who were dancing sinfully well together. "I've always thought you beautiful and smart, but didn't think I stood a chance against the others."

I shook my head and twirled underneath his raised hand. "You are as attractive as they are and one of the kindest Elves I know," I said to him.

He stared at me in shock a moment and then smiled. "Yes, but you are the Death Bringer and I'm just a stable boy."

I started to falter and he helped correct me, making it look as though we'd simply added an extra move to the dance. "You are not a stable boy, but the Horse Master which is an important job. Besides you're the one that showed me that handy portal in the flower fields. It saved my life when I was nine, if you recall."

"Yes, that was a very frightening day," he admitted and his face soured as he recalled the memory a moment. He shook his head as if flinging off the bad memory and his smile returned. "You know for someone who said she wasn't a dancer, you're a natural."

I shrugged. "I never really thought to look at it like a synchronized drill until today. Now it's rather simple." I saw Favian dancing with another Elf whose name I couldn't remember and my happiness diminished.

Alex caught my eye and said, "It's customary for the Prince, when single, to dance with all of the single females."

I shoved the feelings down and smiled. "I know, Alex. I've just had a rough week."

"Well then let me take your mind off of it," he said seductively and suddenly the sweet stable boy I knew was replaced by a man I had not noticed before. He spun us around and then off the dance floor. He led me to a servant who was holding a tray of drinks and handed me one. "You look thirsty," he commented as if that explained why we'd left the dance floor.

I was thirsty, so I greedily gulped the nectar down. Alex led me to the back of the room where other males were gathered and kept his hand on my lower back as we approached. I knew it was a sign of possessiveness, but it made me smile instead of feeling angry as I would have if another had done it. I expected him to stop and chat, but he simply walked passed them and to the hidden back door used for emergencies. He looked around to ensure no one was watching us and then pulled me through it and out into the main hall of the castle. "Where are we going?" I asked curiously.

He put a finger to his lips and whispered, "A surprise."

I lifted the side of my dress and followed him out the secret door of the castle. The moon was shining brightly overhead and the stars glistened like diamonds in the sky. It was one of the most beautiful nights ever. I tripped on a root and Alex caught me. My hands had grabbed onto his arms and I realized how much more muscular he was than other Elves from his work with the animals. I pulled my hands back and stood up. "Sorry, I'm not used to walking in these heels."

He put my hand on the bend of his arm and smiled. "I'll keep you from falling."

I wanted to run my hand along his arm as we walked, but I kept it still. We approached the barn and then he led me to a back stall where I could hear soft whickering and neighing. He waved me forward. "Ladies first."

I peered over the top and a smile split my face as I saw the twin foals lying beside their mother in the stall. They were palominos and judging by the mother, a very sturdy war horse breed. "They're beautiful," I whispered so as not to startle them.

He stood next to me and beamed as though the proud parent. "They're why I missed dinner. I had to help the mare get the second one out. His hindquarters had gotten a little stuck."

"Have you picked names yet?" I asked.

He shook his head. "I always wait until the next day to pick names so that their individual attitudes can come out."

I giggled. "If we did that with Elves you'd be 'Quiet, but lethal'."

He laughed. "You only say that because I scared the crap out of you last year."

"No one can sneak up on me," I said.

"Apparently, I can," he said with a smile and then brushed a strand of hair behind my ear. "You really do look amazing tonight, Marin."

"Thank you," I whispered before turning back to the horses.

The sight of the mother with her babies was wonderful and yet brought up my hurt feelings. I shoved the feelings down, but apparently not quickly enough because Alex put his arm around me and kissed my cheek. "Did you know that the King and Queen always look forward to the ball because it means that you'll be returning?"

"I'm sure they look forward to Favian returning," I said as I watched the mare stand to feed the foals who had started nickering for food.

"Of course they look forward to Favian returning, but you are the jewel of the Elves."

I recalled him telling me that he would welcome me here and I hugged him. "You have been exceptionally kind to me and I fear I have not returned the favor. If you ever need anything, let me know."

He smiled and kissed my cheek. "You are too kind to this humble stable boy."

"We should go sneak into the kitchen and get you some food. You must be starving," I said as I headed out of the barn.

He put my hand on his arm and we made it to the castle kitchen without me falling. I hopped up onto the counter and told Alex some of the funnier missions I'd been on while he made himself a salad and ate it.

We went back to the ball since it was a celebration for my birthday and I curtsied to him as we separated on the dance floor. "I had a great time tonight," I said to Alex.

Alex kissed the back of my hand softly. "I did as well. Thank you." I started to walk away when he asked, "Would you like to help me name the foals tomorrow?"

I turned and nodded my head. "I'm leaving tomorrow, but I'd like to do that before I leave."

"I'll meet you at dawn," he said, beaming happily as he disappeared into the crowd.

I was asked to dance by Balon and a few others and then even more I did not know. Luckily, no one tried to ask to court me, but I had an incredibly fun night filled with flirting and laughter. Sebastian stole the most dances with me, but I knew it was mainly to make Favian jealous. Favian had not once tried to dance with me, but then again, I could not remember a single time we had danced together except during practice sessions with mother.

I had just crested the stairs when I had finally decided I was too tired to continue when Favian said my name softly behind me. I walked the last few feet to my door and then turned to face him. "Hello. Did you have a nice night?"

"You look beautiful," he whispered as he walked closer to me.

My heart beat faster as he moved closer. His hair was shining brightly as though a part of the moon, and his shirt and pants hugged his body in all the right places. "You look great as always," I whispered back.

"I've never seen this dress before," he said as he ran a hand down my arm slowly.

His touch burned, as if he were on fire. "I've never worn it before," I said in barely a whisper.

"Why did you avoid me all night?"

The question snapped me back to reality and I stepped back from him. "I was giving you space to court Emily. You could have come and asked me to dance."

"I'm not courting Emily," he said calmly.

I rolled my eyes. "Your mom explained everything and you giving her a gift is your way of showing interest in courting her."

"The gift wasn't for her," he said as he watched me. "Where did you go? I saw you leave, but couldn't see with who."

"Alex took me to see the new foals."

"Alex?" he asked in shock and then frowned, deep in thought.

"I'm tired, I'd like to get to bed, so if you have nothing else you'd like to discuss…"

"Did you accept a gift from him?"

"No, no one offered me any."

"Favian!" a female called from downstairs. "Where are you?"

He exhaled in frustration. "I've got to see her out. It's proper etiquette."

I opened my door without looking at him. "You can call it whatever you'd like."

"Marin," he said in exasperation. "It's not like that." I started to close my door and he stepped inside. "Why are you being so cold to me?"

"Your father told me that since I'm a demigod that I'm better suited for an eternal as a mate."

Favian's eyes widened in shock. "Oh. What else did my father say?"

"Nothing I need to repeat. Go attend to your duties," I said pushing him out the door.

He let me push him out and then grabbed my hand in his. I watched in shock as he bowed over it and kissed it softly. "Good night, Marin."

I couldn't move or breathe or think. He slowly dropped my hand, smiling happily, and then walked down the stairs. It made me recall the one time he had kissed me when we were at the Academy and it made my stomach flutter. I shook my head and shut my door. It didn't matter that I wanted him; he needed a full-blooded Elf for a mate for when he succeeded his father, no matter what Father said. I had to keep remembering that.

CHAPTER FOURTEEN

I said goodbye to Mother and Father as the sun rose the next morning and then hurried to the stables. I hadn't spoken to Favian or advised him of my plan to leave because I knew he wanted to stay longer at the castle. I on the other hand needed to find something to kill. The stables were noisy as the animals voiced their hunger. I could see Alex inside tossing hay and apples into each stall. I walked inside and then blinked as my eyes adjusted to the light.

"Good morning," Alex said cheerfully as he fed the last steed.

"Good morning," I said as I pet Fire on the nose.

Alex led me to the foals' stall and folded his arms over the top as he looked in at the horses. "I think I have a name for the colt, but I'd like you to pick the filly's name."

I leaned next to him, touching shoulders with him as I looked at the now rambunctious foals. "What's the colt's name?"

"Hero," he said. "A very large spider was crawling towards his sister and he hopped up and then stomped the spider to death."

"That's a good name." I looked at the filly who was pushing her head against her brother's side and trying to get him to play, but he wasn't having it. She didn't give up though, and continued to butt him with her head. She reminded me of me. "Morrigan," I whispered.

Alex looked at me a moment in contemplation and then smiled. "It's beautiful." I looked one last time at the horses before walking to mine and starting to saddle her. "Are you sure you have to leave so soon?" Alex asked.

I nodded my head. "I need to head towards my house to check on the ogre problems."

"Shouldn't you wait for Favian then?" he asked as he helped me adjust the saddle pad and saddle.

"Yes, she should," Favian said as he walked into the stable and began saddling Ice.

I cursed softly and stepped out of my horse's stall to look at him. "You don't need to come. You should stay here."

Favian turned and looked at me and I saw the anger and tightness in his posture. "Why should I stay here?"

"Because you aren't home often and I'm sure Father has more to teach you about being King."

He set the bridle back on the hook where he had just taken it from. "Are you saying you don't want me to come with you?"

I noticed Alex finished bridling Fire and was acting as though he wasn't listening. I met Favian's eyes. "It has nothing to do with whether I want you to come or not. You should start learning from your father and trying to court one of the females."

"I'm coming with you and that's final," he said angrily as he picked the bridle back up.

I hated when he was so stubborn. I tied my bedroll and pack

to my saddle and then waited until Favian walked Ice from the stable before turning to Alex. "Thank you for last night and for allowing me to name one of the foals."

He kissed my cheek and put something into my hand. "Thank you, Marin. And please be safe."

I looked down at the bracelet made of horse hair. "Is this…"

"It's not a courting gift. I never have the opportunity to give you a birthday present, so I thought you'd like this. It's hair from the foals' tails, so you'll always remember me."

I slipped the bracelet on and then kissed his cheek. "I have never forgotten you." I led Fire out of the stable and mounted her, waving to Alex as I rode towards the gate.

Favian looked down at the bracelet and I heard his teeth grind together. "Courting?"

I shook my head. "No, it's for my birthday."

He didn't look like he believed me, but some of his tension eased out of him as we rode. The silence was awkward and I tried to think of a way to disperse of it. I never got the chance though, because a group of goblins jumped us. They were silent and the only warning I had was the shifting of leaves before one jumped onto Fire behind me. I elbowed him in the stomach and then pulled my reins, signaling Fire to stop and rear up her front legs. She did as commanded and the goblin fell off and then she kicked out with her back legs, sending him flying backwards. Favian had been knocked from his horse and was battling three goblins at once. I dismounted and ran to assist him, slicing the goblin's head off that was closest to me. Favian's blade flashed in the sun three times and then we were alone.

"Are you alright?" he asked.

I nodded my head and then pointed to the unconscious but still alive goblin Fire had kicked. Favian walked towards him and punched him in the face to wake him up. The goblin groaned and rolled onto his side. "Why did you attack us?" Favian asked.

The goblin looked up at me and whispered, "We were hired to kill her."

"Who hired you?" Favian asked as he jerked the goblin up.

"Karr."

I cursed and then kicked the body of one of the dead goblins. "That rat!"

Favian dropped the goblin and mounted his horse. I did the same and we ran our horses until we reached the nearest town. The stable owner promised to cool the horses and dry the sweat from them for us.

I could see the rage simmering beneath Favian's calm exterior and wondered when he was going to snap. We paid for a room for the night at the Inn and I sat on the bed, waiting for him to speak. He paced back and forth across the room with his hands clasped behind him. It was the same thing his father did when angry.

"I knew he didn't like you, but I didn't think he'd stoop so low as to hire assassins to kill you."

"They aren't very good assassins," I noted. "Maybe he was just trying to keep me on my toes."

Favian turned and glared at me. "Do not make light of this situation." I raised my hands in surrender and flopped backwards onto the bed, running my finger over the bracelet. "Do you like him?" Favian asked.

"Not particularly, but if he's hired assassins against me I won't feel bad..."

"Not Karr," he said. "Alex."

Oh. "He's nice and attractive, but so are ten other Elves I know. Besides, we both saw what happens when I try to have a relationship."

Favian lifted my feet up and sat on the bed next to me. "Father told me most of what you talked about."

I closed my eyes and swallowed. "What did he tell you?" I asked, refusing to look at him.

"Everything I pretty much already knew, that you think you can't have a relationship because you think they'll end up getting killed because of you."

"Alexandre..."

"Alexandre is not an Elf," Favian said.

"I don't know if I can be with an Elf," I admitted softly.

He pried open one of my eyes and stared into my pupil. "Why not?"

Of all the times, I needed to be honest, I figured now was it. "Because I can't have the one that I want and I don't want to watch him with another female the rest of my life."

He released my eyelid and stared at me in shock. "Who?"

I just stared at him like he was dumb.

"Who is the Elf you want?"

Apparently, Father hadn't told him that bit of information. "It doesn't matter," I said as I stood up and walked to the window which looked out over the town.

"Is it Maddock?" he asked, sounding mad.

"No," I said exasperated. "It's not Maddock."

"Balon?"

I laughed. "Of course not!"

"Then who?"

"It doesn't matter! Not even he knows!" I yelled angrily. Six large shapes moved through the alleys of the town and my fear skyrocketed. I couldn't let Favian get hurt. I shouldn't have even let him come with me while a contract was out on my head. "I'm going to my house," I said with as much steel as I could muster. "Do not follow me."

He grabbed my arm, stopping me before I reached the door. "Do you love me?" he asked.

It was the hardest thing I had ever done in my life, but I knew I had to lie to him to keep him safe. I kept my face even and said, "No." His eyes blazed with hurt and fury and he released my arm.

I opened the door and whispered, "I'm sorry," and then hurried down the stairs and ran to the stables.

"She's not ready to be ridden yet," the owner said.

"Can we trade for a week? I need to leave, but will return for her when I can."

He looked over my mare and then pointed to the end stall where a mare similar to mine was standing. "We can trade for her."

I nodded my head and saddled her quickly before racing out of town. The ogres caught my scent and charged after me, but luckily, they weren't distance runners. I galloped for a few miles and then slowed my mare to conserve her energy.

For three days I rode, only letting my mare stop for short naps and for food and water. The rain started the second day, and the third day as the sky unleashed buckets of water. a goblin jumped me. I was pulled from my saddle and onto the muddy ground. I rolled away from the goblin's sword only to have him kick my ribs. I grunted in pain, but rolled up and pulled my sword. He charged forward and I sliced at his body, but he dodged and then slammed me against a tree. A broken off branch stabbed into my leg, making me cry out in pain. Fury overrode my senses then as I tried to ignore the pain and I stabbed my sword through the goblin. He pulled a dagger and sliced open the top of my sword hand, making me release my sword, but the damage was already done. He staggered backwards and then fell to the ground.

I used my other hand to pull my sword from his body and then limped over to the mare. I quickly bandaged my leg and then screamed as I was forced to put weight on my leg to mount her. Thankfully the mare stayed still and after a little encouragement, took off down the road again. Every step she took sent a huge spike of pain up my leg. I urged her to go faster and almost cried out in joy when I finally saw my house. I corralled her and then hobbled into the house to treat my leg and hand.

My body and mind were exhausted and I fell asleep on the bed before I realized I had even lain down. I woke up sometime later, though I wasn't sure what time of day it was or how many days later it was. I ate some dried meat and then walked to the window. It was pitch black, but I somehow knew it was day time. I walked back to bed and fell asleep again until the sounds of snarling ogres woke me.

The rain pounded against the roof, making an eerie song in the dark. The night sky was black with rain clouds, not even the moon or a star shining through. I looked out the window and waited for the flash of lightning to expose the scene in front of me. Thunder rumbled and then a bolt of lightning appeared.

At least fifty ogres stood amongst the trees, snarling at me and frothing at the mouth. I cursed and kicked the chair beside me. I could handle fifty ogres if I was fully healed, but I yet had a swollen leg and a large cut on my sword hand. I might be able to kill them all, but I had no idea what I was capable of in my current state.

If only I hadn't argued with Favian. If I had kept my mouth shut and not lied to him, then he would be here. I regretted my decision, but I would not be able to correct it now.

I grabbed my sword and held it in my left hand. I would just have to try my hardest and hope that by some massive miracle I survived. I grabbed three light sticks and snapped them, turning them on. I opened my front door and tossed the light sticks in a triangle out in the center of the yard. This way I could see partly around me while they attacked.

The ogres growled happily as I hobbled out of the protection of my house and into the downpour of rain. I gripped my sword tighter and yelled, "Come at me then, you scoundrels!"

The ogres needed no urging, and after issuing a war cry to scare any human, they charged. I blocked the first sword and slid mine across his throat before spinning and sliding underneath the blade of an ogre at my back. I slid my blade through his gut and gagged as the foul stench of his innards filled the air. I stopped controlling my movements and allowed my body to protect itself. My blade whirred through the air like an angry wasp, sinking its pointed end into flesh again and again.

A blade bit into the edge of my skin, releasing blood from my shoulder. I sliced off the offending arm and ducked just as an axe soared towards me. The axe imbedded in the skull of an ogre behind me and ended his attempt to stab me in the back. I stared at the axe in shock for a moment before the sound of dying ogres came from in front of me. Favian had come!

I only had a moment of cheer as more ogres surged towards me in hopes of ending my life. I attacked with weakening strength, receiving three more cuts on my arms. I had lost count of the ogres I'd killed and had no way of knowing if I was winning or not now.

Lightning flashed and I saw Favian twenty feet ahead of me, slicing through ogres left and right with the ease of the warrior he was. His silver hair flashed in the light, making him look as regal as any royal Elf should. At least twenty ogres' bodies lay at his feet, a testament to his incredible power. I blocked one sword from an ogre to the left of me, but saw the ogre to the right of me too late. His blade speared through my stomach, sticking out my back. I screamed in pain and cut off the blade owner's arm before pulling the sword from my body.

A shield smacked me in the back, forcing me down to my knees. I swayed as pain and dizziness vied for priority in my skull. "Marin!" yelled Favian from somewhere nearby.

A blade slashed down at me and I brought my blade up in just enough time to block it. Two more blades came at me and I only blocked one, the second finding purchase in my shoulder. I screamed and rolled away from the attacker and right into the presence of another. The ogre's sword sliced through the tender flesh of my stomach, making me scream again in pain.

Favian's sword zipped by several times and then he picked my head up into his lap. "Marin, talk to me."

"I'm sorry I lied," I whispered. "I should have told you the truth long ago."

He lifted my shirt to examine my wound. "What did you lie about?" he asked quietly.

"Not loving you," I whispered as pain gripped my throat.

He ripped a strip of material from his shirt and pressed it against my stomach. "You're delirious," he whispered.

I shook my head and took his face between my hands, forcing him to look me in the eyes. "I love you, Favian. I know now is an awful time to tell you, but I wanted to tell you before I..."

He stopped my words with a kiss, his lips warm against my cold ones. "I've always loved you, Little Death Bringer. Do not give up, I can heal you."

I shook my head and looked at the pointed ears which were the only noticeable difference, besides his hair, when compared to a human. "You cannot heal this. Only the Gods, if they saw fit, would be able to heal me. Do me a favor?" He nodded his head, kissing the inside of my palm. "Kill Karr."

Favian smiled. "I had planned on it."

"I am sorry that I caused us so much turmoil, but I was afraid if I told you that I loved you and you did not love me back, that it would ruin our friendship," I admitted to him.

"This is what you have been hiding since the Academy?" he asked as he tried to heal my wounds. I nodded my head. He laughed bitterly. "You silly, blind girl. I've always loved you. That's why it bothered me so much when you flirted with the others."

I laughed bitterly at this. I had wasted these years with him and all because I had been afraid to tell him. I relaxed against him and exhaled, my final breath leaving me in a silent rush. The world stilled and I welcomed death's embrace.

CHAPTER FIFTEEN

"Little Death Bringer," a deep voice said from the darkness. "We are surprised you gave up so easily. You have been born with a task that you have yet to complete and here you are, dead."

"What task?" I asked as I fought to open my eyes.

A soft voice, like Amadis' said, "To rid the world of the ogres once and for all. We made them, but the others have twisted them. Your goal is simple, eradicate the race of ogres. We are merciful and will give you one more chance to redeem yourself. Do not fail us. And remember, we are here if you remember to speak to us."

"Who are you?" I asked.

"Don't you know me, Daughter?" the deep voice asked. "Don't you even recognize the voice of your Father?"

"You sound different," I whispered back.

He laughed and said, "Open your eyes and work on this task."

"Can I see you first?" I asked him.

"Tomorrow I will come see you and I will discuss your task."

Light flashed and I opened my eyes to find Favian bent over me. "Favian," I whispered in shock.

His head whipped up and he looked at me with a tear streaked face. "Marin." His arms wrapped around me and he kissed me fiercely. "I thought you were dead."

"I was," I whispered. "Now I'm just wet and cold."

He picked me up and carried me into my house and set me down next to the fireplace. "I'll start the fire while you explain why you think you died if you are still alive."

"My father and the Goddess gave me a second chance."

He lit the logs he'd just put in the fireplace and wrapped a blanket around my shoulders, rubbing hard to dry me. "You spoke to them both?"

I nodded my head. "I couldn't see them though because my eyes wouldn't open, but they told me I had to complete a task." The fire started crackling and I sighed happily as the warmth seeped into me.

My mind was refusing to admit that I'd just died and the Gods had resurrected me, even though I knew it had to be true since I was breathing and I'd just said it out loud. It was also refusing to admit that Favian had told me that he loved me. Favian started checking me for wounds and I slapped his hands away. "I'm fine."

He sat down in front of me and I realized I was alive. I was alive and I had told Favian I loved him and he had kissed me! I leaned forward, letting the blanket slide off of my shoulders and kissed Favian on the lips. He kissed me back and then slowly pushed me backwards until I was lying on top of the blanket. His kiss went from soft and tender to rough and passionate as he lay down on top of me. I had always wanted this! His tongue slipped between my lips and I moaned as his sweet taste filled my mouth. It was everything I had ever dreamed of. His hands roamed along my sides as mine explored the contours of his chest and back. I had always wondered what they felt like. I had always wanted to touch him like this. I had always wanted him to make love to me.

I jerked my head back, smacking it into the floor. "Ow." I couldn't do this. What was I thinking!

He didn't seem to notice as he kissed his way from my lips to my jaw to my throat. "Don't you ever die on me again," he said in a commanding voice that his father would have been proud of. He sat up and stared into my eyes. "It felt like a piece of me had shattered."

I couldn't believe this was happening. I was probably dead and imagining all of this. "We can't do this," I whispered. Despite the fact that this could be a dream, I had to stop on the chance that it wasn't.

He ran his hand up until it rested just under my chest and caused an aching need I had never experienced before. "You're alive, Marin. We can do whatever we want."

"But you're courting someone else," I whispered as he kissed my throat and bit down just enough to make me shiver.

He stopped and sat up. "No, I'm not."

"But the dagger..."

"Is for you," he finished and then smiled at me. "I made it for you, but wanted to show it to Emily to see if I needed to change anything."

I felt like a fool. I needed to apologize to Emily next time I went to the castle. "I don't want you to die," I whispered.

He hugged me tightly and whispered, "As long as you live, so shall I."

That wasn't completely reassuring seeing as how I had died just a moment ago. "You need a full-blooded Elf to be your Queen. And I can't be Queen!"

"Why would I need a full-blooded Elf? You are the favored

daughter in our realm and of course you can be Queen. Mother's been training you for years."

I stared at him in shock as I realized what all of the etiquette lessons had been about. No other female Elf had had to learn so many rules and had had to act so proper. It wasn't because they had adopted me, it was because they had been training me to be Queen. "Oh, no," I whispered in shock. "I never paid attention to why... I just thought... Oh no."

"You're the perfect mate for me, Marin, and the only one I want. I don't have your gift because it's at the castle, but will you let me court you? Since you won't let me mate with you."

I frowned at him. "Mother would be very disappointed in me if I ignored all of the etiquette lessons she had taught me and gave in to my desires."

Favian laughed and kissed my lips again, nipping my bottom lip before letting go. "You're right." I shivered and he rolled off me, sticking another log on the fire and then wrapped us up together in the blanket. "You would get warmer faster if we had skin contact."

"Favian," I said with a blush on my cheeks.

He laughed and kissed my cheek. "I don't think I've seen you blush before," he teased.

I playfully punched his arm. "I don't need your teasing. I deserve some rest after dying."

He pulled me close against his body and ran a fingertip over my curved ear. "You deserve the stars and the moon, but sadly they are out of my reach." I pushed his hair back behind his ears and kissed the pointed tip, another thing I had always wanted to do. He shuddered and his voice dropped an octave as he said, "You shouldn't do that if you're making me wait."

"Sorry," I said with a smile. I dropped my head to his chest and listened to the steady beat of his heart and the rain pounding the roof. I was alive. The full ramification of the events hit me and I started crying. Although I had been given another chance, I had been killed by the ogres just like my human parents, but now I had a reason to hunt them all down. No matter how long it took I was going to exterminate the ogres.

Favian picked me up and took me to my bed, lying down behind me. With the blankets pulled tightly around us to seal in our warmth, he started singing the lullaby Mother had sung to us when we were little. My tears slowed and then finally stopped as I fell asleep in the arms of the man I loved and lived to fight another day.

ALSO BY CATHERINE BANKS

Little Death Bringer Series

Mercenary

Protector

Artemis Lupine Series

Song of the Moon

Kiss of a Star

Healed by Fire

Taming Darkness

Artemis Lupine The Complete Series

Ciara Steele Novella Series

True Faces

Barbaric Tendencies

Pirate Princess Series

Pirate Princess

Princess Triumvirate

Daughter of Lions

Bitten, Beaten, & Loved

Demonic Contract

The Last Werewolf

Dragon's Blood

Anja's Secret

Lady Serra and the Draconian

Connect With the Author

I really appreciate you reading my book! Here are some ways to connect with me:

Join my newsletter for deals and snippets:

http://www.subscribepage.com/c6d3i2

Website:

www.catherinebanks.com

Like my author Facebook page:

http://www.Facebook.com/CatherineBanksAuthor

Follow me on Twitter:

http://www.Twitter.com/catherineebanks

Follow me on Goodreads:

http://www.Goodreads.com/catherine_banks

Additional Links

www.Turbokitten.us

www.Turbokitten.us/catherine-banks

http://Etsy.com/shop/TurboKittenInd